DEAD CAT BOUNCE

A C.T. FERGUSON CRIME NOVEL (#11)

TOM FOWLER

Copyright © 2021 by Tom Fowler

Editing by Chase Nottingham

Cover Design by 100Covers

Published by Widening Gyre Media

For Lisa and Isabel.

CHAPTER 1

MY SECRETARY—TWO words I never thought I'd string together—stared at me. "It's been almost a month. I think I've done a good job."

"You have," I agreed.

"When you've actually let me do things." T.J. crossed her arms. "I know you were a one-man show for a few years, but you don't have to be anymore."

"I'm working on it. Old habits and all." Integrating her into my spotty processes proved a challenge. T.J. was smart and a hard worker. She craved having important things to do in her first actual job—which doubled as the first successful placement for my friend Melinda's Nightlight Foundation. I wanted things to work out almost as much as they did.

"Then, you need to lean on me a little more," she said. "I may not be a keyboard wizard like you, but I'm learning."

"I don't need you to do what I do." T.J.'s interest in education shouldn't have surprised me. There were abundant resources available online for anyone who wanted to teach themselves how to be a hacker. "I need you to handle the rest."

She pushed a lock of blonde hair behind her left ear. "Maybe you should get some more clients."

"It's been a slow few weeks since I opened this location," I said with a nod. Thankfully, Melinda paid half of T.J.'s salary for the first six months. This job had been easier when I enjoyed the patronage of my parents' foundation. Now, I needed to eke out a living like most people, and the jury remained out on how successful I'd been. At least I didn't have any overdue bills. Yet.

"I know you didn't expect to have an employee all of a sudden," T.J. said. "I'm sure it was a favor to Melinda." She looked down at her mostly bare desktop. "Still, I appreciate the opportunity."

"It wasn't just a favor." She glanced up at me. "If Melinda brought some random girl in here, I probably would've told her no. You'd proven yourself before, though. I knew you were smart and tough. The issue was whether my job generated enough work to need someone else here. I'm still not sure it does, but I'm going to give you a shot."

She perked up, and a wide smile played on her pretty face. T.J. was nineteen and had already lived a rough life. She could've gone on to be yet another depressing Baltimore statistic. Instead, she turned things around with Melinda's help, and her reward was a job in a detective agency which didn't see a lot of foot traffic. I felt bad for her, which required me to feel bad for myself, too.

I would need more coffee to get through this. As if sensing my imminent caffeine crisis, T.J. got up and brewed a half pot. As the sweet smell of java flooded my office, T.J. stared at me again. "Hit me with the scenarios. I'm ready."

"All right." I kicked my feet up on my desk. "What if someone calls and wants me to look into a cheating spouse?"

"Decline with extreme prejudice," she said.

"Excellent." I gave her a thumbs up. "How about when an insurance executive wants me to poke around one of their customers?"

"The same."

"Almost," I said. "Is there something beyond extreme prejudice? If so, use it then."

"How'd I do, boss?" she asked as she poured coffee into a mug.

"Very well." T.J. added cream and sugar to the mug and then carried it to her own desk. "You still have some areas of improvement, though. Namely beverage delivery."

While she returned to the slow work of being my secretary, I fixed my own hot drink. Voices rose up from below. My office occupied the second floor above a car repair shop. Loud talking constituted the most tolerable of the noises I heard in a typical day. Still, I enjoyed my own entrance, and Manny gave me a break on the rent after I secured his website for him.

Footsteps came up the metal stairs leading to my door. "Maybe we're about to get a client," I said. "You ready to earn your keep?"

"I have a dose of extreme prejudice ready to go," T.J. said.

I smiled. "That's my girl."

———

The door opened a few seconds later, and a man who filled most of the frame walked in. He looked to be about six-four, giving him two inches on me, and both his jeans and hoodie stretched across his large stomach. The newcomer's eyes flicked back and forth between T.J. and me. They lingered on her a little, which I understood. She was pretty easy on the eyes. It soon became apparent, however, this fellow never let his gaze linger on anything for long. He took in me, the room, T.J., the desk, me again, and the room in fits and starts. T.J. frowned and inched closer to her desk phone. "You the detective?" the man asked in a gravelly voice.

"I am. Want to sit at my desk?"

"I'm all right here," he said as if potential clients standing in the middle of the office were an everyday occurrence.

I doubted I could drag him to a chair, so I went along for now. "All right. My name's on the door, so you know who I am. Who are you?"

Wide blue eyes kept scanning the room. "Call me Irish." He ran a hand through short blond hair. "Call me Irish," he repeated as if trying to rewrite the classic first line of *Moby Dick*. I'd read the book once and didn't need to relive it.

Normally, I might've answered with a request to call me English, but our visitor didn't appear to be playing with a full deck, so I tried to keep it professional. "OK, Irish. What can I do for you?"

"I think I saw a murder."

His comment made T.J. sit up straight in her chair. She grabbed a notebook and pen. "Quite an accusation," I said. "Where was it?"

"Not around here." I tried focusing on Irish's neck to avoid looking at his constantly-moving eyes. I wondered if he had some sort of disorder before his head turned back toward the entry in a panic. "Who's there?"

"No one. You'd hear them coming up the metal stairs. Maybe it's one of the workers in the place below."

"Maybe," he said without turning around. When he did, he marched to my guest chair and sat.

T.J. mouthed, "Cops?" at me, but I shook my head and joined Irish at the desk. "Sure, help yourself to a seat," I said.

"Thanks. You been here long?"

"In this space? No. I'm in my second month, I think. Came from Canton Square."

"I saw a murder," Irish said, refocusing the conversation if not his gaze, which remained as elusive as ever.

"Let's talk about it. Do you mind if my assistant takes notes?" I'd never referred to T.J. this way before, but it struck me as a better word choice at the moment.

Irish shook his head. "Someone should write it down. A man died."

T.J. wheeled her chair closer, crossed her very nice legs, and held the notebook and pen atop her left knee. "Ready when you are."

"I think he knew too much." Irish didn't elaborate. I didn't much care for questioning people, but this would be the most maddening interview ever.

"People get killed quite a bit for what they know," I said. "Who was the victim?"

"I don't know his name. He was smart, though. Had access to a lot of data, and I think it's what did him in. It's fine to know a lot . . . but not too much."

Somehow, T.J. found something worth transcribing in our guest's word salad. I tried to keep us on topic. "You told us it wasn't around here. Where did you see it?"

"Tech company," he said. "But they're not just a tech company. What would happen if a wolf dressed up like a sheep?"

"It'd make for a short Halloween on the farm," I said.

T.J. glared at me. Irish didn't seem to notice or mind. "They took him out the back. I'm pretty sure he was already dead. Looked frozen."

"Maybe we can narrow it down, then. Refrigerators and freezers are common in restaurants. Did you maybe see him there?"

"No." Irish shook his head so hard I thought it might unscrew from his neck. "No restaurant. Tech company."

"But not just a tech company?" I asked.

"No," he said. "Something else, too. Problem is I don't know what." His eyes focused on me for a few seconds. "You ever lose a job?"

"Sort of. Let's say my circumstances changed recently."

"It eats you up, man. You get used to going into the office. The work. The routine. The people." He smiled for a moment before continuing. "Then, one day, you get told it's all done. Sold. Years of work and effort . . . just gone because someone wanted to make a quick buck."

Downsizing had been a part of American business life for decades, but I didn't think Irish would react well to a lecture on basic economics. Getting fired from his job could have been the incident which sent him over the edge. "I'm sure it was difficult to handle."

"I wanted to know more about them," he said.

"We have a common interest, then," I said. "Where did you see all this happen?"

"Miles away . . . behind the building."

"Whose building?"

"It's not as tall as I thought it would be," he said. "They're a smaller company than I figured. Gotta be careful, though. They're wolves."

I glanced at T.J., who shrugged. Her paper was mostly empty. We didn't have anywhere near enough to go on. I couldn't even make a phone call or do a web search with the scattered non-story Irish conveyed to us so far. "I'll be sure to take care," I said. "Before I can, though, I need to know who I'm going to be looking into."

"They killed him." Irish's head wagged again. "I should've figured on it." He slapped himself in the forehead, and it sounded like a hammer smashing into a tree. "I should've seen it coming." Another whack. "Maybe I could've done something about it." T.J. wheeled herself away, slipped out her cell phone, and took it into the corner. I didn't want her calling the cops, but I also couldn't let this man have a meltdown in my office.

"There was probably nothing you could've done." I put my hands up and tried to sound reassuring. "If people want someone dead, they don't take too kindly when you interfere in their plans. Take it from me." Across the room, T.J. hung up the phone and gave me a quick nod. She scooted her chair closer again but maintained a healthier distance from Irish.

"Maybe," he said. "Can you help?"

"I need you to tell me some more first." When it looked like he wanted to answer, I kept talking over him. "I don't know where this happened. You've referred to the victim as a man, so there's one piece of information. How long ago was this? Was more than one person involved? What kind of tech company has a freezer on site?"

"Not just a tech company. I've told you. I figured out who they really were."

"My question stands," I said.

"You can't help," he muttered. "They couldn't help me, either. Deputies are useless."

The presence of deputies put the crime in a county. This didn't narrow the field much—Maryland has over twenty of them—but it was a tiny nugget of information. Before I could say anything else, footfalls rushed up the steps, and four uniformed officers threw the door open. T.J. pointed to Irish, who groaned in protest. She backed away as he stood and started moving toward the cops. One of them tased him, and he fell with a thud. The police assured us it would all be all right as they handcuffed Irish and checked his vitals.

CHAPTER 2

"THAT GUY WAS A NUT." T.J. set her notebook and pen down. She shuddered before looking at me. "I've seen my share."

"I believe you," I said. I'd first met T.J. on a case when she worked as a hooker. Her former occupation probably exposed her to many questionable men. "I'm not convinced we needed the police, though. He didn't seem like a threat."

"I'm not big on taking chances." She crossed her arms. "You saw him smacking himself in the head. It could have escalated."

I shrugged. Irish may have flogged himself, but it didn't make him a threat to T.J. or me. "My concern is the police aren't always the best at handling mental illness." My argument didn't seem to dissuade my secretary whose posture didn't change a whit. "Does he count as a client?"

"I don't know." T.J. scanned her notebook. "I didn't write much down, and what I did doesn't really mean much. He didn't exactly give us a ton of specifics."

"If he knew the whole story, he wouldn't need us," I said.

"He's crazy," she said.

"Maybe. It doesn't make him wrong, though."

"What do you mean?"

"There's a great deal to unpack in his story. We don't know where or when it happened. He didn't give us any information about the victim other than he was a man. Supposedly, the guy was frozen, but it may or may not be how he died. It's not enough to go on yet."

"Because he's a nut," T.J. insisted. "Why are you taking what he said seriously?"

"It might have happened," I said. "Irish could have actually seen the murder he described. We don't know, and we won't until we look into it."

"Good luck." T.J. held up her scant page of notes. "He didn't tell us enough to get started."

"I know. He mentioned a deputy, which puts it somewhere in a county."

"You're going to try and figure this out?" she asked.

"No one else is beating down our door. Let's give it a try. You can search counties for unsolved murders of men."

T.J. rolled her eyes but turned back to her laptop. "Sure. And I'll just untangle Irish's identity while I'm at it, too."

"Good thinking," I said. "It'd be nice to get paid for all this work."

———

While T.J. conducted her research, my cell phone rang. Caller ID showed Rollins' name. It was rare for him to call me out of the blue, so I picked up right away. "You know who might have a tail on me?" he asked once I answered.

"Not a clue, but I'm sure you can lose him."

"Sure. Exactly like I did yesterday and the day before."

Rollins sometimes helped me with my cases. I originally

hired him as a bodyguard when I went up against a band of international sex traffickers. He got paid well for his work then. Since our initial encounter, he generally worked *pro bono* like I used to. "I don't have much going on here," I said, "so it can't be whatever I'm tangled up in. You must've pissed someone off all by yourself."

"Lucky me," he said. "I'm in the same boat as you. Pretty quiet here, too. Hell, I only got back from vacation a few days ago."

"Wow," I said. "I didn't know you took time off. I figured you slept an hour a night and drank the blood of your enemies to keep looking young."

"I'm over forty now. I could probably use a new skin care routine."

"You get much of a look at the drivers?"

"Yeah. Dark hair. If I had to guess, I'd peg them for Italian."

"Maybe they're very aggressive pizza delivery guys," I said.

"I don't eat pizza," Rollins said.

"Even more reason for them to follow you. You're a philistine."

His pickup's powerful engine revved over the connection. "I'm ditching this guy. They're persistent, though."

"Do they know where you live?"

"Probably," he said. "The last two guys acquired me a couple blocks from home."

"I know this is a bit of role reversal," I said, "but do you need a hand?"

"Nah. I can deal with these amateurs." He fell silent for a few seconds, and the sounds of screeching tires and a howling engine replaced his voice. "He's gone. Three in a row. I don't like them knowing where I live, though. Only a matter of time before some shit goes down."

"Maybe I should tail one of these guys. *I* don't even know where you live."

Rollins snorted. "May be better you don't right now. I don't know who these guys are or what they want with me. Doesn't seem like you do, either."

"Not a clue," I said. "Sorry."

"No worries. I think I'm gonna lie low for a few days until whatever this is blows over. I got a burner phone. I'll text you from it later in case we need to keep in touch."

"You sure there's nothing else I can do? Maybe run a plate?"

"They never followed me close enough for me to get one," Rollins said. "These guys aren't very good, but they're not terrible, either. Just keep your phone handy."

"I will," I said. Rollins hung up. I set my mobile down. Since he retired from the army a few years ago, Rollins worked for himself in private security. He tended to stay in the shadows when helping me, which is how he preferred it. If whatever mess he'd landed in stemmed from one of my cases, someone went to a lot of effort to ferret out his involvement. It suggested a dedicated and resourceful adversary.

It also suggested I could find myself in the crosshairs next.

———

After a not-very-hard day at the office, I drove to my home in Federal Hill. Mine is an end-unit rowhouse with a tiny yard and a parking pad in the rear. I left my Audi S4 beside the red rocketlike Mercedes coupe Gloria Reading drives. My girlfriend lounged on the couch with her laptop when I got home. She closed the computer, stood, and greeted me with a proper kiss. "How was work?"

"Only had to shoot ten people today," I said. "Kind of slow."

"I'm sure you'll make up for it tomorrow."

I hung my jacket in the closet and removed the holster and gun from around my torso. "Where did you book us for dinner?"

"Nowhere, actually," Gloria said. "I guess I didn't think about it. Sounds like you're cooking tonight."

"Lucky me." I kissed her again. "I'll see what looks good in the kitchen." Gloria returned to the couch, and I assessed the stock on hand. Thankfully, I'd been to the grocery store this week. If I had more time and inclination, I would've made a pasta sauce from scratch. Instead, I cracked open a jar of my favorite marinara and put the contents in a saucepan over low heat. I found some fresh Italian sausage in the fridge, chopped it, and added it to a skillet. A few minutes and some seasonings later, I drained the cooked sausage and stirred it into the sauce.

About twenty minutes later, Gloria closed her laptop again and joined me at the table. I wondered if she would tell me what she worked on. Maybe over a nice meal. We sat down to a dinner of linguine and sauce with a large salad. Gloria cut her pasta into small bites. By contrast, I twisted it around my fork and ate it properly. "I think I got a new client today," I said once we'd each eaten a little.

"Good." She smiled. "I know it's been slow going recently."

"I'm not sure this is going to be much better. The guy's insane."

"You mean . . . like, really crazy?"

"I'm not qualified to make an official diagnosis," I said, "but yes. He was so erratic T.J. called the cops, and they took him away."

"Wow." Gloria frowned. "How are you going to work with him?"

"I'm not really sure," I admitted. "He told us he saw a man getting murdered, but he couldn't say who the guy was, where it happened, or even how long ago. It's not a lot to go on."

"But I'm sure you started anyway."

"We're trying. He mentioned a deputy, which puts the crime in a county. Lot of those to sift through, though, and T.J.'s first search didn't turn up any likely hits."

"What are you going to do?" Gloria asked.

I used the salad utensils to add some to my bowl. I'd already tossed it with the dressing. "I'm not sure, really. Just because he's probably crazy doesn't mean he's wrong."

"How do you know what he saw wasn't some sort of delusion?"

"I don't," I said. "We're going to look into it and see if there's a match. If not . . . I guess I'm looking for a new client again. Hopefully one the police don't drag away."

"Even if you find something," Gloria said, "it doesn't sound like this guy is in a position to pay you."

"I know." I sighed. "One good client a month can cover the bills. I simply need to find them a bit more often."

"Tomorrow is a new day. You never know who's going to walk through your door."

I nodded. So long as the potential new arrival didn't work for an insurance company or want me to look into an adulterous spouse, I was all set. My principles conflicting with my bank account made for some inconvenient times. "True." I took another couple bites of pasta. Gloria indulged in a few nibbles. I always felt surprised it didn't take her an hour to eat. "What were you working on earlier?"

She shrugged. "Some fundraising stuff. I guess I'm trying to find a good match the same as you are."

It seemed like something more, especially when Gloria didn't elaborate. She shared her work stories much like I did. It made me wonder if something bigger were going on. She would tell me in time, but I'd be curious until she dropped the news, whatever it was. I raised my glass of iced tea. "Here's to good matches, then."

Gloria clinked hers to mine. "Hear, hear."

CHAPTER 3

THE NEXT MORNING, I woke up before Gloria, which was basically an everyday occurrence. This time, she didn't even stir when I got out of bed. I put on a warm running suit and left the house for the mean streets of Federal Hill. A few laps around the eponymous park has always been a great way to get the blood moving and the brain working. After getting shot a few months ago, I didn't run as fast as I used to, and I got tired a bit quicker, but I kept at it. My stamina improved a little every week, and I hoped to be back to a hundred percent—minus my spleen and one node of a lung—someday.

About thirty minutes after I set out, I walked back into my house, showered, and got dressed. The smell of brewing coffee wafted upstairs, and Gloria's feet soon hit the floor. She joined me in the kitchen as the pot finished and planted a minty kiss on me. I worked on breakfast while she poured us each a mug of java and carried them to the table. A little while later, I took in two plates of two waffles each, set them down, and joined Gloria.

She added enough butter to concern a cardiologist, and the fumes from her syrup threatened to give me diabetes from across the table. It always mystified me how she could slather her pancakes and waffles like she did and still maintain her terrific body. The tennis must have made the difference. Gloria turned herself into a good player over the years, and she'd even won a couple local tournaments. She also handed me my behind whenever we got on the court together. "You going to keep looking into that murder?" she asked when she'd taken enough tiny bites to finally finish a waffle.

I nodded. I was halfway through my second and debated whipping up more batter for a third. "Unless something else pressing comes up. Maybe T.J. will uncover something."

"You showing her how to do some of what you know?"

"Some," I said. "She's a pretty quick study." Before becoming a PI, I'd been quite a good hacker. Not good enough to avoid the notice and reach of the Chinese police almost four years ago, but few people have escaped their clutches. Unlike many of the people they arrested, I was lucky enough to get kicked back to the States nineteen days later. Since then, I'd focused on not getting detected, and I tried to pass on some of what I knew to my secretary, who was eager to learn.

Gloria worked on her second waffle. She glanced at me a few times, and I again got the feeling she wanted to tell me something. I hoped her parents were OK. Her dad broke his hip a few months ago, but he'd been doing well last I heard. Might she be pregnant? I couldn't imagine her being coy about telling me such big news. I finished my breakfast and poured us each another cup of coffee. She didn't say anything else.

I walked back upstairs to freshen up before work. When I emerged from the bathroom, Gloria grabbed me and shoved me onto the bed. "I know this is the time you normally go to work," she said as she kissed my neck. "Does T.J. have a key?"

"Yes."

"Good." Gloria grinned. "I'm sure she can live without you for a while. I don't think I can."

I pulled her down tight atop me. "I can show up whenever I want. I'm the boss."

Gloria nibbled my ear. "It sounds like you're not in a hurry, then." Her hot breath sent a shudder down my spine.

"Definitely not."

"That's what I like to hear," she said.

———

When I arrived at the office, T.J. was already there. Her car, a battered Honda Civic which probably came into the world the same year she did, sat in one of the two spots Manny tried to reserve for me. I parked beside her and hoofed it up the stairs. Inside, T.J. sipped from a mug of coffee. I used my vast sleuthing powers to detect a mostly full pot remaining. "You're late again," she said with a smirk.

I poured myself a cup. "The good thing about being the boss is setting your own hours."

"Uh-huh. Let me guess . . . Gloria got frisky after breakfast, and you couldn't resist her?"

"Am I really so predictable?" I asked despite knowing the answer. The day I fended Gloria off would likely coincide with the heat death of the universe.

"Most men are," T.J. said.

I couldn't summon a counterargument, so I focused on work. "Any luck with the county searches yesterday?"

T.J. shook her head. "I couldn't find anything. Sorry."

"Don't be. There may be nothing out there to uncover. I'll take a look."

While my secretary was competent and smart, she lacked

experience. Part of it stemmed from her lack of time on the job, and the rest came from the fact I'd only taken a few cases since she arrived on board. Those involved clients who walked in with credible stories, and the police didn't need to storm the office and drag them away at the end. I maintained Irish might have been telling the truth, but with all the gaps in his story, finding matching details would be a challenge.

Searching each individual county would take too long. Luckily, the state police maintained a database of crimes across Maryland. It didn't update as often as the local versions, but what Irish described clearly happened at least a couple days ago if not longer. T.J. wheeled her chair beside mine to see what I did. I fought the urge to shudder at someone reading over my shoulder and kept going. "What are you looking in?" she asked.

"The state police catalog crimes from all over Maryland," I said. "If you don't know where something happened, it's a good place to start."

"Can you send me the link?"

"Already did."

"Thanks," she said with a nod.

I entered the criteria I wanted to search under, pausing when it came to a date range for when the incident happened. We really didn't know. Too short a window would leave it hidden, and too long may give us more cases to sift through. I settled on a hundred twenty days and submitted my search. "Anyone come in before I got here this morning?"

"You mean before the workday officially began?" T.J. asked.

I grinned and figured I would need to check the carpet for the sarcasm dripping from her tone. "Yes."

"No, but someone called . . . a man who thought his wife was cheating. I told him we don't do domestic cases."

"Excellent."

"Why don't we?"

"I never told you?" I said. T.J. shook her head. "My first client was a woman who was sure her husband was cheating on her. Turns out he wasn't. The whole thing was a mess. It didn't end well for anyone." Especially Alice's husband Paul, who got beaten to death and thrown out of a window.

My results popped up. I set pretty loose parameters to cover the gaps—or the craziness—in Irish's story. My screen displayed a bunch of partial matches. Nothing matched all the details. I re-ran the query for a hundred eighty days and got the same result. "Now what?" T.J. said.

"There's not enough here." I shrugged. "We can't run all these down. Most of them are wrong at first blush, anyway."

"The great client search continues."

"Maybe Manny will let me fix a couple cars for a break on the rent."

T.J. scooted back to her own desk. "Would you know what you're doing?"

"I can change oil," I said. "Not much else."

Before she could point out my mechanical limitations, her desk phone rang. She answered it, provided the usual caveats about what work we did, gave me a thumbs up, and told the caller we would be here in an hour. "We just might have a client."

"Great. Roll out the red carpet."

"Can we afford one?" she asked.

"No," I said.

———

The door opened, and a woman walked in. She wore a smart brown leather jacket which matched her shoes. I liked her already. I guessed her to be a few years older than me. Her blonde hair hung past her shoulders. T.J. took her coat and hung it on the rack near the entrance. My latest potential client was pretty, though her red and puffy eyes told me she wasn't happy—a common trait among people who came to my office. "Thanks for seeing me," she said.

T.J. smiled as she collected her notebook and pen. "We had a slot open up unexpectedly."

I gestured toward the guest chairs in front of my desk. The still-unnamed lady sat in one, and my secretary slid onto the other. "What can we do for you?"

"I'm Amy Napier. I'm married . . . well, I was . . . to Jason." She paused, and I knew what would come next. "He's dead. Murdered."

"I'm sorry," T.J. and I said at the same time. She demurred, and I continued. "How long ago?"

"About three weeks." Amy Napier took a small pack of tissues from her purse and plucked one to wipe her eyes. "It seems so much more recent. Nothing from the police so far. I guess that's why I'm coming to see you."

"I hear it a lot." She sniffled again. "When you're ready, tell us what happened."

Amy nodded and dabbed at her nose once more. "My husband is . . . was a DBA. Database administrator." I knew what she meant without the clarification, but it probably helped T.J. "He worked for a company in Frederick. He'd been there a few years. Recently, he told me he thought something weird was going on."

"Weird how?" I asked.

"He didn't go into a lot of detail." She showed a self-deprecating smile. "I don't have much of a head for the tech stuff, so a lot of what he told me went in one ear and out the other."

"Which company did he work for?"

"Research and Technology Partners," she said. I'd never heard of the place, but I also didn't get to Frederick very often. The city served as the seat of the county of the same name. I'd ventured there about a year ago for a case involving several dead girls. I didn't come away with a positive impression of the sheriff's office. "They don't do much research these days, but the name has stuck. Now, they focus on IT services for other companies."

"Did your husband have access to information from those companies?" I asked.

"I guess." Amy frowned. "Like I said, I didn't follow a lot of the tech talk. He mentioned things were locked down pretty well . . . service-level agreements, I think. If you're wondering if he saw something he shouldn't have in a database, I guess it's possible, but I don't think it's likely."

"We've established you two didn't talk shop. Did he mention any concerns he had? Maybe something of a non-technical nature?"

"I don't know." She furrowed her brows. "A couple weeks before he died, he told me he thought some guys were double-dipping."

"I presume he didn't mean with the chips and salsa . . . though it would still be bad."

"He didn't go into a lot of detail," Amy said while T.J. scribbled a bunch of notes. I wondered why she didn't use her phone or a tablet. She texted at light speed. If this case paid off, I'd have to upgrade her transcription system. "I didn't ask, honestly. He kept a lot of stuff like that close to the vest."

Irish's words played in my head. *Not just a tech company*. It didn't tell me anything else, however, and Amy Napier hadn't exactly filled in the gaps. It occurred to me I expected a grieving widow to plug the holes in a crazy man's story. I might as well fly to Vegas and play roulette. At least the payoff would be large if I hit. "Whatever the double-dipping was might've gotten him killed, then," I said. "He could've been on to the wrong people."

"It's something I've thought about." Amy reached into her purse again, this time pulling out a business card and sliding it across my desk. "This is the CEO. He loved Jason. I told him I was hiring a PI, and he said the company would do whatever they could to help.

"How big is RTP?"

Amy shrugged. "I'm not sure, really. Maybe three hundred and fifty employees?"

"Seems pretty small to have C-level executives," T.J. said, echoing my thoughts.

"Jason thought the same thing when he started. He said they wanted to convey they were professional. A CEO sounds more official than a president."

"I guess it depends how many idiots are on your client list," I said.

"You should call him," Amy said, jutting her chin toward the card. "I believe him when he says he'll be supportive."

I considered the possibility Devon Knott, CEO, might have been in on the murder. Hopefully, Amy did, too, but she also had other worries. Either way, talking to the man wouldn't hurt. "I'll be sure to call him. One more question, and I know it might be hard. How did Jason die?"

Amy took a deep breath before she answered. "The coroner told me he froze to death. It doesn't make any sense." Her eyes welled. "It never did." T.J. and I exchanged a look.

Maybe Irish wasn't crazy after all. "Does this mean I'm hiring you?"

"We're available if you want to. T.J. can go over the rates with you if you didn't see them online."

Amy agreed, and the two adjourned to my assistant's desk. I stared at the business card. They'd printed it on good paper, and the corporate logo clearly conveyed the business RTP conducted. My experience with presidents and CEOs was largely negative, however. Devon Knott could open a lot of doors and help the investigation, or he could resent my meddling and try to have me killed exactly like Jason Napier.

I hoped for the former but needed to be prepared for the latter.

CHAPTER 4

AMY AND T.J. worked out anticipated expenses, and she paid a quarter up front. I'd quoted people half before, but it still represented a sizable sum. "You should deposit it before she changes her mind," my secretary said.

"She's not going to." I took the check and dropped it on my desk. "I'll do a mobile deposit after I call this CEO." I punched in the numbers and reached an executive assistant with a pleasant voice. I hoped T.J. didn't want her title. It sounded more expensive. At first, she told me Mr. Knott couldn't possibly be disturbed, but when I clarified the reason for my call, she promised to get him right away. A moment later, he came on the line.

"Devon Knott speaking."

"Mister Knott, Amy Napier gave me your business card."

"Yes, I'd hoped she would find someone to assist her," he said. "Are you some sort of private investigator?"

"The official sort, yes. My name is C.T. Ferguson. Amy told me you wanted to help us figure out who killed her husband."

"So terrible. I loved Jason. He was the first person I hired back when I served as the CFO."

"Anything you can tell me about him would be useful," I said. "His wife couldn't do much for us on the tech stuff. She doesn't speak the language."

"I'll certainly do what I can. Jason originally came on board as an internal DBA. Maybe a year later, we started using him to audit our clients."

"Financially?"

"Sort of," Knott said. "We do a lot of good work here, and we have clients from all over the world." I rolled my eyes in preparation for the company CEO to read from their latest brochure. He kept the pitch light, which I appreciated. "In the grand scheme of things, we're fairly small. Many of our competitors could buy us out pretty easily . . . and a few have tried. So we do all manners of audits from financial to IT security to compliance. Jason could handle all of them."

"He sounds like a valuable employee."

'Most definitely."

"Maybe he was a little too good at his job," I said. "Or perhaps he saw something in an audit he shouldn't have. Someone killed him for a reason."

Knott sighed. "I understand, and I wish I knew why. Jason didn't report to me anymore. His position still falls under the CFO. I asked her to tell me everything about what he was working on. None of it raised any suspicion."

"Maybe you could tell me. I'm at least fifty percent more suspicious than most people."

Silence filled the line for a few seconds. Then, Knott said, "A lot of it is confidential client data. I have an idea, though. It came into my head when Amy told me she wanted to hire a PI. What did you say your name was again?"

"C.T. Ferguson."

Knott tapped some keys. He was probably Googling me. I

was almost impressed he didn't make his assistant do it. His impromptu research meant it took him a few seconds to talk again. "A couple of these articles mention you're quite handy with computers."

"Significantly underselling my skill set," I said.

"Do you think you could work on a database?"

I didn't care for where this conversation was headed. However, I couldn't miss an opportunity to toot my own horn. "I'm rather overqualified for most IT jobs. Let's say I'm a specialist at the darker side of computer security and a generalist at the rest."

"Here's my idea," Knott said. "We need someone to take Jason's job. Technically, I shouldn't be the one hiring you, but I'm the CEO."

"Rank has its privileges," I said.

"It does. I can get you in here, and you can conduct your investigation from the inside. If someone connected to RTP killed Jason, I damn well want to know about it."

Amy told me Knott would want to help, and it certainly seemed like he did. If he were involved, though, he'd be able to keep a close eye on me while I worked in the building. He could even direct whoever killed Jason Napier to do the same to me. Still, this represented a unique opportunity. I felt confident I could exceed whatever limits RTP tried to put on my access and dig into what Jason last worked on—which may have been what got him killed. "It's a little unconventional . . . but I'm interested."

"Great," Knott said. "Can you come in tomorrow morning?"

"Sure."

"You'll probably need some kind of cover identity. One of the early articles about you has your picture."

"I know," I said with a sigh. I've tried to avoid being photographed since—precisely for this reason. While I'd never gone undercover in the manner Knott proposed, having my picture plastered all over the place would complicate things. "I'll come up with something."

"Great. See you at nine."

"Make it ten. Long drive."

Knott grumbled a little but agreed, and we hung up. "You're going to work there?" T.J. asked as soon as I set my phone down.

I nodded. "Looks like it."

"You know you could be walking into the lion's den?"

"Make sure you pack me a whip and a stool, then."

"I'm serious." She crossed her arms. "What am I going to do while you're out in Frederick?"

"Keep coming in," I said. "I might need you to do some things for me. I'm not worried about getting around their access controls, but if they monitor their computers, they'll know the kinds of things I'm looking for."

"Be careful," T.J. said. "It might look bad on my résumé if my first boss gets horrifically murdered." The corner of her mouth turned up.

"I'll be sure to keep your future employment prospects in mind," I said.

———

A couple hours later, I got a text from Gabriella Rizzo. *Can you meet me for lunch at the restaurant today? Have something I want to run by you.* My longstanding policy is to accept invitations from the head of organized crime in the city, a position Gabriella recently inherited from her father. I replied in the affirmative, and she said I could come anytime. I stood, shrugged my jacket on, and told T.J. I was heading out for lunch. "I'll bring you back something."

"You're so good to me," she said. "I really hope they don't murder you in Frederick."

"Me, too," I said as I left the office. Our location sat just off Eastern Avenue, and it was about a mile walk into Little Italy. At certain times of the day, hoofing it could be faster than driving. The weather was pleasantly cool, so I went on foot. After about fifteen minutes, I closed in on Rizzo's. Gabriella changed the name—for the better in my opinion—from *Il Buon Cibo* when she took over her father's legitimate business, too.

With no maitre d' for the lunch crowd, I found Gabriella on my own. She'd remodeled the place, and while her father liked a first-floor table by the fireplace, his daughter carved out her own spot on the second level. This early in the day, there would be no one else up there. As I climbed the stairs, I saw Gabriella was all alone save for two large goons sitting at a table nearby. She smiled as I approached. They did their best to look menacing, and it wasn't very good.

My hostess smiled and stood as I approached, and we shared a quick embrace. "Good to see you," she said as we sat. "You still feeling all right?"

"I'm not sure I'm a hundred percent yet. I feel like I've settled somewhere in the low nineties."

"Still an A in the gradebook."

I grinned. "And still good enough to do my job."

With the boss lady's table now occupied, a waiter strode beside us to take our orders. Gabriella didn't want lunch, but I've always enjoyed eating on someone else's dime, so I ordered chicken parm with a side Caesar salad and an iced tea. "We're expanding the menu," she said when the server left. "A few more healthy options to bring in the younger crowd."

It was a tactic her father had been loath to try. "Still balanced by things like fettuccine alfredo, I hope."

"We can't get rid of the classics."

"If someone wants to order a heart attack on a plate," I said, "this is America."

The waiter returned with my salad—onto which he cracked some fresh black pepper—and drink. Gabriella let me take a few bites before she started talking again. "I'm . . . concerned about something."

"I'm sure the two gentlemen sitting at the next table can handle a wide variety of problems."

She smirked. Gabriella knew my opinion of the guys she hired. They were no better than her father's goons, though they were a little younger on average. "This might require a different approach." She took a deep breath and leaned in. "I think someone murdered my father." When I paused with my fork halfway to my mouth, Gabriella filled in the conversational gap. "I know the police report says he killed himself. I'm just not sure I believe it."

I set my utensil down on the plate and wiped my mouth. "You should believe the police report."

"Why?" she asked, still angled toward me. "Do you know something you haven't told me?"

I knew a great deal I'd never told her—mainly my presence in the room when Tony put a pistol to his head and pulled the trigger. Gabriella didn't have any way to know this, however, and I wanted her to remain in the dark about it. "I read the report."

"You did?"

"Sure," I said. "I'd known your dad most of my life. It's not like the cops can keep reports hidden from me. I went looking for it, and I found it." I told her the truth—I'd gone hunting for the official writeup, located the file, and read it. Nothing inside proved surprising.

"Do you agree with what it said?" Gabriella asked.

"I do." I figured she'd already seen a copy. Her father kept some cops on the payroll, and there was no reason for his daughter to discontinue the practice. "It's pretty easy to shoot someone and put a gun in their hand after the fact. It creates the appearance of suicide. What you can't fake is the gunshot residue. His hand was covered in it."

"Couldn't someone have held his hand and fired another shot?"

"Sure," I allowed. "Except there was only one round missing from the gun, and no one found another hole anywhere in the room." Gabriella crossed her arms. "I'm sure it's hard to believe."

"It's *impossible*," she said. "I know what my dad did. I've known for years. Despite all that, he considered himself a good Catholic. He wouldn't kill himself."

I spread my hands. "I can tell you I read the report, and I couldn't find fault with it."

"I'm going to keep looking." I figured she would. It made me wonder if Gabriella ordered any of her guys to tail Rollins. He'd driven me to and from Tony's house on the fateful night. Did Gabriella know more than she let on? If so, she did a great job of keeping cards close to her vest. As the waiter approached with my chicken parm, I realized I'd never finished my salad. I took a couple quick bites, pushed it aside, and dug into the main course. "I was hoping you might be able to tell me where to start."

"I wish I could be more help," I said, "but I really think you're barking up the wrong tree here."

"The guy who was with my dad that night swore he heard another voice in the house."

He did, of course. At the time, Tony played it off as making a phone call on speaker. I didn't know if I could use the same excuse, but I couldn't devise another in the heat of the moment. "Maybe he used his phone on speaker?"

"At such a late hour?"

"Let's not pretend your dad worked a nine-to-five job," I said.

Gabriella grunted. "I guess it's possible. It doesn't feel right, though. I'm going to keep looking into everything."

I shrugged. "It's your time." I nudged half my chicken parm and spaghetti to the far side of the plate. It would make a nice lunch for T.J.

"It is," Gabriella said. "Thanks for stopping by. I might need to ask your opinion again at some point."

"Sure," I said. "Happy to help." She maintained a neutral expression. I wondered again how much she knew or suspected, if she'd sent any guys after Rollins, and how she might treat an old friend who stood in her way.

CHAPTER 5

I WALKED BACK to the office and handed T.J. the plastic container with my leftovers. She accepted them with a smile. I told her I was heading out again, and I drove to the headquarters of the Baltimore Police Department. My cousin Rich worked out of the Central District in an adjoining building. I found him in his office and knocked on the door. "You're going to get splinters in your ass being a lieutenant."

He rolled his eyes. "My chair is padded."

"Your waistline will be, too, after a few months. Maybe you can get a volume discount on getting all your suits tailored."

Rich adjusted the lapel of the gray one he wore today. "Did you have an actual reason for coming in this afternoon, or are we just discussing my fitness?"

"You might be getting a couple gray hairs, too," I said. Rich was almost seven years older than me, so he would turn forty in about two years.

"I'm fine," he said. "It's really not much more stressful than being a sergeant. I passed the exam a couple weeks ago, so I'm official now."

"I must have missed the invitation to your coronation." I sat in one of Rich's guest chairs and hoped the one he occupied provided more comfort. It would struggle to provide less.

He shrugged. "I didn't really do anything. It's not like I got a pay raise when the results came in." Rich checked something on his computer. With him being behind a desk more, he needed to coordinate the activities of the homicide detectives who worked for him. I knew he missed being on the streets, and I wondered how often he ventured back out. "What's going on?"

"You have much of a relationship with anyone in the Frederick County Sheriff's Office?"

"Not really," Rich said. "I haven't worked with them a lot. The last time was . . . what, almost a year ago? The serial killer case?"

"Sounds right."

"Deputy's name was Dunn, I think."

"It was," I said.

"He'd be the one I know best, and I can't say I'd remember what he looked like if I tripped over him." Rich paused. "Why? What's going on in Frederick County?"

"I caught a case out there. I'll be going back tomorrow to start looking around." I declined to mention my potential cover as an employee of the company in question. Rich would either think me a fool for walking into the lion's den or laugh at me for joining the workforce, even in a nonstandard capacity. I turned both thoughts over in my head already, and I didn't require him to amplify either. "It would be nice to have some official support if I end up needing it."

"I'd reach out to Dunn if I were you," Rich said. "He probably remembers you."

How fond his memories would be was a matter of conjecture. I recalled not being especially complimentary of the department's work. "All right," I said. "I'll see what he can tell me."

"Good luck." Rich turned back to his computer and started tapping keys. I left and wondered how much I'd be on an island out in Frederick.

———

At my office, I tried to find information on Irish. Using my vast sleuthing powers, I deduced his nickname stemmed from his nationality. This alone wouldn't narrow it sufficiently. His physical characteristics could help. I presumed him to be a Maryland resident. He could have lived out of state and worked in Frederick, but other than Fort Detrick, it lacked the big draw of a city like Baltimore or one closer to DC.

A little over six million people lived in Maryland, and over three and a half million of them were white. I could narrow further from there, but I'd still be fishing in a large pool. Finding some more numbers and figures did nothing to fill me with optimism. Without more information to feed into the search, I held little chance of figuring out who Irish actually was. "You have any luck with the crazy guy?" I asked T.J.

She shook her head. "I didn't even know where to start. I looked around for a while, but I think his identity is beyond me. Sorry."

"Don't be. It's beyond me, too, I think."

"Maybe we can figure it out together."

"Worth a try," I said. "If we presume he's a Maryland resident, there are about one point eight million white males living in our fair state. Nationally, about ten percent of the population identifies as being of Irish descent."

"Now, we're down to a hundred and eighty thousand," T.J. said, doing her best to sound cheery for both of us.

"It might be a tick higher in Maryland, but sure. We'll use your number. How old do you think he is?"

T.J. pursed her lips. "Pretty old . . . at least thirty-five."

"I'll be thirty-five in four years," I pointed out.

"And if I'm still working for you, I'll buy you an 'over the hill' card for your birthday." She smiled.

"It would be your last day on the job." T.J. kept the smile on her face, which forced me to shake my head and laugh. "All right . . . If we put him in the thirty-to-forty group, it's about thirteen percent. Now, we're looking at twenty-three thousand or so."

"Still a big pool."

"It is. I didn't see how height breaks down, but he's taller than average. Let's say we've reduced our population to ten thousand."

"Hair and eye color," T.J. said.

"Let's test your detective powers. What are they?"

She squinted to concentrate. "Blue eyes," she said after a few seconds. "I remember because he kept looking around the room. His hair was short . . . and blond, I think." T.J. blinked and looked at me.

"You're right. High school biology taught me both are recessive genes, so we've dropped from ten thousand to maybe three. It's a seventy percent reduction, but it's still a lot of people to comb through."

"Like you said, he was crazy."

I bobbed my head. "Healthcare privacy laws make a lot of medical factors difficult to search for."

"But *you* could," T.J. said.

"Maybe." I waffled my hand. "It's not like there's a national registry of people who've spent time in the psych ward. If he even has."

"It sucks not being able to figure this out. We've done a lot of work to narrow it this far. I wish we had some more data."

"Welcome to being a detective," I said. "Still want to do this?"

"I have to stick it out four more years." T.J. grinned. "Someone needs to get you an 'over the hill' card."

"You're fired," I said.

———

"You're going to have an actual job? In an office and everything? When did my boyfriend get so domesticated?"

Gloria smiled and poked me in the side as I finished cooking dinner. I took my cast-iron skillet out of the oven. Two chicken breasts lay over a bed of mushrooms, onions, peppers, and minced garlic. I set the pan back on the stove, added rice to two plates, and served the entree with a simple sauce I'd whipped up from chicken stock. The vegetables sizzled from their time in the stove as all the smells rushed to my nostrils. "I guess I can't protest the domesticated bit as I make dinner," I said.

"Not really, no."

"Then, I'd like to point out I already work in an office." I set the plates on the kitchen table, where Gloria joined me. It was small, perfect for two diners and strained to accommodate four. "I even have a secretary. It makes me sixty percent more official."

Gloria cut a piece of her chicken small enough to require

an electron microscope to find it on her plate. She ate it with the rice, veggies, and sauce, and nodded. "Very good."

I remained unconvinced the two molecules she sampled gave her enough of the flavor, but I accepted the compliment. "Thanks. And before you ask, I've already considered the possibility the job is a setup."

"It doesn't concern you?" she asked.

I sliced off a proper amount of my entree and tried it. Gloria's evaluation was spot-on. "It does. Sometimes, though, you need to walk into a trap to see if it really is one. I'll be prepared. Joey's going to set me up with a different appearance. It should fool anyone who sees my picture online. If I run into trouble, I'll have a gun in my bag."

"You think it'll last long?"

"I'm not sure," I admitted. "Part of me thinks I'll be able to crack it pretty quickly. The more rational side realizes companies are often good about hiding evidence of their own malfeasance, so it'll probably take some digging."

Gloria frowned. "All while the killer might be in an office at the end of the hall."

"It's a possibility. I don't even know if the gig will get off the ground. The CEO seems supportive now. Let's see how he feels when I'm in his office tomorrow, and the prospect of having an outsider investigate his company and his people—including him—really hits home."

"You think he'll back out?"

I cut up the chicken breast and stirred it in with everything else. "No idea. If he does, it saves me a bunch of trips to and from Frederick."

Gloria's brows remained knitted as she ate. I knew she felt concerned. I did, too. I'd be The New Guy at a company small enough for people to notice my status, need to blend in while still conducting an investigation, try to stay off the killer's radar, and do it all without the support of the two police departments I normally worked with.

If the meal I'd cooked weren't so good, I might have lost my appetite.

CHAPTER 6

WHEN I LEARNED I might be going undercover, I needed a plan. Part of it involved reaching out to my old friend Joey Trovato. Like me, Joey possessed prodigious computer skills, but he used his to create new identities for people and help them disappear. Sometimes, this required a change in the person's looks, so I drove to the Greektown area of Baltimore to meet my friend and his "appearance girl" as he called her.

Greektown sits in the shadow of the Johns Hopkins Hospital Bayview campus. The address I wanted lay immediately off Eastern Avenue near Ikaros Restaurant. I vaguely remembered the place I parked behind being an eatery at some point. Now, it served as a costume shop when Joey didn't use the owner to help his clients. I knocked on the rear door as instructed. It cracked open a moment later, and Joey's large frame filled the gap. "What's the password?" he said.

"Breakfast."

"Good enough." He smiled and let me in. Joey was a black Sicilian of good humor and better appetite. His girth hid a surprising amount of athleticism. He could have played college football if he'd been so inclined, and he probably would've made a good lineman on either side of the ball. Joey eyed the brown paper bag in my hand, its right side growing translucent from a grease spot. "What's in there?"

"Bagel sandwiches," I said as I looked around the cluttered back area. A lot of cardboard boxes lay strewn about. Racks of clothes lined most of the walls and intruded on the room itself. A small table with a large mirror sat off to the side. "One each for me and your expert and three for you."

"Sounds like the right ratio."

The star of the show walked into the room. She was a tall, slender woman who looked to be in her forties. A mess of black curls spilled down her face and onto her shoulders. She wore a shapeless dress and kept a pencil tucked behind her ear. Her glasses sat on her forehead, and I wondered how many times she would misplace them while we were here. "Are you disappearing, too?" she asked me.

"I just need to not look like myself," I said.

"This is Cynthia," Joey said in a belated introduction. "She's worked in makeup and theater for years."

"And what are we doing for you today?" Cynthia's voice sounded airy and light . . . exactly like I figured it would. "Are you on the run?"

"No. I'm walking into a hornets' nest." Joey frowned as I continued. I hadn't given him the full details of my predicament when I called him last night. "I'm investigating a murder and might be working in the same office as the killer. I need to not be recognizable as the handsome PI who's had his picture in the paper." Cynthia furrowed her brows and scrutinized my face. "I'm sure you've never worked with such a pristine canvas before, but I trust your talents."

She chuckled. "How badly do you need to fool these people?"

"If they see my photo in the article," I said, "I want them to think the guy in the office is someone else."

"I can definitely get you there," Cynthia said. "Sit at the makeup table." I grabbed the vacant seat and waited. She brought a platinum blond wig and held it up to my head. "It's much lighter than your natural color and a few inches longer." She held my chin and turned my head with a strength belying her slight frame. "If we change your eyes, too, it'll fool a lot of people."

A few minutes later, I looked at myself in the mirror. Now, instead of my short dark brown hair, I sported a blond mop which touched the collar of my Polo shirt. Thanks to colored contacts, my eyes went from green to a muted blue.

"Let me take a picture for Gloria," Joey said as he reached for his phone.

"I'll strangle you with a lacy sweater," I said. "There are enough of them around."

He snapped the photo anyway, of course. "She'll be thrilled to know her boyfriend aced his audition for the Aerosmith cover band."

I gestured in the direction of the water. "Why don't you walk this way into the harbor?"

"You two are incorrigible," Cynthia said, trying and failing to suppress a giggle. She stared at me in the mirror. "I'm not sure it's enough." She flittered away to a different area of the room and returned a moment later. "One more feature." Cynthia removed a small dot from a pad and stuck it onto my face. "There. Now, you have a mole. You can put a new one on every morning. Just remember where it is." I took note of it--below my left eye directly in line with my nostril. Easy enough. She handed me what looked like a small sheet of stickers. It held eleven replacement moles. "Better. We've changed three different factors. It should fool most people."

I turned my head to evaluate my new appearance from all angles. "Let's hope the killer is among them."

"If not, we could play a power ballad at your funeral," Joey suggested. "A good choice might be 'Cryin'.'"

"Maybe you'll choke on a bagel," I said.

———

I approached the headquarters of Research and Technology Partners. It sat a short distance off Route 15 in Frederick, and my commute time was about an hour. I hoped I wouldn't need to make too many trips here. The building stood four stories tall. I did a circuit of it in the parking lot. It had the length and depth of most supermarkets. Finding a spot was easy, and I left the S4 under a light stanchion.

Inside, I told the receptionist I came to see Mister Knott. She checked something on her computer, apparently found everything to be in order, and made a phone call. A couple minutes later, a man in a decent suit stepped off the elevator. He stood about my height but looked slender enough to cross into gaunt territory. Silver hair and wrinkles on his face put him somewhere in his sixties. "You must be the new DBA." He extended a hand. "Devon Knott."

"Trent Gustaffson." Knott looked confused for an instant, but he recovered quickly and nodded. I couldn't use my real name. It would render my appearance change pointless. A couple years ago, Joey made me a patchwork identity whenever I might need one. I'd used it a few times to pose as a reporter. It wouldn't stand up to the scrutiny of a proper hiring process—I didn't want to pay him his rate—but considering Knott was basically sweeping me in, it would hold up.

We walked into the elevator, where Knott gave me a brief rundown of what happened on each level, including the basement. "This was a meat processing plant years ago. There's still a freezer down there. We use it as the old computer graveyard."

Another point for Irish's theory. "You always lead off with totally random facts?" I asked.

The CEO grinned but didn't answer. Once the elevator began its rise to the fourth floor, Knott said, "New name and looks. Smart."

"Thanks. I hope I only need to fool people for a few days."

The doors opened, and we moved down the hall. Large offices lined the walls. These must be the executive suites. Sure enough, Knott greeted his secretary and walked into the largest one. He shut the door after I entered. Despite being the biggest office, the room was probably only fifteen feet square. Knott's huge desk took up a good portion of the rear half. I dropped into a guest chair. "I've worked out all the hiring details," he said. "Remember, you technically work for the CFO. You'll meet her soon. She wasn't pleased to be frozen out of the decision, but she'll get over it. Try to be nice to her."

"I will," I said.

"For stuff related to the case, you'll obviously want to keep everything on the down-low." I fought the urge to roll my eyes. What else would I do? Trumpet my intentions at an office where the killer might occupy the next cubicle? "Whatever you find, you bring directly to me. No one else."

"If I uncover the mother lode, I'm duty bound to go to the police, too."

"Fine, fine." Knott waved a bony hand. "I just want to be sure I'm in the loop where the company is concerned. To think we have a murderer here in the building . . ." He shook his head. "It makes my blood run cold."

"Will I have access to Jason's files?" I asked.

"Yes. Normally, a PC gets reimaged once someone leaves. Considering how Jason died, though, I ordered IT to leave it connected in an unused cubicle. They've also taken a backup of it."

"If someone in their shop is involved, though, you can't trust the work."

"I can only do what I can do." Knott shrugged. "I trust the guy who did it. He liked Jason."

The assurance would need to be good enough. If the fellow did everything right, I could access the old computer over the network. "All right," I said. "What's next?"

"You need to meet Pat. She's your boss. Then, we'll go to HR and get your accounts and stuff squared away. There's a staff meeting just before lunch. We'll introduce you."

"I'll try to be pleasant while scrutinizing my new coworkers to see which one is a killer."

Knott chuckled. "You been to a lot of staff meetings before?"

"No. Let's just say I prefer working for myself."

"You might be in for a few surprises, then," he said.

I'd already presumed as much.

———

Once we finished, Knott went with me to the third floor—this time, we took the stairs—to meet my boss and teammates. Patricia Ritter, the CFO, sat at her desk, and another man stood behind her as they chatted. "Pat's husband," Knott said. "Good guy. He comes in every so often to drop off flowers or something for his wife." Sure enough, a bouquet of roses sat in a mediocre vase on the CFO's small conference table.

"What's he do?" I asked.

"He's something of a finance whiz." Pat's husband rubbed her shoulders. As someone who hated having anyone stand behind me while I worked, I wondered how she tolerated it.

The husband left, shaking hands with Knott and offering me a polite nod as he headed for the elevator. "Is this my new DBA?" Pat asked, eyeing me up and down. Joey's barb about the Aerosmith cover band found the mark. I looked more like a guy belting out "Sweet Emotion" in a beer-soaked bar than a professional IT worker who could administer the hell out of some databases. Pat's gaze told me she probably thought the same. I hoped she wouldn't ask me to sing.

"In the flesh," I said as I walked into her office. I pegged it as a couple feet smaller on each side than Knott's. Rank had its privileges, one of which was square footage. She kept her hands on her keyboard, so I kept mine at my sides.

"You have a lot of experience?"

"Enough."

Pat grunted. Knott poked his head in and said, "I'm going back upstairs. Pat, you'll still need to take him to HR."

"I know how the hiring process works, Devon," she said. Knott left, and Pat rolled her eyes. "I'm sure he means well. It's just weird for my boss to tell me he hired someone who reports to me."

"I'm not trying to get in the middle of a turf war," I said.

"Devon must have recommended you for a reason." She narrowed her eyes. "Have you worked with him before?"

"I think someone who worked with both Jason and me before passed my name on."

Her expression softened. "Fair enough. Let's get you down

to HR for the paperwork and badge." Pat stood, showing herself to be a short and squat woman. She was definitely younger than Knott, probably by a decade or more. My new boss and I rode the elevator down to the second floor. The offices of human resources occupied a good chunk of the floor space. I completed all the paperwork. Trent Gustaffson might get revealed as a phony, but I hoped to be out of here with a killer in jail before it happened. Joey did the basics, so I hoped it would be enough to keep me here until I solved the case.

Next, I got my badge. "It's also a smart card," Pat said after a bored employee snapped my picture. "You'll use it to access certain areas of the building, and it serves as the login token for your computer."

"I understand," I said. The onboarding process required me to provide a fingerprint which went into making the digital certificate embedded on my new ID card. I'd also need to provide a PIN when I logged in or accessed certain areas of the building. Two-factor authentication. For whatever faults the company may have, RTP got this part right.

"By now, your accounts should be ready," Pat said as we walked back toward the elevator. We stepped off on the third floor and stopped in the cubicles outside her office. "Here you go." Fabric walls enclosed the small space. A laptop, keyboard, mouse, and monitor sat in the middle partition of the U-shaped desk. A chair which promised more utility than comfort waited for me to sit. "You know where my office is. Check everything out. The calendar invite for the staff meeting should be in your email."

"Thanks," I said as Pat walked away. Logging in with the smart card proved simple. The basic Windows wallpaper—enhanced only by the company logo and a build version number—stared back at me. My email held the promised meeting announcement plus instructions on how to use my DBA privileges.

Nosing around seemed like a good start. The company required me to launch the application via the "Run as different user" option and enter my PIN again. I wasn't a different user, but even basic account control measures stopped a theoretical rapscallion who swiped my card but didn't know the PIN. I checked out my access. The schema broke the databases down at a high level. *Financial-External. Audit-External. IT-Internal.* A few clicks and some basic SQL commands told me I possessed unfettered access to all three. It was more than I expected. Maybe Knott made sure I could see everything. Regardless, I hoped it would make my job easier.

I looked at my watch. An hour remained until I would be paraded in front of my new—and very temporary—coworkers. I used the time to exploit my access and poke around. Nothing jumped out at me. I needed an epiphany before my identity raised red flags . . . or before someone tried to kill me.

CHAPTER 7

A LARGE CONFERENCE room on the second floor housed the meeting. From what little I knew of the company, the attendees consisted of Knott's executive team and everyone who worked for Pat. Another crew I'd never seen walked in scant minutes before the witching hour. My phone vibrated at a text from T.J. *How's it going, boss? Hope they didn't kill you yet.*

I dashed off a quick reply. *Not yet, but the day is still young. This staff meeting might just do me in.* Knott called everything to order. He opened the shindig with a brief recap of projects the company worked on over the past two weeks. Despite his best efforts to lull me to sleep, I managed to stay awake. A couple minutes later, he changed gears. "We have a new DBA joining us as of today. He'll be working on Pat's team replacing ..." Knott trailed off but recovered. "Anyway, he has some good experience, and I'm glad we were able to get him. Trent."

I stood and offered a polite wave around the room. "Hi, everyone. I'm Trent Gustaffson. I'm still learning everything here, but I hope to be up to speed soon." A couple of the guys who strode in an instant before the bell crossed their arms as they stared at me. It made me wonder if they disliked newcomers, or they'd played a part in the murder of my predecessor. Or both. No one glared at me with open hostility, but I also didn't get the warm and fuzzies from anybody.

Once everyone murmured their lukewarm greetings, I slipped my phone from my pants to the pocket of my shirt. The top—including the camera—protruded. Below the table, I opened an app on my watch. It would enable me to take pictures without touching my phone. I shifted in the seat, turning a little each direction and snapping about a dozen photos in all.

Once Knott wrapped up his overview of the company, Pat talked about the value her DBA team brought, especially on external audits. She didn't mention me or Jason. Next, a man named Louie Eckert talked way too long—which is to say more than ten seconds—about the company's mergers and acquisitions branch. Knott leaned forward during the segment, while Pat sat with her arms crossed. It struck me as odd for the CFO not to care about something right in her professional wheelhouse. For his part, Eckert didn't look like a numbers guy. He was pretty short, but even past his shirt and sweater, I could tell he knew his way around the gym. I made sure to get his picture, too. The other men who walked in under the wire fist bumped him when he finished. Maybe they all studied accounting while maxing out their bench presses. *Spot me, bro. What's the formula for ROI, bro?*

The gathering wrapped up by going around the table and giving everyone a chance to say what they'd worked on. Most declined the chance to speak. I joined them . . . in part because I hadn't done anything of note yet, and in part because two hours in the workforce taught me the uselessness of meetings.

I took the stairs back to the third floor. Most people waited for the elevator. As I walked, I texted T.J. *I'm going to send you some pictures shortly. Run them through the usual channels and tell me what you get.* At my cubicle, I plopped onto the mediocre chair. T.J. sent a reply.

Sure thing, boss. Glad you're not dead yet.

I sent a quick response. *Same here, but one of these guys might feel differently.* The whole mergers and acquisitions team may have, in fact. At least it gave me something to look for in the databases and when combing through Jason's old files.

———

I scrolled through the pictures I took at the staff meeting, trying to find the best ones to send to T.J. Before I could select any, someone knocked on the opening to my cube. A short, thin man with glasses too large for his face stood there, and he showed an awkward smile. "Hi. You must be the new guy. Jason's replacement."

"I hear I have big shoes to fill."

"Yeah." He made a point of looking at my guest chair to the right of the desk. I gestured toward it, and he sat. "I'm Brent. My spot's two doors down from yours."

"Nice to meet you. I'm Trent." We shook hands.

"Rhyming names," he said, and the awkward smile became a little less so. "You're kind of lucky, I guess. You started on password change day."

"It's the same for everyone?"

"Yeah. Every two months, we all have to make a new one."

I'd never heard of the policy hitting everyone the same day before, but I doubted Brent knocked on my wall to discuss corporate *diktat.* "How long have you been here?" I asked.

"Three years and two months."

"And twelve days and two hours?" Brent frowned, so I

changed gears. "You know, I haven't heard much about the guy I'm replacing. Everyone seems pretty tight-lipped about him. Did he make a run for the border with a bunch of client money or something?"

"He died."

"Oh." I tried to act surprised and hoped it worked. My high school drama teacher told me I had no future in the theater. I took it as a compliment at the time. "Now, I get it. Maybe it's why the guys from the other team gave me the side-eye a little while ago."

"Mergers and acquisitions?" he said, and I nodded. "They're all right. I know they look like meatheads, but I wouldn't worry about them." Brent leaned forward and lowered his voice. "It's Pat and Knott I'm not so sure about."

I paused so as to not pounce on his comment. "Why?"

"They've both been here a long time. Way more than me. Knott hired Pat years ago, and she's basically followed him up the chain ever since. I don't know what Jason was working on. He and I were on the same team, but we dealt with different clients most of the time, and he was pretty hush-hush."

"You think it might've gotten him killed?"

Brent sat back upright again. "Who said he got killed?"

Shit, I chided myself. I wasn't supposed to know anything about this. "I guess I inferred it from our conversation . . . plus how no one has talked about the guy."

"I don't know." Brent spread his hands. "All they told us is he died. I don't like to read the news, but I looked for any stories about someone being murdered. Couldn't find any to match Jason."

"You seem a little suspicious," I said, "and you clearly don't trust your boss or the CEO. Why are you still here?"

"Pay's good," Brent said. "I looked for a job about a year ago doing the same thing. I woulda been driving farther and making about seven grand less. I have a good amount of work experience but not a college degree. Lots of companies hold it against me."

My new colleague didn't trust his bosses and felt trapped at the company he—on some level—suspected of murdering a coworker. I needed an ally in the workforce, but keeping Brent on my side required walking a fine line. I couldn't know too much, be overly suspicious, or ask a ton of probing questions. Basically, I needed to lose myself in the role of the handsome overqualified new employee. My high school drama teacher be damned. "Thanks for stopping by," I said. "I definitely have a lot to take in and learn. Do you mind if I ask you some questions along the way?"

"Not at all," Brent said. "We're all on the same team."

Not all of us, and I still needed to find the rogue.

———

Due to Brent's admitted suspicions—which I couldn't rule out —I found good pictures of Patricia Ritter and Devon Knott on the company website. I generally believed institutions rotted from the top down, so including the two executives fit my own worldview, too. Once I added them to the batch I took at the town hall meeting, I sent them all to T.J. along with some instructions. *I need you to run these through the facial rec program I showed you. Let me know if you get any hits.*

She'd only used the system a couple times, so it might take here a while to get back to me. I settled in to do some actual work and frowned at the thought. I'd gotten used to being my own boss, and even this temporary role chafed at me. Despite the real reason I was here, I couldn't simply kick my feet up and loaf around all day. I needed to appear to be a legitimate employee, and the unfortunate side effect of this meant doing the work.

My DBA account provided a high level of access, so I used it to keep poking around. Trying to do it without raising an alarm limited my curiosity. I needed to know what kind of monitoring the company used, but I couldn't ask without drawing suspicion. Maybe smart surfing would tell me. I browsed the network file share for documentation and found what I wanted after a few minutes. All workstations were monitored in accordance with policy. Network access control booted off potential rogue devices after five minutes without verification. Any machine out of update compliance got shunted to a separate segment in a similar amount of time. Firewalls and a proxy server watched and limited internet traffic. From what I knew of the corporate world, this struck me as standard.

My phone vibrated, and a text from T.J. popped up. *Got some results. Can you talk?* I told her I could, and she called a moment later. "You sound quiet," she said when I picked up. "Sure you're not dying?"

"Positive. What do you have?"

"Not a smoking gun, unfortunately. No killers work there . . . at least not according to their police reports. I got three hits on priors. The earliest is Patricia Ritter."

"Really?" I said. I stood enough to peer over the top of my cube wall. Pat sat in her office, staring at her monitor and typing away. "For what?"

"It's from a while ago," T.J. said. "Almost twenty years. She got popped for a DUI. I don't know why she didn't get it expunged. I guess your new employers don't care all that much."

"I guess not. What else?"

"Two guys each got picked up once for assault. Corey Young and Eric LaFave. You may not have names for all the faces yet, so they're two of the gym bros."

And they worked in mergers and acquisitions for their equally meatheaded boss. "Good to know. Thanks."

"I emailed everything to you, too," she said. "I don't know if you can check it there or not."

"Probably best I don't," I said. "I'll reach out again if I need anything."

"I'll be here hoping you don't get killed."

"It's only been a day. Not enough time for my charm to take hold." I ended the call and got back to work—such as it was. With no tasks assigned to me at the moment, I felt free to poke around. A property database told me the name of Jason's old PC, and I pinged it and found it online. My DBA account did not extend to local or domain administrative privileges, however, so I couldn't access it or map the hard drive. As long as RTP left it online, I would get those dominoes to fall.

A short while later, Pat walked to my cube. "I'm headed home. Did you need anything else?" She dragged a bag behind her, and I wondered if she would leave here and drive to the airport. "It's my laptop," she said, noticing my gaze. "You should take yours home, too."

"Are we supposed to work from home?" I asked.

"No." Pat scoffed. "I don't. I give this company all my time during the day. The evening is for me. I take the computer in case something comes up. What if there's a hurricane, and we can't make it to the office? That sort of thing."

I nodded. "All right. I'll take mine when I go. It should fit in my bookbag."

"Good. Tomorrow, I'm putting you to work. I hope you've managed to learn a bit about how we do things here."

I had plenty more to go in this area—namely who killed my predecessor. "I think things are off to a good start," I said as diplomatically as I could.

————

When I arrived home, Gloria reminded me we were due to have dinner with my parents. I sighed and resigned myself to it. Relations between us had been frosty for a few months—with the temperature plummeting after I got shot, prompting them to withdraw their support of my PI business. Recent *détente* thawed things a bit, and things like this routine sit-down meal were the result. If only it felt routine.

"You could let me drive your car," I said as we put our jackets on. "I need something to look forward to."

Gloria grinned and tossed me her keys. "I still think you're being a little rough on your folks. Try to enjoy a nice dinner with them."

"Are they paying?"

"As far as I know," she said.

"Then, my enjoyment just went up twelve percent," I said.

I slid behind the wheel of Gloria's Mercedes coupe. It only had two pedals, but the turbocharged V8 was a blast to drive even without a clutch. We weren't going very far, and city roads didn't give me much chance to get on the gas. Still, I used the paddles to downshift aggressively whenever I could, and zooming around a Prius as we neared Fells Point proved very satisfying. I found a spot not far from our destination at the Waterfront Hotel, and we walked inside.

For once, we were on time, though my parents already

stood near the hostess station. We all exchanged hugs and greetings. The Waterfront has long been one of my favorite places to eat. The interior was mostly brick, dark wood, and exposed beams. Somehow, the owners fit a great bar and restaurant into a wide rowhouse. By comparison, I felt lucky to keep my rooms in order. We sat on the second floor, our table overlooking the small ground-level stage which would thankfully be empty tonight.

A tall, slender waiter with the blackest hair I'd ever seen dropped off water for each of us. My mother eyed his mane, and I saw a hint of jealousy. She wouldn't admit it, but she'd long maintained her dark color with the aid of a bottle. This fellow probably bought his shade at the drug store, too. Maybe they would compare before we left. My parents both ordered Greek salads with breast meat. I opted for the fried chicken sandwich, and Gloria selected buffalo shrimp tacos.

"It's nice to see you both again," my father said.

"Likewise," Gloria answered while I sipped some water.

"Are we still enjoying our *détente*?"

"Are you still playing the part of a failed communist regime?" I asked.

"Grudgingly," my father said.

"Then, yes."

"How is work going for you, Coningsby?" my mother wanted to know.

I shrugged. "It ebbs and flows. I'm working on a case now in Frederick. Makes for some long drives, but I need to keep the lights on."

Neither of them took the bait, which was probably just as well. "Is your secretary working out?"

"She's great," I said.

We lapsed into silence for a few minutes. They then asked

about my health, and I insisted I was fine until the waiter returned with our meals. Following a respite for eating, my father wiped his mouth and sat his napkin down. "We've been thinking."

"I thought I smelled smoke," I said.

He rolled his eyes but otherwise ignored the joke. "I know you were upset about how our arrangement ended." I didn't point out his tremendous understatement. "We think we have something of a solution going forward."

I frowned. This was certainly unexpected. "I'm listening."

"I guess we kind of got used to you helping the kind of people who come through our foundation," he said. Despite my recent opinion of their judgment, my parents were great philanthropists who helped hundreds of people.

"There are times we wanted to refer someone to you," my mother added. "You probably could've helped."

My father bobbed his head in assent. "We'll need to figure out how to make it work. If we can, though, would you want us to refer some people to you? They wouldn't be able to pay you, so we'd pick up the tab . . . kind of like before."

"With the exception you're gatekeeping my potential clients," I pointed out. Both my parents frowned. While I didn't like them being the first stop on the train, this still represented a significant development. They'd washed their hands of funding my work after I got shot, citing the danger involved. Maybe our *détente* might pay off. "It's worth considering, though. I'd be open to it if you were."

Our server dropped off the check and cleared the plates. My father picked up the small leather folder, glanced at the amount, and inserted his credit card. "All right. Let's circle back once you finish what you're working on now."

"I think this is going to be good for all of us, Coningsby," my mother said.

I thought so, too, but I reserved judgment. They'd pulled the rug out from under me once before, and I wouldn't celebrate until we'd finalized something. I joined in my father's ice-water toast because the news represented the best thing I'd heard all day.

CHAPTER 8

THE NEXT MORNING, I woke up shortly after seven. Gloria barely stirred as I headed downstairs. Normally, her feet hit the floor once I put coffee on and start making breakfast. Today, these occurred a good two hours earlier than normal, and my girlfriend remained fast asleep. As the java brewed, I wished I were still lying beside her. I didn't have time for an elaborate breakfast, so I scrambled a few eggs, fried some sausage, and made a quick burrito I could eat in the car. I left extra portions of the proteins on the stove as I walked upstairs to get dressed.

Gloria again didn't move or wake up. I padded back to the first floor as quietly as I could, grabbed my burrito and a Yeti full of coffee, and headed to Frederick. At this hour, there was no way to get there which wouldn't leave me in traffic some-where, so I sucked it up and focused on the road. A white SUV behind me drew my attention. I first noticed it on Conway Street as I neared I-395, and it stayed a few car lengths back and one lane over once we were on the highway. If I changed lanes, the crossover made the same move, attempting to keep a professional distance away.

I lived on Riverside Avenue in Federal Hill. Trent

Gustaffson's address put him on Harvey Street near The Baltimore Museum of Industry. In some people's minds, this area blurred the lines between Federal Hill and Locust Point in yet another neighborhood pissing contest. Regardless, Trent lived farther from the highway, but anyone who plotted a route on a GPS would know he'd be coming the way I drove. There were dozens of little side streets and parking lots to sit and wait for me to go past . . . which meant someone knew which car Trent drove. At least they'd peg him for having good taste.

As I moved through lanes on the Baltimore Beltway, I noticed the tail was a large Ford model. Probably an Expedition. Its engine would be more powerful than the one in my S4, but my car would be quicker and more maneuverable. Moderate traffic negated those advantages, however, and no one following me made any aggressive moves. As we neared the I-70 interchange—the "triple bridges" as traffic reports called the sometimes confusing proliferation of entry and exit ramps— I darted from lane to lane to see if my tail would do the same. The driver kept the Ford steady and followed me onto I-70 headed toward Frederick.

Maybe I was being paranoid. Taking the place of a dead guy plus having T.J. joke about me getting killed all the time could've been wearing on me. Maybe this white Expedition simply happened to be leaving Baltimore around the same time and heading west. In any event, I stopped believing in coincidences shortly after beginning my illustrious PI career. The real test would come when I neared the RTP building.

I got off the highway and drove down the streets of Frederick. The white SUV exited two cars behind me. Getting to work would be a matter of a few turns. Pretty direct. I made it indirect, taking side roads I didn't need to traverse and taking a circuitous route in general. The Expedition stayed in my rearview all the time. If the driver knew where we were headed, he must have figured the jig was up, but he stayed the course. As I turned into the RTP lot and kept one hand on the pistol in my bag, the Ford kept going. I sat in the car a couple minutes after parking it, but the white vehicle didn't return.

A quick scan of my surroundings showed no one waiting for me. I got out of the car and headed to work.

———

The coffee at RTP was aggressively mediocre. Still, it was caffeine, and since I'd consumed my travel mug full on the interesting drive to work, I felt pretty desperate. Brent stopped by as I sipped my hot beverage, but he didn't stay and chat. Once I logged in and checked email, I saw a message from Pat. I'd been setup in the corporate ticketing system, and until she assigned me to any external projects, working the queue would be the best use of my time.

I sharply disagreed with her on the last point, but here, I needed to play the part of worker bee, keep my head down, and sniff out a killer without attracting ire or suspicion. Considering I'd already been followed from Baltimore after my first day on the job, I couldn't feel confident about keeping a low profile. The hope someone dispatched the guy in the Ford to tail Trent Gustaffson and not C.T. Ferguson would have to sustain me for now.

RTP used a program called ServiceCounter to manage their incidents, change requests, and other pointless minutiae they bundled under the umbrella term of tickets. Pat expected me to read service-level agreements about resolving—or at least attempting to—certain categories of issues within a predetermined length of time, but I couldn't be bothered. My commitment to keeping up appearances at the job went only so far, and going down a boring corporate policy rabbit hole was beyond the pale.

I resolved the first item in the queue within a few minutes. Someone wanted a few queries run and the results furnished via email. I marked the ticket as resolved and moved on. Before I could read the second one, my phone rang. Caller ID showed Rollins' name. Considering what he'd told me the last time we spoke, I picked up and kept my voice low. "The small crow squawks at midnight," I said.

"What?"

"You're the one in hiding. I figured we were doing some spy shit to make sure you're really you and I'm really me."

"Of course," Rollins said. "But the large raven beats its wings at dawn."

"Excellent. Do you bring news from the front?"

"I'm still in the wind. Not sure how it fits with your Cold War fantasy this morning, but I thought you'd like to know."

"No change?" I asked.

"Saw a couple guys surveilling my house," Rollins said. "They definitely know where I live."

"I'm still a little jealous."

"Maybe I'll invite you for a beer when this is all over. I got a couple cameras on the exterior and in the yard. Snagged a few good looks at these clowns."

"And?"

"I'm pretty sure they're Italian," he said. "You piss off any more mob bosses recently?"

After my conversation with Gabriella, I felt confident these were her men tailing Rollins. Hell, what if they followed me this morning? I figured someone at RTP got suspicious of a handsome and overqualified DBA starting so quickly, but it could have been Gabriella keeping tabs on me. "Maybe," I admitted. "Gabriella is looking into her father's death."

"Well, shit."

"Pretty much my thoughts, too. She's convinced someone killed him or was at least in the room with him. I mentioned I'd read the police report and agreed with the findings. Even something so minor made her suspicious."

"You think she's gonna have you followed, too?" Rollins said.

"It's a possibility," I said. "I don't think she trusts anybody on this one. Old friends included. The goon in the house thought he heard someone when I was there. Tony played it off, but he probably remained suspicious. We have to figure he basically owned the block. If anyone saw or heard anything, Gabriella will know about it."

"She living in the old man's house?"

"Far as I know."

Rollins fell silent for a few seconds. Then, he said, "Someone on the street could've had a camera. I doubt it would've gotten a good look at us as fast I was driving, but you never know. You might want to watch your six, too."

"Maybe you know a bodyguard I could call," I said.

"Very funny. Just be careful. I'm going to remain in my undisclosed location for now. Let me know if anything changes."

"I will." He hung up. The thought of Gabriella sending the Expedition after me this morning made me shudder. She'd been a friend for years. We'd practically grown up together. She was her father's daughter, however, and if coming after me meant getting what she wanted faster, I knew she would do it.

———

I couldn't access Jason Napier's old PC, so I went hunting for databases or tables he might've created. He'd worked here for years, so this provided a lot of material to comb through. On top of it all—and despite my speed at resolving issues—Pat barked periodic reminders about the service ticket queue. The afternoon cemented the fact I never wanted to work for anyone in the first place. My tenure at this blasted place couldn't end soon enough.

In the times my boss didn't bellow from her office, I combed through Jason's handiwork. In addition to databases, he'd written some scripts and simple programs. They were all saved to a common location. I focused on the programming side. It was easier to use comments—which wouldn't execute when the developer compiled the code—to make notes, provide versioning information, or maybe identify someone at work who might be a murderer.

Unfortunately, nothing Jason produced held any such information. As far as I could tell, he'd been a competent programmer, and his comments contained brief technical info and notes to himself about potential future versions. It left the databases to slog through, and finding nuggets in them would prove more challenging. A couple hours into my futility, Pat approached, dragging her ridiculous laptop bag behind her again. "Looks like you resolved quite a few tickets today."

I shrugged. "They were pretty easy."

She peered around the cubicle wall to see my screen, but I'd only left my email up. "All right. We should be getting you fully up to speed next week. I think you'll be able to handle it. Good night."

I didn't tell her I had no plans to be talking to her next week. Instead, I flashed a quick smile and said, "See you tomorrow."

The extra half-hour I remained at my desk proved no more fruitful than any others. I wrote a query looking for specific words like *kill*, *murder*, and the like, and ran it against a bunch of Jason's databases. No hits. If he felt suspicious about anyone at RTP, he either didn't leave an electronic record of it, or he stored them all on his computer. I couldn't access any of his files yet, but a plan to make it work tomorrow formed in my mind. I would need the unwitting assistance of the company's help desk, but this seemed a small hurdle to clear.

I packed my bag, adding the laptop at the end, and slung it over my shoulder. As usual, I eschewed the elevator and walked down to the first floor. The sun had already begun its descent into the western sky when I reached the parking lot.

It provided plenty of light to see the two goons standing at my car.

CHAPTER 9

MY TREK through the third floor to the steps revealed most people already left. At least three-quarters of the spots in the lot were empty. The pair of musclebound cretins eyed me as I approached. One stood a few inches taller than the other, and part of his height advantage stemmed from his absurd blond mohawk. I hoped he carried a razor in his pocket so I could take it and shave his head while he lay semi-conscious. The other, whose black hair was a much shorter and more reasonable basic cut, practiced his glower and snarl.

I stopped a few feet away. "Did I forget to valet my car this morning?"

"What?" the taller one said.

"Look, if you guys are in a union, I get it. It's like trying to pump your own gas in New Jersey. I don't want to tell you how to do your job, but you might want to have someone here when I pull in."

"We're not the fucking valet," the shorter one said.

"I hope not," I said. "People in the service industry shouldn't swear at their customers."

Blond Mohawk rolled his eyes. "Look, asshole, we're here to

deliver a message. We can either tell you what it is, or we can show you."

I shrugged and dropped my bookbag onto the grass behind me. "I'm not a very good listener."

"Have it your way." I took a defensive stance as the shorter of the two men advanced. A couple months ago, I'd developed a flinch which manifested itself in physical confrontations—another wonderful side effect of getting shot and nearly dying. In the time since, I'd worked on controlling it, but the slow-down in cases left me with few opportunities to practice. My foe drew his fist rearward for a haymaker.

I rocked onto my back foot, and his fist whizzed past my chin. He frowned. I smiled. He tried another punch, but I blocked it and hit him with a short jab in the solar plexus. He backed away sucking wind as the other one stepped up in his place. My new adversary's height meant he had longer arms and more reach than his shorter friend. He tried softening me up with a few jabs, all of which I turned aside. I also blocked the big hook, took a small step forward, and drove my elbow into his face.

He cursed and stumbled away from me. By now, the darker-haired goon had recovered, and he came at me with a barrage of punches. One skimmed off my arm and thudded into my chest rather than my midsection, but it still put me on my heels. He tried to capitalize, but I grabbed his arm and flipped him onto his back. Before I could put him out, the larger one grabbed me from behind, pinning my arms to my sides.

The guy on the ground shook his head to clear the cobwebs. I struggled to break out of the bear hug. Blond Mohawk pulled his left hand away and drilled me in the kidneys with a hard punch. It hurt like hell, but it also meant I could use my arm. Before he could hit me again, I slammed an elbow into his face.

It didn't put him down, but it stunned him enough to let me do it again. This time, his grip fell away. I planted a hard side kick in his gut, folding him in half as the air left his lungs in a loud groan. I then grabbed his stupid hair and drove my knee into his face. His nose cracked with an audible crunch, and he sagged to the sidewalk.

The shorter goon, back on his feet now, glanced at his fallen comrade. "Walk away now," I said. "You won't get the offer again."

"He was soft." The guy surged forward again, leading with his fists. None slipped past my parries this time, though. I grabbed his wrist and elbow with both my hands and twisted. The muscleman grunted in pain. While he struggled to free himself, I kicked him in the gut, then gave him a harder boot to his jaw. He dropped to the grass and lay still.

The taller one grunted and cradled his nose. I stood over him. "Who sent you?"

"Go to hell," he muttered.

"Have it your way." I dropped to a crouch quickly, punching him hard in the face and turning the lights out for real. With both of them down for the count, I rummaged through their pockets but found no wallets, money, or identification. The shorter one held a set of keys to a car. No fob with buttons, so it must have dated from at least fifteen years prior. I scanned the lot as a white SUV with flashing yellow lights approached. A security company I'd never heard of plastered its logo on the doors.

The portly fellow who stepped out wouldn't have fared well against either of my adversaries, let alone both. "The hell happened here?" he roared as he climbed from the Escape.

"They attacked me."

"You sure? They're the ones lying on the ground."

"You know many people who pick a fight with a pair of gym rats?" I asked. "They attacked me. I defended myself. Turns out I'm better than they are."

"What the hell am I supposed to do with these two?"

"You work in security." I picked up my bag and slung it back over my shoulder. "I'm sure you have a procedure to follow."

"You're gonna need to stick around," he said.

If he called the cops, I didn't want Trent Gustaffson to be involved. I fished my actual ID and badge from the bag and showed it to him. "I'd appreciate being left out of it," I said. "You can always tell the deputies the other guy split. Feel free to get my description wrong."

"What's in it for me?"

I tossed him the car keys. "Must be an older model somewhere. No wallets on them, so my guess is you'll find them in the car. Whatever money you see is yours."

He shrugged and gave me a nod. I climbed into my S4 and drove away.

———

I made it back home to Baltimore. The goons definitely didn't look Italian. Even if Gabriella's men followed Rollins, the two in Frederick didn't come from her roster. It meant someone at RTP didn't want me nosing around. Now, I needed to know if they merely wanted to intimidate new DBA Trent Gustaffson or if they saw through the facade to who I really was. I'd instructed T.J. to decline cheating partners and insurance cases with extreme prejudice. Anything requiring me to go under-cover might need to be added to the list.

Gloria's coupe occupied half the parking pad, so I slid the

S4 in beside it. I unlocked the back door and walked in via the kitchen. Gloria sat on the couch with her laptop open, a pair of earbuds in, and she was chatting with someone. I caught something about a certificate before she looked up in surprise but recovered to smile at me. "I need to go," she said. "See you later." Gloria tapped the screen and took the small headphones out of her ears.

"Talking to your other boyfriend?" I said as I dropped down beside her on the couch.

"I need something to do during the day when you're at work," she said with a wink.

"You have another fundraiser coming up?"

"Not anytime soon." She shook her head. "How did your second day at the office go?"

I wondered why she was being cagey about her Zoom call, but I didn't want to pursue it now. She would tell me in time if it were important. My joke about her other boyfriend notwithstanding, I trusted Gloria. "For about eight hours, it was mostly boring and uneventful. When I left, though, two enforcers stood near my car."

Gloria's hand found mine on the sofa, and she squeezed. "What happened?"

"I came home to my beautiful girlfriend," I said. "Those two are probably going to see a paramedic and a doctor."

"Does someone at the company know who you are?" she asked. "Who you really are, I mean."

"I've thought about it." I pulled the blond wig off carefully. My budding rock career sputtered and died as I removed it. "I guess it's possible. My picture has been in the paper, but it's something you'd need to search for." I shook the hairpiece. "This and the contacts definitely change my appearance, but my disguise isn't exactly foolproof."

"You can't hide handsome," Gloria said.

I grinned. "I told Joey the same thing. I don't think he understood."

"How could he?"

"Someone would need to be suspicious . . . probably in general but also of the newcomer. They'd also need to have seen my picture at some point. I don't think my cover is blown. My guess is someone is trying to keep Trent the capable new DBA from finding something he shouldn't."

"But you don't know," Gloria said. "You might've been found out, and if so, you're an hour away with no safety net."

"I'm carrying a gun in my bag," I said. "Thankfully, the company policy is to not search them. I can also take care of myself in a fight."

"I know." Gloria squeezed my hand again. "I worry about you, though. This is way more than you've done before."

"I'll be all right."

Gloria put her head on my shoulder and nestled into me. "I sure hope so. My other boyfriend isn't as good-looking as you."

"How could he be?" I said.

———

While I rummaged through my fridge and contemplated what to make for dinner, my cell phone rang. Amy Napier called. The upside to having clients in my new arrangement was getting paid. The downside was dealing with calls and requests for status updates. Before, when they didn't pay me, I could brush these off. Now, as much as I hated doing it, I felt compelled to tell someone how well I'd been spending their money.

"Devon tells me you've been working at RTP for two days," she said following the initial exchange of pleasantries.

I found it interesting she was on a first-name basis with the CEO. He struck me as the kind to prefer being called Mr. Knott unless drinking beers at a baseball game. "They even introduced me at an all-hands meeting."

"You have a line on anyone yet?"

"No," I said. "I've been combing through a lot of the work Jason did, and I haven't found any notes or nuggets he might have left behind. What I haven't been able to do is access his old laptop, but I think I'm going to have a workaround tomorrow."

"If I knew his password, I'd tell you," Amy said. "Jason was always fanatical about that kind of stuff. He didn't want to know any of my passwords, either, even to stuff we might share."

"It's a good practice. I'm pretty sure I'll have what I need tomorrow. Then, I need to hope he made a note somewhere."

"He definitely didn't say anything to me." She paused. "Has everyone at RTP been nice to you?"

"Yes, but they think I'm the new DBA. No one except Knott knows who I really am." I hoped at least this much was true.

"Jason mentioned feeling like he was being followed a few times. Has it happened to you?"

"You mean while he was driving?" I asked.

"Yes."

"Not yet, no." While I didn't know who tailed me on the way to work, I pondered whether to tell her about the welcoming committee waiting for me at my car. I didn't think she'd get scared and pull the plug. She came to me because she wanted justice. "A couple guys waited for me in the parking lot after work today, though."

"Oh, my gosh," she said, and her voice went up an octave. "What did they want?"

"They weren't exactly seeking donations for the local Four-H," I said. "Someone sent them to dissuade me. I think it means they wanted to keep Trent from getting too close to something. I can't prove it either way, but I think my cover is intact for now."

"Be careful, C.T. I knew there was some danger in this, but I'd hate for you to get mixed up with whoever killed Jason."

"If I'm going to figure out who did it, getting mixed up with them is inevitable. Don't worry about me. Those two won't be bothering anyone again for a while."

"All right. Please let me know when you have something."

"I will," I said, and we hung up. I didn't know what to make of Amy's chumminess with Devon Knott. He seemed like a good guy, and he certainly professed his fondness for Jason at every opportunity. He'd also be the perfect person to try and quash my investigation before it started. Maybe the access I planned to get tomorrow would enable me to poke around his computer, too.

CHAPTER 10

THE NEXT MORNING, no one followed me on my too-early run around Federal Hill Park or on my drive to Frederick. I arrived at RTP just before my appointed time and took the stairs to the third floor. No sooner did I log in and check my email than an instant message from Devon Knott popped up. He wanted me to stop into his office. I wondered if he and Amy chatted after my conversation with her last night.

I glanced at the bookbag I'd placed under the desk. It held my 9MM. If Knott were involved, he might have a welcoming committee waiting for me on the top level. He could use the right kind of guys to make it appear legit, and no one would question the popular CEO of a small company. Still, I couldn't walk up there with a gun in my waistband if it turned out he really just wanted to talk. People would see me coming and going, and I didn't wear the right kind of clothes to hide the tell-tale bulge of a pistol.

After a moment of deliberation, I left the gun where it was. A quick jaunt up the steps took me to the fourth floor. I stepped out of the stairwell and looked both ways along the corridor. No goons waited nearby. I walked the wrong way around the floor to get a peek at Knott's office. It was empty other than him. I kept going and checked the nearby cubes as I strolled past. They were either unoccupied or staffed by the people who were supposed to be there.

I knocked on the boss' door. He waved me in, and I closed up shop behind me. "Good morning, Trent," he said, keeping up appearances. "Anything to report?"

"Nothing yet." Another conundrum now hit me. If Knott didn't send the enforcers to menace me yesterday, who did? How would he react? I figured there was only one way to find out. "I'm getting the feeling someone doesn't want me nosing around, though."

His brows knitted. "What do you mean?"

I told him about the pair of goons waiting at my car—a vehicle registered in my real name for anyone who possessed the means to do the research. "Either someone was worried a new DBA would uncover something he shouldn't, or you're not the only one here who knows I'm working undercover."

"I haven't told anyone," he said, and he held my gaze the entire time.

"The only other person involved who knows is Amy, and I'm pretty sure she didn't put them onto me."

"Do you think your cover is blown?" Knott asked. "Should we try something else? Maybe you work from home for a while?"

"I don't want to draw any more attention to myself," I said. "For now, I should appear to be like any other employee. I'll keep watching my back."

"Is there anything you need?"

"Access to Jason's old computer. His local files in particular."

"I don't know what he kept here," Knott said. "It could be

confidential data. We often work under nondisclosure agreements, and I can't let information fall into the wrong hands."

I shrugged. "You seemed to know my reputation when you agreed to let me work here." Knott frowned and nodded. "It would be easier to get what I need with your support. If you won't provide it, though, I'll go around you. I'm not really here to administer a database, and I don't give a shit about the agreements you've signed with your clients. I'm trying to catch a killer, and I'll do what I have to."

Knott spread his hands. "Don't tell me about it, then. Do what you need to do, but leave the details out of our conversations."

I knew he did this for plausible deniability. If anything untoward happened as a result of my investigation, he could claim ignorance of my methods, brand me a rogue, and try to keep the company's reputation intact. In the end, I didn't care. I didn't really need Knott to help me, but I did need him not to oppose me. "I understand. Anything else?"

"I think we've covered it all," he said.

I left his office. No one lay in wait for me.

———

I worked on the next part of my plan to gain access to Jason's old files. My DBA powers did not extend to the operating system. I couldn't access anything under another user's profile or in a folder where I didn't have permissions. The local administrator account, however, could do all these things. For convenience, most enterprises used the same credentials on every PC. Local security policies prevented me from plugging in a flash drive, but they allowed my phone to both charge and appear as a data device.

My help desk ticket for a software installation sat in a queue waiting to be resolved. About an hour after I returned from my meeting with Devon Knott, Adam from IT emailed to ask if I would be at my desk in a few minutes. I said I would. I technically didn't need the app I requested, but whoever tried to resolve the problem would need to use a privileged account to do so. After telling Adam I was ready whenever he was, I sent a text to T.J. *I'm plugging my phone in. Be ready with the script.* She replied in the affirmative.

I covered the black USB cable tethering my phone to the back of the laptop with a magazine from the break room. A few minutes later, someone rapped on my felt-lined cubicle wall. A fellow about my age appeared at the opening. He stood shorter and heavier than me, and thick glasses dominated his face. "I'm Adam," he said as if it weren't obvious. "You ready for the install?"

"Sure." I figured I would feign ignorance for most of the process. "You need me to logoff?"

"Yes," he said with a tinge of impatience in his tone. I didn't envy him the job he did. Answering occasional computer questions from people I know felt like torture. I couldn't imagine it basically being my job. I signed off and moved aside so the technician could sit in my seat.

"I'm surprised you don't do this sort of thing remotely," I said.

Adam shrugged. "The boss likes us to get out and meet the users." His tone suggested he'd rather jump into a pool of battery acid, and I couldn't blame him. It was difficult for me to pretend to be a common user, so I opted not to talk much. Adam signed in with a local administrator username and password. My phone remained on my desk, so I used my watch to tell T.J. she was on the clock. She sent a thumbs-up emoji.

As Adam browsed a network file share, my watch screen showed another incoming message. This would be T.J. sending the script. It was designed to copy itself to the local drive and run in the background. It would run with the permissions of the current user, which was exactly what I needed. A tiny DOS box appeared and disappeared in the taskbar, the only indication the script ran. If Adam noticed it, he didn't say anything.

He double-clicked the executable for a code compiler I didn't really need. As it installed, he leaned back in my chair, which creaked under the greater strain. "You pretty new here?"

"My first week," I said.

"I don't think you need this program." He shrugged. "Not my job to tell you no, though. If your boss is cool with it, I don't care. I couldn't do your job, and I don't think you could do mine."

He was a thousand percent wrong on the second count, but I didn't need to debate the point with him. I knew his type from college—guys who were better with computers than other people, especially those of the opposite sex. They often ended up in some tech support role and grew frustrated when their lack of soft skills prevented the advancement they felt they deserved. "Good thing I'm a DBA, then," I said in a moment of diplomacy.

The compiler finished a moment later. Adam fired it up to make sure it ran, which it did, and he then logged off. "I'll mark your ticket closed. You'll get a survey over email." He stared at me but didn't ask me to fill it out favorably. Yep. A definite lack of people skills.

"Thanks." Adam left, and I logged back in. A small text file now sat in the Temp folder. In it were the local administrator name and password. I smiled and sent T.J. a text. *All good. Thanks for your help.*

She replied a moment later. *You got it, boss. Good luck.*

With these credentials, my luck took a turn for the better.

———

Of course, it quickly took a quirky turn for the worse. Pat needed all hands on deck to resolve some issue with an external client accessing data. It didn't strike me as a crisis, but she marched around and yelled like we were all on a ship which was about to disappear under the waves unless we stopped it. Brent didn't help much. I eventually sorted out the problem as a permissions issue thanks to a stored static password. The customer updated his credentials, didn't want to change the access method, and failed to thank me for my assistance.

In addition to not wanting Adam's job, I didn't want my own anymore.

Resolving this chewed up most of the afternoon. I mapped a folder to the hard drive on Jason's old computer to make sure I could. Copying his data might take a while, and the clock neared quitting time. I didn't want someone at RTP to pull the laptop offline, however. I logged in with the local admin account and copied all relevant files and folders to my hard drive. Using the privileged credential masked who actually moved the data. With an unknown number of people knowing the username and password, none of the actions were attributable.

It took an extra forty minutes for everything to finish, and I signed off with glee when the last file traversed the Ethernet cables. I packed up my stuff and headed to the S4. No one waited for me in the lot this time. I climbed in and headed home. Thanks to staying longer than normal, traffic slowed my progress. It took over an hour to make it down I-70, onto the Beltway, and into Baltimore.

I noticed the tail as I drove through the city.

There was enough traffic to blend into, and a smarter vehicle choice might have escaped my notice. Only one red SUV remained in my rearview mirror, however, and it mimicked my movements every time I changed lanes. This was getting old. I still didn't know who followed me. It could have been someone at RTP who killed Jason, or it might have been Gabriella obsessing over her father's death and anyone whose involvement she suspected.

I weaved in and out of traffic, using my smaller and nimbler vehicle to my advantage. The large SUV might have kept more ponies under the hood, but it couldn't change lanes as quickly as my S4. I blew through a signal on Light Street and pulled into a parking lot. The red SUV idled. I got out of the car with my phone in my hand. When the light changed, I zoomed in on the passenger compartment and snapped a few pictures. The driver didn't bother pulling over. He got away as quickly as the other cars on the road would allow.

The drive back to my house was fairly short. I did a circuit of the neighborhood and didn't see the red vehicle anywhere. Gloria's car sat on the parking pad, and I pulled in beside her. Before I got out, I looked through the photos I'd taken. The driver and the passenger both had dark hair and classic Italian complexions. I recognized them from Rizzo's.

They worked for Gabriella. What the hell did this mean?

CHAPTER 11

I MADE it back to Frederick the next morning without being followed. In case things escalated, I drove my second car. It was a fairly ugly late 'eighties Chevy Caprice. The chop shop owner I acquired it from dropped a Corvette V8 into it and fortified the body against small arms fire. I used it when the chances of getting shot at were higher than normal, and all indicators headed in this direction. I wondered if someone at RTP or Gabriella's goons would be the ones pulling the triggers.

While I needed to deal with Gabriella, my current case demanded attention. At my desk, I checked the network for Jason's old laptop. It didn't answer any ping requests. Either someone took it offline, or the company removed it entirely. So much for Knott telling me it would remain available. Good thing I copied the files I thought I would need last night. Now, I hoped I hadn't left anything important behind in my desire to get out of the office. I wouldn't get a second chance to find anything.

Unfortunately, the demands of my fake job intruded on doing my real one. Pat bellowed about the DBA ticket queue ballooning after we focused on one major issue yesterday. I worked a couple while poking around Jason's folders. My initial hunt didn't reveal any smoking guns. He struck me as a cautious fellow, and this made it likely he would bury incriminating files deep in a directory tree . . . probably under names designed not to draw attention.

Later in the morning with the queue under control and my boss working quietly in her office, I got back to the real task at hand. Jason organized his folders with great care. They were broken down by client name, ticket requests, and the nature of the database query he ran. On some level, I appreciated the commitment to detail, but it made my job tedious. I needed to check everything to make sure he didn't hide something vital in a random folder only he would know to check.

He didn't, and it took me a while to find anything potentially useful. In the internal folders broken down by query, I found some general financial information on RTP. It didn't seem to correspond with any official request for information. Maybe Jason conducted his own research after stumbling on some disturbing details. He probably didn't tell Amy, so I didn't see the point of asking her. I moved anything I wanted to send to T.J. into a separate directory. Lunchtime came and went as I pored over boring files. Nothing jumped out as super incriminating, but I identified a bunch to pass on and look at later.

Emailing them to myself or my secretary seemed a poor method. I nosed around in the corporate services and found a secure file transfer protocol site. I could use it to transmit the info I wanted to my server and tell T.J. how to access it. I opened the connection, attached what I wanted, and initiated the transfer.

Once the files were away, footsteps approached my cube. I didn't see anyone, so my hand slipped inside my bag and closed around the grip of my gun. A moment later, Brent strolled by, offered a polite nod, and kept going. I released a deep breath and my hold on the pistol.

———

A few minutes later, I walked outside the building and called T.J. "You're not dead yet," she said when she picked up.

"I haven't eaten lunch. I could still choke on a chicken bone."

"It'd be a crappy way to go."

"I found some files I might want to look at later," I said, focusing her away from my possible demise. "The company runs an SFTP server, so I sent them to myself. I'll tell you how to access them."

T.J. asked me to hold while she wrote down my instructions. I told her how to log in to my Linux server using an account I created for her, where to find the data, and how to transfer it to her own computer. "It's a good thing I'm young and smart," she said.

"Don't forget being cheap. Melinda paying half your salary might be your best attribute."

"And you wonder why I keep asking if you've been killed yet." I grinned as T.J. tapped on the keys. "All right, I'm in. I see the folder you were talking about." She paused long enough to move the files I'd sent there. "I'll check on my laptop now." After another short delay, she said, "I got them. Now what? You want me to look them over?"

"I'm not sure," I said. "I don't want you to get used to sleeping at work."

"That exciting?"

"I haven't gone over a lot of them in depth yet, but I'm not expecting anything riveting. A lot of it looks financial, which might be beyond either of us."

"You have an expert in mind?" T.J. asked.

I ran through old acquaintances and past cases in my head. Thankfully, I hadn't taken any which required a great knowledge of bookkeeping, mostly because I hated being bored. I recalled an accountant who helped me with one of my earlier cases. "Actually, I do. You'll need to look him up, but he's an accountant named Marvin Bernard. It's been almost three years now, but I'm sure he'll remember working with me before."

"OK, I'll find him. What if you're not as unforgettable as you think?"

"Then, I'll be wounded," I said.

"You realize this guy might want to charge us for his time and expertise, right?"

"Good thing we have a paying client, then. We can pass on the expense."

"You're getting pretty used to this whole business thing," she said.

"Yeah," I said. "Now, I just need to live long enough to enjoy it. I'll check in later and see what Marvin said."

"Good luck surviving the day," T.J. said.

I hoped I wouldn't need it.

———

Toward the end of the day, Brent approached my section of the rat maze again. "Hey," he said in lieu of knocking. "I think a couple of the mergers guys want to take you out for a happy hour."

"Are you their party planner?"

He frowned. "No."

"To whom do I RSVP in the negative, then?" I said.

"They can be kind of fun. Besides, they'll pay for the drinks. It's something they do for all the new people."

"Did they take you out?"

Brent's brows remained knitted. "No . . . . but it's been a couple years since I started. I don't think any of them were here at the time."

"Are you going today?" I asked.

"I can't make it," he said.

"So it's going to be me and a few gym bros? What if they invite me to a bench press competition?"

Brent shrugged. "You'd probably lose."

I didn't much like the idea of going. With Brent not joining us, the whole thing smelled like a setup. Still, this could be a chance to sit down and talk to people who might have been involved in Jason's murder. Maybe a few beers would loosen them up. "Fine. I'll go."

"Cool. I'm sure they'll come by when they're ready."

"Can't wait," I said with as much enthusiasm as I could muster. I returned to work, wondering if I could bring my bag with me. Taking it into the bar would be obvious. I'd packed a smaller 9MM I could more easily conceal than my preferred .45. So long as no one stared at my butt, putting it in my waistband would work. My sweater and jacket would cover it. I made a mental note to look for a secret James Bond holster for occasions like these.

A few minutes later, Louie and his two meathead subordinates appeared at my cube door. "Brent tell you about happy hour?"

"Yep."

He put on a grin I spotted as fake right away. "Just a little something we do for the new folks we work with. We're not on the same team directly, but I think you'll find your group interfaces with ours a lot."

"Sounds fascinating," I said and hoped I injected it with enough sincerity.

"Come on." Louie jerked his head toward the elevators. "You can ride with us. The place we're going is pretty close. We'll drop you back here when we're done drinking."

I rode the elevator down with them, expecting an ambush the whole time. None materialized. After dropping my bag in my car, I climbed into Louie's black BMW X5 SUV. The interior gleamed like he'd recently gotten it detailed. On the drive through Frederick, he introduced me to the two guys I saw at the staff meeting. Corey Young rode up front with the boss. I could tell he was tall and lean even when seated, though the slope of his shoulders suggested he went to the gym on the regular. Eric LaFave occupied the back seats with me, and he fit the classic goon physique so well I wondered if he'd been sent over from central casting. I shifted in my seat to better hide my back from his view.

About ten minutes after we left RTP, we pulled into the lot of a bar with the ominous name Dead Eddie's. It looked rundown on the outside. The exterior screamed for a fresh coat of paint, and whoever degreased the windows would indeed be an unfortunate soul. Louie parked near the back door, and we walked around to the main entrance. It reminded me of a dozen neighborhood taverns on the inside. Scuffs and small chips pockmarked the wooden floor, but the rest of the interior remained in better shape than the exterior. The bar itself must have been the newest feature in the place. It dominated the right side in the back half of the floor space, and most stools were occupied.

Louie found us a table. A waitress dropped off four menus and a beer list. The lager selection redeemed the place a little. A couple guys shot pool when they weren't standing around watching a sports show playing on a nearby big-screen TV. It reminded me of playing in the dorm in college. I'd never been great, but I got about eighty percent better when I realized I didn't need to hit the cue ball as hard as possible all the time.

We ordered a round of drinks, and Louie took it upon himself to make a selection of appetizers for the table. A few minutes later, our brews came out along with plates of mozzarella sticks, onion rings, and jalapeño poppers. "The four main food groups," I said.

"Good stuff, right?" Louie said, raising his voice a little to talk over the din. "Look, me and the guys want to welcome you to the company. We don't see a lot of turnover, so we don't get to do this too often." For their parts, Young and LaFave nodded as their boss spoke. "It was a shame what happened to Jason, but I think you're off to a good start." He raised his mug. "Keep it up, and maybe you can work with the big boys at some point."

I clinked my stein against his. "I'm not really sure how mergers and acquisitions fits in with the company. It doesn't seem to go along with the other avenues of business."

"Started a couple years ago. Some of the companies we partner with, especially on the tech end, are barely staying afloat. We acquired one, kept a few people, and sold off the rest. I guess Knott liked doing it, so he added the branch."

"Why not just be smarter in picking clients?" I asked.

Louie shrugged. "Above my pay grade."

The other two glanced at the back door. Corey picked up his phone and keyed with his thumbs. They shared a look. Louie didn't give any indication he saw it, but I figured he did. They were up to something. I slipped my cell out, opened a

Bluetooth hacking app, and set it loose. Corey's phone—cleverly named *Corey's Phone* as it turned out—popped up. I initiated the pairing, let the app do its work, and broke into his device in a manner of seconds.

He exchanged texts with someone named Bryce. The gist of the conversation was Bryce and a couple friends would be ready outside the back door. Corey and his crew simply needed to get me to leave via the rear. Despite the strong aroma of grease in the air, I knew I'd smelled an ambush. It had been a while since I tangled with three guys . . . probably several months before I got shot. I needed an equalizer.

"I'm going to the men's can," I said as I stood.

"I'll order another round," Louie offered.

I finished my first. Leaving my beer out for them to add something to struck me as a poor way to walk into an attack. I could always not drink the second. On the way to the restrooms, I walked by the pool table. Using my gun against three guys trying to beat me up would be a last resort. Even with this limitation, I could even the odds in other ways. Both players' eyes were on the TV, and my tablemates paid me no mind. I reached down and plucked the 12 ball out of the return and headed into the lavatory. Once inside, I walked into a stall and shut the door.

I took off my tennis shoes and slipped both my black socks off. They were long dress models which went up over my calves. I'd thought they were a little much with the Dockers, but I was glad I decided to wear them this morning. I put one inside the other, dropped the hefty ball with the blue stripe inside, and tied the top with a strong double knot. Now, I carried a long and very powerful sap in my pocket. After slipping my shoes back on, I returned to the table.

Our second round came out a moment later. I sipped mine

but didn't drink much of it. Bryce texted Corey and said they were in position. After getting the message, Corey said, "Don't we need to finish prepping the White acquisition?"

"You're right," Louie said, setting his mug down in mock haste. "Shit. I forgot all about it." He took out his wallet and handed me a company credit card. "Can you settle up with the waitress? We're gonna head to the car. Meet you out there."

"Uh-huh," I said. I paid the tab, left a generous tip, and slipped my sap into my jacket pocket. I walked into the men's room again. It sat just past the back door. I stood on tiptoes to look out the window. A large and lifted pickup shone its headlights on the area, and three large men stood nearby. I remembered what I said to T.J. about entering the lion's den sometimes, and I wished I wasn't always so damned smart.

With my hands in my jacket pockets, I walked out the rear door.

CHAPTER 12

THREE MEN of imposing stature stood near the front of the truck. Its massive headlights bathed the area, lifting the intruding dusk. I noticed Louie's SUV leaving the lot, removing any tiny shred of doubt this was all a planned ambush. I didn't know if they set it for Trent or for me, and I wouldn't have time to think about it until later. The pool ball felt heavy in my hand as I stopped a few paces from the trio of would-be assailants. They were all at least my height and much wider and broader. The bearded one with a black bandana over his stringy hair took a step forward. "You Bryce?" I said.

He frowned. "How do you know my name?"

I shrugged. "Doesn't matter." I bobbed my head at each of the other two in turn. "Last chance to beat it."

"We got you outnumbered," the one on my right said. He was also a member of the bandanna club, but his was purple. The third fellow wore nothing on his head.

"For the moment." They all glanced at one another. I projected calm despite hearing my pulse in my ears. "Guys, we all know why we're here. Leave now if you want your evening to go well. When we get down to business, I won't be so generous."

Bryce made a show of laughing. I turned enough to present my profile to him. My hand—still in my pocket—moved to grip the end of my makeshift sap. The mirth ended as Bryce's leg tensed. When he drew his arm back, I pulled out my weapon, turned my hips, and swung it directly at his head. It landed home with a loud crack. Bryce dropped like he'd been shot, and if I hadn't seen what happened, the sound alone would make me think he had.

"Jesus Christ!" the one to my right yelled. He stood about half a step closer than the other goon, so I moved in his direction. The guy possessed enough sense to raise his hands at my approach, but I swung the 12 ball and blasted him right in the midsection. At least one rib cracked, and he stumbled backward, falling onto his ample butt as he held his stomach.

The third guy had plenty of time to get his wits about him. As I faced him and readied another swing, he grabbed the end of my sap, twisted it from my grip, and threw it into a bunch of trees at the back of the lot. No matter. It did its job. Bryce was down for the count, and the second guy would be limited if he got back to his feet. My new opponent threw a wild punch, which I blocked. He launched another. I moved closer as I turned it aside and elbowed him in the side of the head. It didn't put him down, but it stunned him long enough for me to give him a sharp kick in the family jewels. With him folded in half, another hard elbow to the noggin put him on the asphalt.

I stalked toward the one who remained conscious. He clutched his midsection and struggled back to his feet. "Still have me outnumbered?" I said.

My foe put up a hand. "Hey, man. We were just trying to scare you. It was nothing personal."

I grabbed his hand and twisted it hard enough to snap his wrist. The man howled in pain. "I took it personally." A kick to his injured ribs bent him over, and I drove my knee into his face. All three of them lay behind the building. No car or foot traffic came by, and unless someone exited via the rear door anytime soon, they would all go unnoticed. The only thing back here was a dumpster, and if I'd felt more industrious, I would have tossed all three of them into it. Instead, I wanted to visit my coworkers and tell them what a grand time I had at Dead Eddie's.

I verified Bryce was still alive, searched his pockets, took the cash from his wallet, and snagged the keys to his truck. His unconscious form lay in the path. While squashing him with his own truck felt tempting, I wasn't a killer. I dragged him out of the way, climbed into the raised pickup, and fired up the engine.

———

I've never cared for trucks. I don't like riding in them, and the more obnoxious ones raise my ire as someone who drives a normal car. In Bryce's absurd pickup, I felt like I was riding way too high. The engine rumbled louder than it should have, probably thanks to an aftermarket exhaust. It definitely pulled the truck forward with a great deal of haste. In this way, driving it felt like being behind the wheel of Rich's Camaro with its powerful V8.

I made it back to RTP quickly enough. As it was well past quitting time, the lot sat mostly empty. I made a sharp right and approached the wall separating this property from the next. It was stone and about four feet high. Thanks to Bryce raising the suspension to absurd levels, the mirrors sat higher than the top of the barrier. I smiled. It took a little finagling thanks to the truck's size, but I finally got it in position directly next to the partition. I drove down the length of it, scraping the paint along the way. When I finished, I threw it into reverse and backed into the corner of the wall hard enough to damage the bumper.

Louie's nice BMW SUV sat by itself under a pole light. I performed the same maneuver as I did along the stones, though this one proved much easier to line up. Bryce's truck scraped along both sides of the X5. When I'd finished causing thousands of dollars in damage, I upped the bill. I pulled ahead of the Bimmer, threw the truck into reverse, and backed into it with my foot on the floor. The backup camera gave me a nice shot of the rear bumper blasting the black hood and folding it like an accordion.

When I'd finished, I did the same thing on the driver's and passenger's sides. Before going back into the building, I checked my disguise in the mirror. Everything looked in order. I climbed out of the truck while its mangled rear bumper still sat amid the marred metal of Louie's passenger doors. As usual, I eschewed the elevator and took the stairs to the third floor. It took a moment to find Louie's office, but the stunned expression on his face when I strode through the door made it all worthwhile. "I … uh … I …"

"Oh, fuck off," I said. "Call Corey in here now."

Louie hollered for his employee. He approached a few seconds later, and his jaw dropped when he saw me. After hesitating a moment, he kept walking. Once he'd crossed into the office, I punched him in the groin. Before he could bend in half, I grabbed him around the jaw and slammed his head into the nearest wall. "Don't pass out on me, you asshole."

"Leave him alone!" Louie yelled.

I ignored him. "Listen to me. I might be the new guy, I

might just be a DBA . . . whatever. I can take care of myself in a fight. You can ask your friend Bryce when he regains consciousness. *If* he regains consciousness. Try something like this again, and I'll make sure you're lying beside him in the morgue. We clear?"

"Yeah . . . yeah," Corey stammered.

I let go of his face and shoved him through the doorway. "Now, get out of here while your boss and I talk." I fired Bryce's keys at Corey as hard as I could, and they struck him flush in the face. He recoiled and rubbed his cheek. "Go back to the bar and give those to your friend. You might want to call an ambulance on your way."

"I should call security," Louie said.

"Save it for a tow truck," I said. "I had to drive Bryce's pickup back. Not very experienced with such a large rig. I tried to park near you, but I might have hit your car once or twice . . . or six times."

"You son of a bitch." Louie stood.

I got right in his face and matched his glare. "What are you gonna do? I took out the three guys you and your buddy set on me. How do you like your odds one-on-one?"

"You seem awfully capable for a DBA," he said.

"And how many finance guys spend as much time in the gym as you?" I countered. "Let's not pigeonhole each other. I've had some training, and I'm not wired to back down. You want a doormat, buy one at Wal-Mart."

Louie maintained his glower for all the good it did him. "This isn't over, Trent."

"It'd better be." I stomped from his office and returned to my cube. Louie called me Trent. If he knew my real name, he probably would've blurted it out in the heat of the moment. Corey was a cog in the mergers machine. If he knew, he would've learned it from his boss. Bryce and his two buddies were hired muscle. I slipped my bag over my shoulders. My cover probably wasn't blown, but now I'd definitely landed on Louie's radar, and I didn't yet know what this meant.

————

I left the RTP parking lot. My hands clenched and unclenched on the Caprice's steering wheel. I tried to console myself with the fact my cover probably remained intact, but then I went down the rabbit hole of trying to calculate the odds. It only served to raise my anxiety. Some people needed to know about the mergers team siccing three guys on me. I started with T.J. "You almost got your wish about my untimely demise," I said when she picked up.

"What happened?" Her voice carried a serious tone at the news.

"A few of my new coworkers took me to a bar for happy hour. While we were there, they arranged an ambush in the parking lot."

"Sounds like you sniffed it out."

"With a little help from Bluetooth," I said. "I ended up driving a big pickup back to work and got to run into some asshole's car in the parking lot." T.J. didn't say anything. "Long story. Maybe you had to be there."

"Do you think they know who you really are?" T.J. asked.

"I can't say for sure." My hands flexed on the wheel again. "My best guess is probably not. One of the guys called me Trent after the fact in the office. If he knew who I was, I think he would've blurted it in the moment."

"I hope you'll be careful out there. It's weird having you so far away."

"It's a little odd for me, too."

"I found that accountant you told me about," said T.J. "He remembered you. I sent everything to him. You can call him tomorrow afternoon."

"Pretty quick turnaround," I said. "Thanks." We ended our call, and I punched in Amy Napier's number. "I feel like I might be getting on to something."

"Are they going after you?" she wanted to know.

"Yes. Yesterday, I got access to Jason's old laptop. Not authorized . . . let's just say I found a way on my own. I copied a bunch of files. Good thing I did because today, his PC was offline."

"They're circling the wagons." She snorted. "And to think he gave years of his life to this damn company."

"I also got treated to an ambush after work." I told her about the happy hour cover and what waited for me in the parking lot.

"Wow." Amy blew out a long, deep breath. "They must know who you are."

"I don't think so," I said, "though I can't claim it with certainty. It seems like this is all in response to me being on to something. Which means Jason must have been, too, and he was farther down the road. Did he ever tell you anything about a guy named Louie or the team in mergers and acquisitions?"

"Not specifically," she said. "He might've mentioned the name once or twice. He kept a lot of the work stuff close to the vest."

"I know. These guys might be involved, though."

"I remember Jason telling me he didn't like the fact that the company had a mergers and acquisitions team. He thought it went against the core mission. Even as the company got away from research over time, they did a lot of work with technology services. I don't think he felt Louie's team fit in very well."

"They do seem a bit like an outlier," I said, "even with RTP doing financial audits."

"What do you think is going on, C.T.?"

"I'm not positive yet. Louie has at least one boss, so even if he's dirty, his orders might be coming from above. I think I'm going to keep rattling cages and see what happens."

"Are you sure it's a good idea?" Amy said.

"It's what I do," I said. "At the end of the day, I poke around, annoy people, and figure things out. I don't put the process on my business cards because I like to keep a little mystery for the clients. Don't tell anyone."

She chuckled. "I won't. Thanks for letting me know . . . and please be careful. I'd hate to see something bad happen to you, too."

"You and me both." I hung up. Amy really hadn't clarified anything for me. I would be driving back into the lion's den tomorrow.

CHAPTER 13

I WOKE up even earlier than normal the next morning. Yesterday evening's parking lot encounter still played in my head, and I felt a little amped up when I thought about it. Might as well blow off the excess energy with a few laps around Federal Hill Park. Gloria stirred as I got dressed, and she rubbed her eyes and sat up. The sheet fell from her shoulders, revealing a small tank top, and my resolve to exercise wavered. "You sure going out is a good idea?" she asked in a sleep-induced husky tone.

"No, but I need to. I'll have a gun with me."

My comment made her frown. "I hope you don't need it. Be careful."

"Always." I approached the bed, leaned down, and kissed her goodbye. She snuggled back under the covers, and I hit the mean streets of Baltimore for my morning constitutional. After a brisk walk to the park to loosen up, I settled into a nice rhythm. As I crossed the halfway mark in my first lap and ran away from the harbor, I spotted the red SUV which tailed me the other day. It didn't stop, but it drove by at a slow enough pace to make sure I could see it.

Message received.

I popped earbuds in and called Joey Trovato. After a few rings, he answered in a tired mumble. "Rise and shine," I said, slowing to a brisk walk again. "We have some work to do."

"How's the disguise?" he asked, sounding more alert.

"It's fine. I don't think they're on to me yet. You know who is, though? Gabriella."

He paused and eventually said, "Rizzo?"

"The same."

"Holy shit."

"Yeah," I said. "It might not be good for the home team."

"What's she after you for? I thought you two were pretty tight?"

"We are . . . or we were at least. She's obsessed with looking into her father's death because she thinks the police report is inaccurate."

"Is it?" Joey said.

"No."

"But she thinks something else happened?"

"Gabriella is convinced someone was in the room with him. There's also the stuff about him being a good Catholic who could never kill himself. I'm sure Tony would've needed nine hours for a proper confession, so I don't think his faith kept him from doing bad things."

"What do you need?"

I kept an eye out for the SUV but didn't see it again. A couple people jogged past me, and I waited for them to get out of earshot before answering. "I don't know what she's planning. She has it in her head I know more than I've told her."

"You do," Joey pointed out.

"Sure," I said, "but I'd prefer she stay in the dark on the whole thing. I'd like you to be around more. Normally, I would ask Rollins, but he's noticed some of her people tailing him. Check on Gloria while I'm gone during the day. I don't think Gabriella would involve her, but I'm not willing to put a wager on another Rizzo's stability."

"I still call dibs on Gloria if you get killed," Joey said.

"I'm sure she'd be honored. Between you and T.J., I can expect a heck of a funeral. Too bad I wouldn't be able to see it."

"Don't worry," Joey said. "I'll be around."

"Thanks," I said and clicked off. I resumed my running pace. About ten minutes later, I saw the red SUV again. This time, I was close enough to get a look at the passenger. It was the same guy as before. These were definitely Gabriella's men again.

I didn't need the extra complication her vendetta presented.

———

I experienced an uneventful drive to Frederick. No one followed me, and no goons waited in the lot. Louie parked his now-battered X5 away from the rest of the cars. I took the stairs to the third floor, made a deliberate loop past his team, and waved at all three. None of them said anything, though Louie glowered at me as I approached. Before walking to my desk, I stopped near Corey's cube to check my phone. He hadn't sent any messages since texting with Bryce yesterday from the bar.

The morning kept me busy and reminded me why I hated this gig and wanted it to end. One of the perks of working for myself is prioritizing tasks. Pat and I assigned very different levels of urgency to certain things, and the matters she asked me to drop everything and work on often turned out to be minor. Brent didn't strike me as very capable, but he probably could've done a lot of it. Worst of all, she didn't even thank me once despite having me do several allegedly important things for her. I kind of hoped she was involved just so I could watch her get arrested. Maybe being a shitty boss could get bundled in with the charges.

I drove into downtown Frederick and picked up lunch from a local deli. Mostly, I wanted to get out of the office, and a turkey on rye made for an excellent reward. How people managed to toil for others for years on end mystified me. I returned and ate lunch at my desk. Pat stomped up with more requests, but I told her I was eating. She scowled and walked away, and I soon heard her barking orders at Brent. I almost felt bad for him, but my lunch was really good.

Whatever issues Brent resolved got Pat off the warpath. I headed down to the parking lot and called Marvin Bernard. I made sure to be walking in case he bored me with talk of accounting. "I was hoping to hear from you today," he said.

"I'm glad you're willing to help."

"I looked at some of the things your secretary sent over. It was quite a trove."

"I'm dreading being up here," I said. "Working for other people is the worst. Please tell me you have something."

"You'll recall the last time we did this I told you certain things were hard to prove," he said. "I'm afraid I need to issue the same disclaimer again. There's also information I don't have, so it inhibits my ability to draw a conclusion."

"I'll take your best guess."

"All right. First, I think it's irregular for a technology services company to have a mergers and acquisitions team. It doesn't mean the group is shady, but it's questionable."

"I agree . . . for what it's worth," I said. "Having met the people on the team, I agree extra hard."

"I imagine outliers are useful in your line of work, too."

Marvin's stilted tone—which didn't strike me as an affectation—made me smile. It was strangely endearing . . . somehow both very like and unlike an accountant at the same time. "They are."

"I'll give you some details," he said. "Are you familiar with the term 'dead cat bounce'?"

"I imagine it's very unpopular among felines," I said.

"I suppose it would be. Normally, it means a brief uptick in the price of a stock which is in decline."

"RTP is a private company. I guess I don't follow."

"They don't necessarily pick their clients well," he said. "Or maybe they do. I guess it depends on whether you think they're doing some things deliberately. Several of the companies RTP has contracted with were in pretty dire straits. Shortly after signing the contracts, they experienced a brief resurgence."

Marvin was right—I didn't follow. "Then what?"

"The mergers and acquisitions team would move in. RTP would buy some sort of share in the company and sell off a bunch of assets. Then, they'd basically auction off the rest and move on."

"Certainly a strange business model," I said.

"And a relatively new one," he pointed out. "Up until a few years ago, they were all above board. I don't know how they identify the companies they'll work with. Someone is either not doing their homework or deliberately selecting businesses teetering on the brink."

"They're making money on this?"

"Yes. The uptick in value paints a positive picture. It allows them to get more for assets, intellectual property, real estate . . . you name it. I don't think the CEO is going to retire on this scheme alone, but it's definitely adding to the bottom line."

"This might be outside your area of expertise," I said, "but does it seem like the person who compiled the files I sent you caught onto it?"

"I think so," Marvin said. "I obviously don't know if it had to do with whatever fate befell the poor fellow . . . I presume he's dead."

"He is."

"The ball is in your court on the murder. Like I said, this is all very unusual, but it's hard to prove at this point, and it may not be illegal."

"I'll take it from here, then," I said. "Thanks for your help on this one. Send my secretary a bill for your time. I'm actually getting paid by clients now, so I can pass the expense along."

"Will do. Good luck, Mister Ferguson."

He rang off. I wished people weren't in the habit of wishing me good luck so often. I also wished I didn't feel like I needed it.

———

I headed back into the building when Rich called. This would probably be another conversation to have outside. At some point, Pat would notice me missing and bellow for me to come to her office, but I really didn't care. I returned to the parking lot and answered. "Good news," he said when I picked up.

"I just won the lottery?"

"Not exactly. I talked to Deputy Dunn out there in Frederick." I remembered him—and not very fondly in terms of his competence—from a prior case. "He said the sheriff's office is willing to work with you if you get proof."

"There's the rub," I said. "I'm the one who needs to put my neck on the line to get it. Why can't they do an investigation?"

"He told me there's not enough to go on yet."

I rolled my eyes. "All right. Let me run down what I know, and you can tell me if there's something here. Someone murdered my predecessor. He didn't have any enemies I can find. On the surface, everyone here liked him, but the files he kept on his computer suggest he suspected something shady was going on. I can't find anything to indicate he presented his concerns to anyone. A short while later, he was dead. So far, I've had two guys waiting for me in the parking lot after work, and three behind a bar yesterday at an alleged happy hour. They're not exactly rolling out the red carpet here."

"You think your cover is blown?" Rich asked.

"I've considered it, but I feel it's unlikely. For now, I'm staying the course. Do you think I have enough now for Dunn to get off his ass and do something?"

"I doubt it, honestly."

"Rich, I know one of the guys here set up the ambush behind the restaurant."

"Can you prove it in a court of law?" he said.

"Probably not without being cited for something," I admitted. "Then, I'd probably get popped for contempt. Me going before a judge at this point seems like a poor idea."

"I don't think Dunn is going to work with you yet. You'll have to get something tangible."

"I sent the files to an accountant. He agrees with Jason's implicit assertion of something fishy happening."

"Did he tell you it probably got the guy killed?" Rich wanted to know.

"No," I said, "he's a numbers guy. He punted the question back to me. He agrees the company looks suspicious. Jason gathered the information. He was a healthy man around your age. You're not dropping dead anytime soon."

"Let's hope not."

"Don't talk to T.J. too much, then. She's done everything but measure me for a coffin."

Rich chuckled. "She probably just wants you to be careful. I do, too. Someone got killed, and it's clear you're unpopular . . . well, even more so than normal."

"People love me," I said. "Those who aren't murderers at least."

"Keep at it. I told Dunn you'd be reaching out to him at some point. You'll need to give him more than what you have now, though."

I grunted. "Fine. I'll see what I can do."

"I'll give T.J. your height and weight in the meantime," Rich said and hung up.

The joke would be on him. I was sure she already knew.

———

I walked back inside and sat at my desk again. While I was on the phone, Pat sent me three instant messages and two emails asking where I was. I ignored them and got back to work. A ticket about setting up custom views for each member of an office sat at the top of the queue. It would take a while to resolve, so I got to it. While I was in the middle of it, Pat strolled to my cube. "There you are. I was looking for you."

"I was in the bathroom," I said without turning around. "Lunch didn't sit well."

"I'm not sure I believe you."

I sighed and spun around in my chair. Pat stood at the

opening with her arms crossed. "Is there something I can help you with?"

"I want to know where you were," she insisted.

"I told you."

"I don't believe you."

"I don't care."

"Excuse me?"

"Maybe you're out of practice at listening," I said. "You do enough hollering from your desk. It's possible. Anyway, I don't care if you believe me or not. It doesn't change what happened."

She frowned, causing a deep line to crease her forehead. "You're still in your probationary period, you know."

A million uncharitable replies swam through my head, most of them profane. I didn't need her to fire me on the spot, however. Knott might provide cover for me, but I couldn't count on it. He might not want to draw attention to my being here by sticking his neck out for the new guy. Rather than launch into a tirade, I said, "I'm trying to work a complex ticket. Is there something I can help you with?"

"No," she said. "Just try to be available." She walked away before I could say anything else, which was definitely for the best. Toward the end of the day, Knott sent me an email asking me to stop by his office on my way out. I'd finished the request I was working on, and Pat left with her stupid laptop bag about a half-hour ago. I could call it a day, too, so I packed up and headed to the top floor to chat with the CEO.

"Come in," he said and waved me toward a guest chair. "How are things going?"

"I don't like Pat," I said. "I'm hoping to wrap this up soon. Another week of her might be too much."

"She's . . . not very popular." Knott tried to smile, but it didn't work. He might've appreciated Pat's professional acumen, but I guessed he didn't much care for her, either. "How are you making out otherwise?"

"All right, I guess. I've been followed once and ambushed twice, so I must be on the right track."

Color drained from the CEO's face. "Ambushed? Again?"

"Not here at least," I said. "This time, it was behind a local pub. The mergers guys took me there for a happy hour. When I walked outside, three guys were waiting for me, and they weren't very interested in talking about databases."

"Good lord, Trent. What happened?"

I shrugged. "I'm still here, aren't I? I can take care of myself in a scrape. Most guys who are hired muscle get by on size. They usually don't have a lot of technique."

"I can't imagine Louie and his team are involved," Knott said, still frowning. "Are you sure they lured you there under false pretenses?"

"They haven't written any sworn affidavits," I said. "I can do the math, though. Pretty sure you can, too. You can give me all the platitudes you want about Louie and his guys, but someone on the team didn't want me sniffing around. They must think I'd pick up where Jason left off." When he didn't answer right away, I continued. "Speaking of Jason, I got access to his files . . . no thanks to you."

Knott turned up his palms. "I didn't want to create the impression you'd uncover whatever he might have."

"Which is what, exactly? RTP is a technology services company . . . at least most of the time. In its spare moments, the mergers guys buy up failing companies, and you pick the skeleton clean to sell off the bones."

"It wasn't my idea," Knott said. "It was Pat's."

"Another reason not to like her."

"Her husband works in finance. He made the suggestion, and she brought it to me. I thought it was a little irregular, but it's added to the bottom line. We're a small company, and we try to do things like pay good salaries and give bonuses to our employees. Extra revenue matters."

I leaned forward and stared at Knott, who had trouble meeting my eyes. "Even when it gets a good man killed?" He didn't have an answer. "You told me you didn't think Louie and his team were involved. Fine. Let's say you're right. Who is?"

"I don't know," Knott said in a small voice. "I wish I did. I feel I let Jason down."

"You probably did."

"I know." He nodded. "I wish I could think of a better answer for you. Maybe something will come to you over the weekend. I'll see you again on Monday morning."

"No offense, but I hope it's my last week here." I stood and left his office. No one waited for me in the parking lot this time, and I didn't pick up a tail on the way home. They were little victories, but at this point, I would take them.

CHAPTER 14

I SPENT Friday night and most of Saturday decompressing from my week in Frederick. Among the rigors of commuting in traffic, dealing with Pat, the two ambushes, and pretending to hold down a job, I felt worn out. I slept past ten o'clock on Saturday for the first time since I completed rehab after getting shot. Gloria and I enjoyed a leisurely breakfast and day. Later in the afternoon, she said she needed to tend to something and went home. We made plans for me to go to her house tomorrow. Considering the situation in Frederick and whatever threat Gabriella presented, not having to worry about Gloria being in my house alone came as a relief.

On Sunday, I woke up shortly after nine. Because I spent the prior day basically being a couch potato, I went for a morning run around Federal Hill Park, a 9MM under my lightweight Under Armour jacket. I never saw any suspicious SUVs, goons, or roustabouts, so I ended up not needing it. After a shower and breakfast, I thought about what Marvin Bernard told me. The M&A department was suspicious but not indicative of anything illegal on its own. Corey—and probably Louie, too—wanted the new DBA to stay in his lane and stop sniffing around. When I'd connected to Corey's phone, I didn't see anything about the two guys waiting for me after work. Maybe Louie sent them directly. Either way, I found the whole team suspicious.

As much as I hated to admit it, Rich was right. I'd amassed a collection of facts and suppositions which fell well short of representing a smoking gun. Even if someone at RTP were guilty of some financial malfeasance, a county sheriff's office would probably punt the matter to the state or feds. If I were going to put together a case to take to the FCSO, I needed to tie someone to the murder of Jason and the assaults against me.

In the early afternoon, I drove the S4 to Gloria's house in Brooklandville. It was a tony neighborhood in Baltimore County. Rather than the row houses popular in Federal Hill, Gloria's area featured trees, winding roads, and large single-family homes. Hers might have been the smallest on the street, but it would still hold my place at least twice over. Manicured hedges framed every driveway. I wondered if keeping a land-scaper on speed dial was a requirement of the homeowners' association.

Gloria greeted me at the door with a kiss. "I have something to show you," she said. When I perked up, she added, "Not that. Not yet, at least." She led me upstairs. The second level held a massive master bedroom and two smaller ones. Even those were bigger than most rooms in my house. Gloria opened one of the doors and stepped aside to reveal a finished office.

When I was convalescing after getting shot, we set up a desk and laptop in this space for me to work. She'd totally trans-formed it in the months since. A large desk dominated the left wall, along with a leather chair I'd be proud to use. A printer sat atop a new small table. The laptop I'd seen Gloria use a few times was connected to a large monitor. Her bachelor's degree from Brown hung on the wall along with something else beside it. It was a graduate certificate in fundraising from the University of Maryland issued only a few days ago. I didn't have any words to encompass everything, so I opted for a simple, "Wow."

"Yeah." Gloria beamed as she looked at the certificate. "Now you know what I've been doing on my laptop and phone in my spare time."

"You going to finish the master's?"

She shrugged. "Maybe. I don't know if there's a big benefit over what I have now." She paused and clapped her hands together. "The office is for my new business. It's been unofficial for a while, but now I'm a proper fundraiser."

I wrapped Gloria in a hug. "I'm proud of you. You found something you liked doing, and you went after it."

"It means I can ask people for money at my parties," she said with a grin.

"I know you're being funny, but this is a big deal. You're going to do great." I swept my hand to encompass the very nice home office setup. "You couldn't find a car repair shop with a spare top floor?"

"I admit I didn't look very hard."

"You don't know what you're missing," I said. We walked back downstairs to order lunch. "I guess the new office is a good entry for something I need to say." Gloria frowned. "The Frederick case is heating up. Two ambushes, and who knows what might be next? Plus, Gabriella is still sniffing around her father's death, and I don't trust her right now. I think it's best if you stay here for a while . . . just until these things blow over."

"You're probably right," Gloria said with a slow nod. "I hope it's not for long."

"Me, too." I hoped the Frederick issue would be resolved soon, but I had no idea when Gabriella would drop her crusade. She'd already chased Rollins away. With Gloria remaining in her house for the time being, I thought about renting a room in Frederick. It would lessen my commute and remove me from the city while the queen of organized crime employed men who followed me.

"Can we wait a little bit on lunch?" Gloria asked, grabbing my hand and glancing toward the stairs.

"Absolutely," I said.

———

A few hours later, I drove a circuit of my neighborhood to see if Gabriella kept lookouts in the area. I didn't see any. Once I parked on the concrete pad behind my house, I got out slowly, looked in all directions, and kept my hand on my gun. A room in Frederick for a few nights would definitely be preferable to this. It hadn't even been long, and I already grew tired of looking over my shoulder in my own neighborhood. Someone I thought was a friend being responsible only made it a thousand times worse.

My phone ringing snapped me out of my reverie. Melinda Davenport called. "It's Sunday," I said when I picked up. "Shouldn't we both have the day off?"

"I'm not sure I've really had one of those in a while." I didn't doubt it. Melinda's foundation needed to be ready twenty-four-seven to both accept new girls and help the ones they'd already rescued from the streets. I imagined she worked irregular hours, especially because I knew how much she valued being involved in each young woman's life. Crusaders rarely enjoyed down-time. "It's been thirty days since T.J. started in your office."

"Already? Wow." To her credit, my new secretary fit in well and did a good job . . . at least when she wasn't busy preparing for my untimely demise.

"I was hoping you could give me a progress report," Melinda said.

"It couldn't wait until tomorrow?"

"I like to hit milestones when they actually come up."

"Fair enough," I said. "T.J.'s doing great. She shows up on time, she's smart, she asks good questions, she takes great notes. I only wish we could get more clients."

"She's not taking unnecessary risks?" Melinda asked.

"No. I know her history there, and I figure you're still salty at me for giving her the idea of putting herself in danger."

"I am."

"It was her call," I said. "She was brave, and what she did really mattered. In this job, though, I'm not asking her to take risks. She's doing the kind of work you'd expect an assistant to do, and she's good at it."

"Are you teaching her your computer voodoo?"

I chuckled. It was probably an inevitable question, and Melinda wouldn't be the last person to raise it. "A little. She wants to learn more. I taught myself most of what I know, so I don't exactly have an education roadmap handy. I'm showing her things here and there as time allows and cases require."

"All right," Melinda said. "If it's OK with you, we can skip the sixty-day report and just do the next one at ninety."

"One of my mottos is 'the fewer reports, the better.'"

"Ninety it is, then. Thanks, C.T. We've placed a second girl now, too, but T.J. will always be the first. It really means a lot to me that you took a chance on her when it would have been easy to say no."

"I knew you put a lot of time in with her," I said. "It was the only endorsement I needed. Though the six months of paying half her salary helped."

"I kind of figured," Melinda said.

A red vehicle out the window drew my attention, but it wasn't the SUV I'd seen before. "You there?" Melinda asked.

"Yeah. Sorry. I . . . have something I should probably get back to."

"But it's Sunday," she said in a teasing tone.

"No rest for the wicked and all," I said, and we hung up. Thinking about the red SUV soured my mood. I changed into looser clothes and walked downstairs to wail on a punching bag for a while.

———

After a shower, I put respectable clothes back on. Using the exercise area of Gloria's basement was always preferable to mine, and a principal reason was the ability to stand up. At six-two, I exceeded the height limit in my lower level by about three inches. When keeping my knees bent and working over the bag, it didn't present a problem. Walking downstairs to put something in storage and not thinking about the ceiling height definitely led to a few avoidable whacks on the noggin from a floor joist.

I texted Gloria to ask if she was eating dinner. She sent a reply quickly. *Looking over my carryout options. I'm spoiled by my boyfriend cooking for me so often.*

Unable to resist such an opening, I responded. *He sounds*

like a great guy. Probably very handsome, too. Most men who can cook are.

He's all right. I laughed and put my phone away. I lived in a bustling Baltimore neighborhood. A ten-minute walking radius would probably yield two dozen places serving a decent dinner. On a normal venture into Federal Hill, I'd go out unarmed. Gabriella and her goons, however, made this anything but a normal evening. I also couldn't discount Louie and his team tracing Trent Gustaffson back to me. I strapped a 9MM around my waist before venturing out into the chilly evening air.

I passed a few other people who had similar plans at seven-thirty on a Sunday. My basement workout made me hungry, but nothing I passed right away compelled me to stop. The Abbey and its excellent burgers represented an old standby. If nothing else spoke to me on my trek, I could always go there. As I walked farther, I saw a familiar red SUV drive down a nearby side street.

Very few people shared the sidewalks with me. I felt exposed. If the SUV drove back, and someone inside stuck a gun out the window, I would have a problem. It went by once more a moment later, this time driving the other direction. I would swear I saw the same goon in the passenger's seat again. I passed an alley, and footsteps came out of it a moment later.

Before I could turn, something dark went over my head.

This happened once before a couple years ago. I'd taken a hell of a thrashing then and didn't care to go through it again. It only ended when I got a shot off and hit one of my assailants. As a pair of hands grabbed one of my shoulders, I reached for my pistol. An unseen adversary wrapped me in a bear hug from behind, however, pinning my arms in place and keeping the handle of my Glock a few inches away from my fingertips.

Whoever grabbed me also lifted me off the ground. I

thrashed about with my legs but didn't connect with anyone. The man who hoisted me also stayed out of range of a head-butt. Tires screeched to a halt somewhere to my left. I kept kicking and eventually hit someone. It didn't matter, however. The next thing I knew, I flew through the air and landed on a hard surface a second later. Hands held my arms and legs down as a door shut and the vehicle I unwillingly rode in sped away.

CHAPTER 15

DESPITE MY STRUGGLES, I was outnumbered. Getting tossed into what I presumed to be a van meant I was overwhelmed in a very confined space, which didn't make good odds for the home team. Someone bound my hands and feet. I changed tactics and tried to focus on where we were going. Whatever they put over my head blocked my vision completely. It didn't even let any light in.

I tried discerning directions based on where we started, which turn the vehicle made, and how long it went in a particular direction. It soon grew impossible. Maybe the driver took an indirect route on purpose. More likely, what I attempted worked in movies because the script said the hero could do it. After a couple minutes, I had no idea where we were, so I gave up. I would need to get away once we reached our destination. If I moved quickly enough, I might be able to shake off a captor and reach my gun.

My abduction represented bad news on a major front: it meant whoever murdered Jason Napier unraveled Trent Gustaffson's identity and ended up with me. If I lived—and if my bill to Amy allowed for it—maybe I would ask Joey to beef up Trent's identity. It did me no good now of course, so I saved my strength and mental energy. Frederick was a long drive from Federal Hill even on a Sunday night.

The ride came to an end much sooner than I anticipated. No way we'd made it anywhere near RTP. I didn't have a precise sense of time, but the van drove for fifteen minutes at most. Reaching Frederick in such a small amount of time would require going at NASCAR speeds. Wherever we were, it was closer to home than I expected. Someone untied my feet, but my hands remained bound. Smart on their part.

One of my captors herded me out of the vehicle and shoved me forward. "It would be easier if I could see where I was going," I pointed out. No one answered. At least two men walked with me. Probably three. We were out in the open here. Soon, someone would need to take us through a door. It would be a more restricted space. I would make my move then.

Sure enough, a man fiddled with keys, and we came to a stop. The grip on my arm loosened, and I lashed out. My wrists were still bound, so I used my arms together like a club. I hit someone, and an unfamiliar voice cursed. Before I could make any more trouble, a captor punched me hard in the stomach, and I dropped to one knee, sucking wind. A moment later, unseen hands jerked me to my feet and led me inside. "Where the hell are we?" I yelled as my heart raced.

Another door opened ahead. Was this a different part of whatever building we were in? Maybe it was a butcher shop and these assholes would hang me from the meathooks. I made no progress struggling against whomever walked with me. A few seconds later, we stopped, and someone walloped me in the midsection again. I folded in half, and they shoved me into a chair. My gun and phone got taken. The ties holding my arms together separated but only long enough for someone stronger than me to move them behind the chair. A rope soon held them in place there. My legs remained free for all the good it did me.

The hood remained over my head. Without saying anything, my abductors walked out of the room and slammed the door, leaving me alone with my morbid thoughts and pounding pulse.

———

I had no idea how much time passed. It felt like an hour. It could have been five for all I knew. I'd made many attempts to break my bonds, but none worked. The ropes were strong, and whoever tied the knot knew what he was doing. I wasn't slipping out anytime soon. I considered standing and crashing hard to the ground in an effort to break the chair. It felt sturdy. If I tried and failed, I'd be lying down and would need to get up without the use of my arm.

If I grew more desperate, I would make the attempt. For now, I waited. No other good options presented themselves. I was late for dinner, so hunger pangs made my situation even worse. The door opened a short while later. One set of footsteps walked inside, stopped, and locked up again. Was this my executioner? My heart raced anew at the thought. I couldn't even mount a final defense. Whoever entered walked around to the front and lifted the hood from my head.

I didn't recognize the man who stood before me. Nothing stood out about him. I couldn't even guess a nationality from his boring American features. His physique suggested he could do bicep curls by picking up the chair with me still in it. The room I sat in looked maybe eight feet square. Bare concrete walls. No windows. What kind of place was this? My captor's dark eyes held no compassion as he regarded me. "You need anything?"

The question took me by surprise, and he repeated it a few seconds later. "Going home would be nice," I said.

"How about something I can actually do for you?" he said. "We might be here a while."

"Fine. I'm hungry. You picked me up on the way to dinner. And I need to pee."

"For Christ's sake," he muttered. "Wait here."

"Where else would I go?" I asked as he left the room. He didn't lock the door again. Probably not going far. Sure enough, he returned a minute later and set a bucket between my feet.

"I'm going to untie your right hand." He moved behind me. "Your left will get bound to the chair. I suggest not trying anything. I'm stronger than you, and I don't want to hurt you, but I will if you make me."

"Is hurting me someone else's job, then?" He didn't answer. My hands came free a moment later, but he held them in a vise grip. Even if I wanted to make a move, I couldn't. Sure enough, he tied my left to the back of the chair and left my right free.

"I know it ain't the best solution, but it's what we got." He set a small bottle of hand sanitizer on the left arm of the chair. "I'll turn around. Let me know when you're done."

This was the best I was going to get, and I really did need to pee, so I made do. A moment later, I said, "All right."

The burly man moved back in front of me. He handed me a bottle of water and two protein bars. "Ain't got much else."

"Thanks," I said, and I chided myself for it. Why show gratitude to a man whose job consisted of keeping me tied up in a small musty room? Was this how Stockholm Syndrome started? I couldn't take it back, but I didn't need to repeat it for basic acts of humanity. Despite the man looming nearby, I scarfed down the bars and drank the water.

"You good for now?" he said.

"I think so."

He walked behind me again, undid the rope holding my left hand in place, and grabbed my right. I didn't resist. He was definitely stronger than me, and even if we were equally matched, he held the advantage of leverage. I would need to find another time to mount an offense. Within a few seconds, my hands were bound behind me again. There was no give in the knot. "Settle in," he said. "I'd expect to be here a while."

"Where's Louie?" I asked. "Did he put you up to this?"

The only answer I got came from the slamming door.

———

Some indeterminate amount of time passed. The bars took the edge off my hunger, at least. I tried the knot and found it secure. If I managed to escape these bonds, it would need to be a different way. I picked at the ropes themselves and tried to pull a thread loose. This method would take longer, but no one seemed to be in a hurry, and while my chair sat at a weird angle, it mostly faced the door, so anyone who came in couldn't see my hands.

I'd managed to separate a strand and work it when the door opened. The guy who gave me food before entered, joined by another fellow of similar size and build. Both of them stared at me, but the blond newcomer looked especially unfriendly. Sure enough, he closed the distance quickly and pounded me in the midsection. I saw it coming and clenched my abs in time, but it still hurt, and my next few breaths weren't easy. "Tell us what you know," the recent arrival said.

"Everything?"

"Of course everything."

"You might want to find some chairs of your own," I said.

"We could be her a while. I'm a genius. I know an awful lot. What do you want to talk about? Computer science?"

"You're a comedian, huh?" he said. He leaned close to me, and I smelled his stale breath. "You know who I really hate?"

"Dentists?"

He slapped me across the face. It stung, and if he decided to clobber me, I couldn't do anything to protect myself. "I hate people who think they're funny." To accentuate the point, he punched me in the face, and the force of the blow snapped my head to the side. My jaw blazed with pain. "Now, let's get down to it. You need to tell us what you know."

"I'd listen to him," the other said. "He's a lot meaner than me."

"It's a small sample size," I said, "but I have to agree."

"Start talking, then!" the blond goon roared.

I wondered how Louie or Corey figured out Trent was really me. Joey told me the identity wouldn't stand up to the full scrutiny of a hiring process. I got swept in the door by Knott, though, and bypassed whatever systems human resources put in place. Did Louie get pissed and make an inquiry to HR? Maybe Pat did. She seemed salty she didn't get to pick her new hire, and I knew I pissed her off the other day. Either of them could've done it, and it didn't mean they played a part in Jason's demise. "Look, I don't know who put you up to this. Maybe it was Louie. He seems the type." When they both looked at each other in confusion, I changed direction. "Pat, then. Perhaps she's a more interesting woman than I thought." The two goons frowned at me. "Corey?"

"You're oh-for-three, friend," the dark-haired one said. "I don't know anyone by those names."

I tossed out another even though it represented a long shot. "Devon Knott?"

"Quit stalling," the blond said. "The only Corey I ever met was some asshole in high school. None of those other names ring a bell."

"I have no idea what we're doing here, then," I said.

The meaner one waded in and clobbered me in the stomach again. I'd be coughing blood soon at this rate. "You better figure it out real quick. While you do, you might want to confess."

"Fine. I've never watched *Ted Lasso*. I just don't like soccer very much, and I don't think I'd get into the show."

The other one saved me from another punch by talking. "You're in luck." He looked at his phone. "I think you're about to get at least one answer." He unlocked the door and pulled it open.

Gabriella Rizzo walked in.

CHAPTER 16

GABRIELLA REGARDED me with pitiless eyes. I remembered meeting her when we were both much younger . . . before my parents—my mother, really—learned Gabriella's dad ran organized crime in the city. We liked each other as teenagers, though I never made a move or asked her out for fear Tony would have me drawn and quartered. Over the years, I'd gotten used to her brown eyes being full of life and warmth. To have her look at me as if she barely knew me felt jarring. I was but another obstacle on her road to the truth, whatever she determined it to be.

The goons stopped menacing me and waited for instructions from the boss lady. "You haven't been honest with me, C.T.," she said. "After all these years, I expected better from you."

"I told you the conclusion in the police report looked accurate."

"We both know it wasn't."

"You're entitled to your opinion, Gabriella," I said. "You're not entitled to your own facts, and having these two assholes abduct me from the street is way over the line." Both men glared at me but didn't make a move. They still waited for orders. "If you wanted to talk again, I would've come to the restaurant."

"We're way past that point." She shook her head. "I didn't want to admit it to myself. You've been such a good friend to my dad and me over the years." She took a few steps closer, and the blond enforcer mirrored her movements. "I wish there were another way, but I need the truth."

"I've told you the truth," I insisted.

My comment earned me another punch to the midsection. I gritted my teeth and went back to working on the rope. Gabriella being in charge of the two Chads escalated things. If they worked for Louie, they might sweat me out for answers. The link between Trent and C.T. might be tenuous enough to buy me some time. I didn't think I'd get the time now. Gabriella lost herself down a rabbit hole where she sought a version of the truth to fit her predetermined facts. Nothing I said outside her parameters would matter. It would just be another lie in her eyes.

"I'm going to give you a chance now," she said. "You know what really happened. Tell me, and we'll let you go. This will all be over."

I doubted it would be so simple. "The truth is he shot himself in the head. Exactly like it says in the report. Ballistics and gunshot residue don't lie."

"But people do. Like you are now." She looked at the blond muscleman and gave him a quick nod. In turn, he gave me a hard right cross to the face. It rang my bell and rocked me back in the chair, nearly tipping it over. If it capsized, I didn't want to think about what Tweedledee and Tweedledum might do to a mostly defenseless hostage. I needed to get free.

Gabriella leaned down and stared at me. "Why do you do this? What's the point of holding out? Make it easy on yourself."

"Or what?" I said. "These two will beat me to death while I'm tied to a chair? Your father might have been a lot of things, but he was never a coward. I guess you haven't improved operations as much as you thought."

"Don't speak nasty to Miss Rizzo," the blond said, and he gave me a one-two combination in the stomach for my perceived temerity.

"You know I'm right," I wheezed.

"I know you're right about one thing," she said. "My dad wasn't a coward. It's why he couldn't have killed himself. It's impossible. I'm here for the truth, C.T., and you're in the way. If you keep lying, these two will keep punishing you for it."

"I have a case in Frederick. A widow. Her husband was murdered, and I'm close to getting justice for her. I can't lose time with your vendetta."

Gabriella closed her eyes and shook her head. "Do you think I care about someone in Frederick? This is about my father and me. Don't waste my time anymore than you already have."

"I've told you what I know," I said. "You're the one wasting time."

"I'm sorry you feel that way." She walked toward the door. "Boys, get the truth out of him." She glanced at her watch. "Rest if you need to. He's not going anywhere until he tells us what we want to know."

"Or until he dies," the light-haired one added.

Gabriella didn't say anything as she left, and the door slammed shut behind her.

———

I absorbed a few more blows before my two captors called it a night. "Rest up if you can," the blond said, smiling like a predator the whole time. "We'll be back to work you over soon." He shadow boxed near the door. "I love a good morning constitutional."

My midsection ached, and both sides of my face felt like someone left my head in a vise for a few hours. One tooth felt loose as I moved my tongue inside my mouth. I continued working the rope to try and break free. A second thread pulled away. Now, all I needed to do was keep tugging on it to unravel it. The coarse bonds scratched my wrists, and my shoulders grew numb from having my arms pinned behind me for so long. Despite all this—and probably because of the beating I'd been forced to endure—I felt tired, and I drifted off to sleep not knowing what time it was.

I jolted awake an indeterminate time later. After the initial shock of wondering where I was, I remembered everything, especially my interest in getting free. I plucked at the rope more and made some progress. A thread loosened, and I gained a little more mobility in my lower arms. Two sets of footsteps drew closer, and the door opened a few seconds later. Both enforcers walked in. The blond strode close and walloped me in the face. Even turning my head a little before his fist thundered home didn't lessen the impact. I nearly fell over again. "Morning, prick," he said. "Ready to talk?"

"Does telling you to go fuck yourself count?" I said.

He drew his fist back, but the dark-haired guy put a hand on his shoulder. "Let's try something different." He turned his attention to me. "You know why you're here. Make it easy on yourself. Tell us what you know, and this can all end."

I spat blood onto the floor. "I know Gabriella misses her father. The thing is I don't have some piercing insight into his final moments. I read the police report. Over the years, I've seen a lot, and a few have been bullshit. This one was solid. I have no reason to question it. I know it's not what she wants to hear, but like I told her, she doesn't get to make up her own facts."

"You're sure?" he asked. His tone sounded much more composed than his raving friend. We were two guys having a conversation.

"Positive," I said. "There's no point in keeping this up. I don't like being a punching bag, and I've told everyone what I know more than once. Let's just call it a day."

"You don't get to make the call," the blond said. He stepped to me and rocked me with a series of body blows which left me gasping for breath and barely upright. I worked another strand loose, however, and freedom felt much closer. I only needed a couple more minutes.

"I'm trying here," the dark-haired goon said. "You're not helping much."

"You want me to invent something to satisfy your boss' bloodlust?" I jerked my head at the light-haired masochist. "Or his?"

"I thought you might act in your own self-interest." He shrugged. "Guess I was wrong." He walked to the door. "I'm going to leave you two alone to work this out. I'll check back later. Unless I forget." He opened the door and disappeared down the hall.

When it slammed shut again, the blond showed a bare-toothed grin. "Just you and me now, meat. No one to tell me to stop. No one to pause the beating for questions unless I decide to ask you one. Miss Rizzo wants the truth, and I'm gonna pound it out of you. Whether you survive will be up to you."

True to his word, he drew his fist back and hammered me

in the face. The loose tooth came free, and my mouth filled with blood and agony. I worked on the rope with both hands, unraveling a thread even as my deranged captor admired his handiwork. "You still got all your teeth?"

I hocked the one he'd dislodged at his feet. "All but one." He glowered at me. "You want me to flap my gums? Fine. I'm going to tell you something. If you hit me again, I promise I'll break your arm. If you're lucky, I'll stop there, but you're an asshole, so no promises."

"Pretty tough talk for someone who's tied to a chair," he said. As his fist went back, I undid enough of the rope to bypass the knot and get my wrists free. My shoulders pumped with blood again even as I took another right cross to the face. I kept my hands behind my back for now as feeling returned up and down my arms. "Remind me again how you're gonna break my arm. I like it when people get defiant. Makes beating them to death a little more fun."

He went for another huge haymaker, and I rolled to the side out of the chair. When the goon's massive punch left him unbalanced, he spun around and tried to regain his footing. I followed his eyes down to the rope, which lay on the floor unraveled around its knot. When the enforcer looked back at me, fear glinted in his eyes for the first time.

I smiled.

CHAPTER 17

I COULDN'T GET into a long fight with this guy. For starters, he was bigger and stronger. While this never dissuaded me, he also didn't spend the last several hours tied to a chair, and he definitely didn't take a solid pummeling. Adrenaline coursed through my veins, but I knew I operated at far less than a hundred percent. This needed to be a quick fight. Instead of my usual method of playing defense, I pressed the offense.

When my foe recovered from his shock and went for another punch, I hit him with a quick snap kick in the thigh. It stopped his haymaker as he covered his leg. I kicked him in the other one. With both his hands lowered, I stepped forward and elbowed him square in the mouth. It didn't knock him over, but it did stagger him into the nearby wall. I followed and unleashed a barrage of punches to his midsection. Blood rimmed his lips after the last one, and he sagged to a crouch.

He tried to punch me, and I caught his fist. Keeping my right hand on it, I encircled his wrist with my left and applied a painful hold. Sure enough, he grimaced and tried to get free. "The more you fight it, the more it hurts," I told him. Normally, I stood back farther when using this wrist lock, but I wasn't paying much mind to defense. "I told you I was going to break your arm if you hit me again."

"I was just following orders," he said, his voice an octave higher than its usual snarl.

I twisted my hands, and the sound of his wrist bones snapping filled the room. He yelled in pain and lowered his head. "You had a choice." I slid my left hand farther up his forearm. "If I twist again a little harder, your elbow will break, too. I think it's called a spiral fracture . . . I don't know. I'm not a doctor. Have you learned your lesson?"

"Yes," he croaked.

"I'm not sure I believe you," I said. "You told me on more than one occasion how you were going to beat me to death. Maybe you did what Gabriella told you. Maybe you're just a sick son of a bitch. Either way, I don't want you to threaten anyone again." I twisted with more power, and his elbow broke. The enforcer slumped to the floor and cried. When he lifted his head to look at me, I kicked him hard in the face, bouncing his skull off the concrete. He lay still, and I made sure he was still breathing.

A quick search of his pockets revealed none of my things, but he did carry a phone and a knife. I smashed his cell, cut the useless portion of rope, and sized up the rest. A good dozen feet remained. I tied a length around his ankles and slung the other end over a beam in the ceiling. Even feeling weaker than usual, leverage allowed me to pull enough to get his torso off the deck. I stood on the chair and knotted the other end around another beam.

The other goon hadn't returned yet. I didn't know how big this place was, but the blond's screams would've drawn the attention of anyone nearby. I kept the knife, opened the door, and peered up and down the hallway. Coast clear. I approached an open door on the opposite side of the hallway. The room was empty save for a box which held my things. I put my wallet back in my pocket, looked at my phone long enough to see the time—still at least an hour until sunrise—and a bunch of messages from Gloria, and strapped my gun back on. When I stepped out into the corridor again, the dark-haired goon approached. His face twisted into a scowl, and he sprinted toward me.

It left no time to unholster my pistol and bring it to bear, and I suspected he knew this. Instead, while he tried to clothesline me, I dropped to one knee and stuck my other leg out. He tripped over it and crashed to the concrete floor. "Save the wrestling moves for WWE," I said as he scrambled back to his feet. Despite having plenty of time to bring the knife or my gun to bear, I didn't use either. While this guy proved far less sadistic than his friend, he'd still worked me over, and he left me alone with a murderous madman.

He needed to pay.

As with his fellow goon, I focused more on offense in the interest of ending things quickly. I needed to eat, hydrate, and rest, and the man staring me down held the advantage on all three fronts. He blocked my punches, and I returned the favor with his. The enforcer planted his rear foot and launched a high kick. He telegraphed the move, though, and he wasn't very fast. I stepped to the side and drove my foot into his straight rear leg. His knee gave way with a crunch which reverberated up and down the hallway, and he collapsed while screaming and clutching his leg.

I fished his cell phone out and spiked it on the concrete until it broke. The fallen goon muttered curses at me as I looked around for something to tie him up with. I couldn't find more rope, but another mostly empty room held a roll of duct tape. When I approached, the prone muscleman tried to lash out at me. I avoided his clumsy attempt, leaned down, and whacked him in the face. His eyes rolled back and closed. I bound his arms to his sides. With a broken leg, he wasn't going to get up and go anywhere.

His pockets also held a set of car keys. I took them, left the building, and used the largest on the ring to lock the door. Gabriella's men kept me in a small industrial-looking space. I didn't know where I was yet. My phone's GPS indicated somewhere on the west side of Baltimore. As I walked to the van they used to abduct me, I formulated a plan for the rest of the morning.

My old friend Gabriella wouldn't like it.

———

Once my hands steadied from the adrenaline leaving my blood, I drove through the city. The rising sun peeked through buildings as I headed east. I'd texted Gloria before I left and gave her a brief rundown what happened. She called as I neared the center of Baltimore, and the worry in her voice came through on the speakerphone. "Oh, my gosh, are you all right?"

"More or less," I said. "It's not something I'd care to endure again, but on the Chinese prison scale, it was tolerable." My nineteen days of detention in Hong Kong marked the worst time of my life. The goon twins were amateurs compared to my overseas jailers, even though my dentist might disagree.

"What are you doing now?"

"Driving home in the van they used to pick me up. I'm hungry and thirsty, so I'm going to eat a little before I pay Gabriella a visit."

"Don't do anything you'll regret," Gloria said.

"Impossible," I said. "I don't believe in regrets. Besides, after what her men put me through the last ten hours or so, nothing I do in response would be out of bounds."

"I'm worried about you. You sound really hyped up. I want to come by."

"Kind of hard not to be. I'll be fine, though. Let's stick to the plan."

Gloria sighed. "All right. I don't like it, but I know you're too stubborn to change your mind when you're like this. Please be careful. Call me when you can."

"I will," I said. "I love you."

"Love you, too," my girlfriend said, "even when you're a pain in the ass." We hung up, and I approached Federal Hill. I left the van in front of a hydrant near my house, tossed the keys down a nearby sewer drain, and called the towing company listed on a *No Parking* sign. Once inside, I guzzled a bottle of water and ate a protein bar around my missing tooth. I felt a little better but still well short of full capacity. It would take at least one night of rest to get there, and I still needed to drive to Frederick later and pretend to be a good RTP employee.

I brewed a cup of coffee, found some expired instant oatmeal in my pantry, and cooked it anyway. It tasted a little stale, but it was soft, and two packets proved pretty filling. I grabbed another bottle of water for the drive. Gabriella lived in her father's old house. I knew the way there by heart. She would have at least one man on site. By now, she was probably awake, and she might have tried to reach the two goons who held me prisoner.

She would learn their fates soon enough. I walked out the back of my house to the parking pad, climbed into the S4, and sped away.

CHAPTER 18

MY PHONE BUZZED at a traffic light. It was the single vibration of email. I checked, and Devon Knott sent a very generic message wondering when I would be in and where we stood with the important project he'd asked me to work on. I felt my hand clench around the phone. I was still amped up after getting away from Gabriella's goons. I pulled into a nearby parking lot and read the email in full.

Knott did a good job leaving the specifics out of it. He also copied Pat Ritter. I replied to both of them.

Good morning,

Despite being up pretty early, I'm afraid I'll be getting a late start today. There's something I need to resolve with my car before I come in. Look for me sometime in the late morning. I'll be sure to work on all projects once I'm there.

. . .

Cheers,
   Trent

Hopefully, Pat would see her boss' email and not burden me with a lot of annoying busywork. It struck me as something she liked to do, so I'd probably have to deal with some regardless. No one else on the team seemed to be very good. I also wondered about Louie and Corey. They both harbored their suspicions of Trent after the bar ambush of a few days ago. I wanted to stay off their collective radar, too. I expected I would need to dodge a killer in Frederick, but I didn't think I'd also need to avoid ambushing buffoons, barely competent bosses, useless coworkers, and office politics.

More than ever, I felt glad to be my own boss.

Once I sent my reply, I pulled back onto the road and resumed my drive to Gabriella's house. Thinking of having it out with her boiled my blood again, and whatever respite I got from typing an email ended quickly. My hands clenched and unclenched on the steering wheel, and I heard my pulse in my ears as I pushed the accelerator harder.

———

Gabriella lived in the house she grew up in. Her father owned a nice place on Highfield Road in the Guilford area of Baltimore. Nearby, Sherwood Garden would boast of the city's best tulips once the weather warmed up. I never pegged Tony for a fan of the flowers, but his daughter probably appreciated them. Most homes on the street remained dark. I parked across the street and one house down. No one moved outside the Rizzo residence.

Tony never used an alarm system. One of his guys always stayed in the house. Gabriella already modernized certain parts of the operation—starting with the restaurant which let the family claim a legitimate business—but I wondered if she'd gotten to the house. As I crept around the perimeter, I saw no indication she'd made an upgrade in this area. A couple lights were already on inside. Might as well gain entry like a respectable member of society.

I held my pistol in my right hand and knocked on the front door with my left. My face would give me away, but from the rear, I could pass for one of Gabriella's men. I turned and waited. Locks unlatched a few seconds later. I pivoted back in time to see a large goon open the door. Before he could say anything, I hit him with a short jab in the midsection. It wasn't designed to put him down, but it stunned him long enough for me to step forward, grab his head, and slam it into the door frame.

When the first wallop didn't turn the lights out, I did it again, then a third time, and then a fourth. Blood marred the paint, and he slumped to the floor. I locked up behind me, relieved the unconscious guard of his gun, and tucked it into my waistband. The inside looked much like it did when I visited Tony a couple months ago. The chair railings and oil paintings didn't seem like Gabriella's tastes at all.

I walked over the hardwood floors toward the rear. Conveniently, the lady of the house emerged from the kitchen, saw me training a gun on her, and gaped. "Surprised I'm alive?" I said.

"They weren't going to kill you," she insisted.

"We're going to have a strong difference of opinion there." I jerked the gun toward the living room. "In there. Sit down. You and I are going to have a talk."

Gabriella crossed her arms. "I'm good here."

I sighted a cabinet in the kitchen and fired. Gabriella ducked and covered her ears as the bullet blew a hole in the door, which flopped back and forth. "Jesus Christ, C.T.!" she said.

"I'm not fucking around. The next one goes in your chest." I fixed the pistol on her again. "Let's chat."

"You think it's smart to fire a gun in a neighborhood?"

"Let's not pretend the people nearby don't know who you are and what you do. I'm sure your father trained them well."

Gabriella glared at me, but she walked into the living room and dropped onto a brown leather sofa I remembered from when we were teenagers. I stood nearby. "The blond guy told me more than once he planned to kill me," I said. "The other one didn't seem too interested in stopping him. If I hadn't gotten free, I think I'd be dead right now."

"You're being dramatic."

"You weren't there. Sure, you made a little appearance, and you made certain I knew those two assholes worked for you. Once you left, though, it got a lot worse." She wouldn't meet my gaze. "Look at my face."

She did, and her hard gaze softened for a second. "They were only supposed to get you to talk."

"They failed," I said.

"Are they alive?"

"They were when I left." I shrugged. "Maybe they still are. I honestly don't give a shit. They're both hurt, and I broke their phones. Unless someone's going to check on them, you'll need to get them an ambulance." She reached for her jeans pocket. "After we're done here."

"They might die," she said.

"Boo-hoo. They knew the job and the risks going with it when they signed up."

"Fine." Gabriella crossed her arms again, and whatever sympathy flashed in her expression earlier was long gone. "Let's talk. You know more about my father's death than you're letting on."

"He killed himself," I said.

"No." She shook her head. "No. I don't believe it. I can't."

"Did you know he paid Nicky Papers to take me out?" Her face didn't crack even a little. "You did, didn't you?"

Gabriella sighed. "Not at first, no. Not even when he ordered it done. I only discovered it in a letter he left me. I was . . . horrified. It was an overreaction."

"I think I'd go with a much stronger word," I said.

"I never thought he'd do something like that."

"Me, either. But he did, and I found out."

"How?"

I waved my free hand. "Not important." I had a source who fed me the info, but I'd be damned if I gave Mouse up to Gabriella. "I knew, and I spent some time thinking of the best way to deal with it."

"I know you didn't kill him," she said.

"No, but I'll admit I thought about it. If he weren't already dying, I might have." I paused. "You want to know how I'm so certain your father killed himself?" Gabriella frowned, but her head bobbed. "He did it right in front of me. I was in his office when it happened."

She didn't say anything for a few seconds. After some deep breaths, she looked up at me. "You came to the house?"

"Yes. Almost got caught by the guy downstairs, but I made it."

"Gino," Gabriella said. "He told me he thought someone else was here that night. Dad said he was on speakerphone. It was why I started down this road in the first place."

"Why did you think I knew more than I told you?" I asked. I expected my relationship with Gabriella to ice over after this. Today would likely be my last chance to get an answer.

"Dad didn't believe in security systems." She let out a dry chuckle. "Someone up the street has a Ring setup. His camera saw a black pickup speeding away. We put it together from there. Seemed likely to be you and your friend Rollins."

"He only drove me. Hell, he spent most of the trip telling me I was an idiot for walking in unarmed."

"You were."

"Maybe," I said. "I didn't want to be tempted to use a gun."

"Are you telling me the truth?" Gabriella stared with welling eyes. "Did he really kill himself in front of you?"

"He'd been pointing the revolver at me for a while." I replayed the scene in my head, and I almost flinched at the memory. "Your dad was in a corner. I knew what he'd done, and I figured he went after other people, too. The cancer might've been killing him, but he still would've gotten arrested and put through the system. In the end, he stuck the gun up to his temple and pulled the trigger."

Tears ran down each of Gabriella's cheeks. I fought the urge to offer her a tissue or say something to comfort her. She may have been my friend for a long time, but the past few days burned the bridge to ashes. "I know you're telling me the truth, but it's so hard to believe."

"At the end," I said, "he asked me to look after you." She closed her eyes and cried some more. "The fool I am, I told him I would. Maybe it's bad form to break your word to a dying man, but here we are. You left me alone with two killers because you couldn't handle the truth. You can look after yourself."

"You could have been honest with me from the beginning," Gabriella said. She jabbed her finger in tune with her raised voice.

"I was. Your father killed himself. Whether I told you I was in the room or not doesn't change what happened." Gabriella looked away and stewed. "I've given you the truth . . . the entire time. Now, I want something from you."

"You've got a lot of nerve," she said, fixing me with a sharp glare.

"Get over yourself," I said, finally letting my tired arm holding the gun relax. "You're the one who had me abducted and beaten. Here are the terms—you leave me, my family, my friends, and my loved ones alone. No more inquest. No more vendetta."

"And in return?"

"I don't shoot you and the guy by the door on my way out."

"You're not a killer, C.T."

"Try me," I said, raising the pistol again. "Getting shot and nearly dying changes a man."

Gabriella took a deep breath and wiped her eyes with her flannel sleeve. "Fine."

"Good."

"We're not friends anymore, though," she said. "Don't come into my restaurant . . . don't ask me for shit. You stay away, and I'll do the same."

I nodded. "Great. Have a nice life, Gabriella. You actually might if you don't fuck it up." I put my pistol away and left the room. The goon by the door remained down for the count. I tossed his gun in an azalea bush as I left.

———

I arrived home and headed downstairs right away. My basement wasn't full height, so I avoided using it for a lot of things. A while ago, however, I hung a heavy bag in an area where I could more or less stand. Bending my knees helped ensure I didn't bang my noggin on the wood overhead. Today, I eschewed changing into workout clothes.

I simply needed to get out some steam.

The two goons' faces came to mind. I slipped on a pair of MMA gloves and gave the bag a few hard whacks. Bryce, Corey, Louie, and their friends took a turn next. I punched the bag hard enough to make it sway, gave it a few solid elbows, and drove kicks into the head of whoever the canvas represented at the moment.

I replayed the Frederick bar encounter in my head. Getting the pool ball and making a sap had been very aggressive. It wasn't something I would've done before I got shot. I'd tangled with three attackers at a time before, and while I wouldn't file any of those encounters in the *easy* category, I'd come away from all of them as the one still on his feet. Did I not trust myself? Was I still skittish even after getting over my flinching problem? No, I realized as I clobbered the bag some more.

The reality was I didn't want to get injured again. Taking two bullets, nearly dying, and spending time in rehab weighed on me. I realized it as I went through a good punching routine. I'd endured a lot and still hadn't made it back to a hundred percent. Maybe I never would. As much as I dislike the phrase, it remained possible my current level represented my new normal. The new, slightly lesser, me might need an advantage going against three guys in a bar parking lot.

I'd brutalized Gabriella's men. Sure, they took turns

whaling away on me, and the one promised to kill me, but I left them in a bad way. It was angry. Aggressive. Several months ago, I would've been content to knock them out and move on. This morning, I needed to injure them. I didn't care for this level of bloodlust. Even knowing it came from a desire not to be in mortal danger again, I still disliked it. My job sometimes required violence to solve a problem, but I never thought of myself as a violent person, and I didn't want to become one.

My thoughts turned to Doctor Parrish. She'd helped me on-site as the shrink at the Arizona facility where I rehabbed. I'd leaned on her remotely a few times since. She'd have a wise-crack or two, but she'd also be proud I worked through this on my own. My bank account would be happy I didn't need to contact her again. I took my gloves off, walked upstairs, and looked at my bed. Despite feeling exhausted, I didn't want to rest. Too much to do today. Instead, I got a shower. Afterwards, I assessed my face in the mirror.

It looked like I'd gone a few rounds with a heavyweight. Bruises marred both my cheeks, and the beginnings of a shiner showed around my left eye. The missing tooth sat far enough back in my mouth to not be visible. Still, I couldn't go to work like this. It would raise too many questions. Gloria kept a bunch of makeup in the bathroom. She owned enough to start her own company. Much of it proved no help, but some basic skin-tone foundation would cover my injuries enough for now. For the first time in my life, I applied some to my face. I'd seen Gloria do it enough. Once I finished, I looked presentable. I slipped the makeup into my pocket in case I needed to apply more later.

Before leaving, I checked my phone. Shortly after I sent my email, Pat responded in the affirmative. Leaving now offered the perk of not being in traffic. I grabbed water and a couple granola bars, climbed back into the S4, and headed to Frederick, wondering what I'd find waiting for me there today.

CHAPTER 19

AFTER I REACHED my desk and put my backpack down, Pat showed up in short order. "You're late," she said from my cubicle door.

"Good morning to you, too," I said an instant after turning over several extremely uncharitable replies in my head. She remained silent. "I sent you an email to tell you I was running behind."

"I guess I didn't see it."

"You replied."

She frowned and pursed her lips at the same time. "No, I didn't."

"Yes, you did," I insisted. "I sent it to you and Devon both, and you answered."

"You must be mistaken," Pat said, her brows still knitted. "Maybe Devon got back to you. Once I'm off the clock, I don't do work."

While I didn't like Pat, I also didn't think she tried to pull a fast one here. She looked legitimately surprised when I mentioned she responded to my email. It was almost like I accused her of something. "Maybe," I said to try and exit the situation.

"Anyway, you're here now. Make sure you give us a good effort today." Before I could answer, she walked back to her office. Probably for the best, as anything I might've said would have only made the situation worse. I didn't need Pat to like me, but I did need her not to try and fire me. Knott might be able to protect me, but he also risked exposing his role in the arrangement if he stuck his neck out for the new hire. I sat in my mediocre chair and looked at what menial tasks awaited me today.

A few minutes in, I got a reprieve when Knott emailed and asked me to come to his office. A quick trip to the top floor later, I sat in one of the CEO's guest chairs. "How's it going . . . uh, Trent?"

"I wish I could say no one tried to kill me in the last twenty-four hours," I said. "No one from here tried at least." Knott stared at me with his mouth agape. "So . . . how was your weekend?"

"Er . . . fine. It sounds like you've been a little distracted."

"Yes." I shifted in my seat. "And a little sore, actually, with all the excitement well behind me." My jaw in particular ached.

"My secretary can give you some Tylenol." He steepled his fingers. "How are we on the matter of Jason?"

"I shared what I got with an accountant I trust," I said. "He thinks something fishy is going on, but he needs more time to go over everything. If he's right, I think it's reasonable to conclude Jason got killed for what he knew."

"My god." Knott ran a shaking hand through his hair. "I don't want to be a micromanager. I try to trust department heads to keep a handle on things and let me know if something is brewing. Maybe I was too hands off."

"It doesn't matter now. What's important is to be vigilant going forward. I just told you something irregular is probably happening here, and a man likely lost his life as a result. I'm not going to tell you how to run your company, but how you handle this is going to be important."

"You're right," he said. "Keep me posted. Once we know more for certain, I'll meet with the division heads individually. One of them is bound to tell me what happened."

I didn't think his suggested step was the next logical one, but I also didn't serve as the company's CEO. RTP, like any company, dealt with problems, and if Knott couldn't steer the firm back to solid ground, both would likely sink. Saving the place wasn't my job, however. "If I were you, I'd make sure someone keeps an eye on the mergers team," I said.

"What happened to not telling me how to run the place?"

"Do what you want." I shrugged. "If you don't get the company out of this mess, you're probably going to be looking for work, and I doubt RTP can give you a golden parachute. If I were you, and if I were concerned about who might be shady within my walls, I'd be sure I kept watch on a certain team. What you do with my advice or how you decide to implement it is up to you."

"A lot of good people work here."

"Good people work everywhere. It'd be great to save their jobs, but I'm here to solve a murder. I think I'm making progress. If I live long enough, we all just might get through this."

"I'll figure out a way to keep an eye on Louie's group," Knott said.

"Start by asking your IT staff."

"We monitor systems, not people."

"You're the CEO," I said as I stood. "Who better to change a policy in a moment of need?"

———

I collected the Tylenol from Knott's secretary when I left his office. About a half-hour later, the pain in my face and midsection eased. While working at my desk over lunch, I called T.J.

"You've survived a whole week there," she said. "I'm impressed."

"I'm about ready to pull my hair out," I said. "I hate doing office work. We need to wrap this up ASAP."

"You got anything else?"

"Soon." I paused to survey the area. The only person in earshot was Pat, but she sat in her office with the door closed. "Speaking of surviving . . . you should know. Someone abducted me last night."

"Holy shit. Was it related?"

"No," I said. "Something else. I'll fill you in later. It's resolved, though." I remembered Rollins leaving town to get away from Gabriella's men. He should hear the good news, too. "Anything else from Marvin Bernard?"

"He sent me a message this morning." I waited while she paused to pull it up. "Said nothing changed from his conclusion last week, but he can't give you anything else until he gets more data."

"I'm working on it. I have the admin credentials. We'll see what else they can get me into here. Most places don't lock down their privileged accounts very well."

"Hurry back," T.J. said. "I'm getting bored chasing off insurance men and aggrieved wives."

"Sounds like you're doing great," I told her, and we hung

up. I called Rollins next, and as usual, he answered right away. "Cloak, this is Dagger," I said when he picked up.

"You've seen too many spy movies."

"You still lying low?"

"As best I can," he said. "Haven't seen any suspicious Italians in SUVs for a couple days."

"Good," I said. "I don't think you will, either. I took one for the team."

"What happened?" I heard the concern in his voice. Rollins proved to be a big help in my rehab after getting shot, and I knew he wanted me to stay on the good side of the grass.

"Someone threw a hood over my head last night." The fact these events happened when I went walking for dinner eighteen hours ago felt surreal. "They took me to some place and worked me over. Eventually, Gabriella showed up. She told me I was holding out on her, and the two gentlemen she hired were going to get it out of me. One of them promised to kill me, and if I didn't manage to get free, I think he would have."

Rollins blew out a long breath. "What happened to the guys?"

"Injured but alive," I said as I imaged Rollins shaking his head. He would've killed them. "Once I dealt with them, I went to see Gabriella. She got someone's video doorbell footage showing a truck speeding away after her father died. I didn't think someone would trace it back to you, but she managed to."

"Is she still alive, too?" Rollins asked.

"She is. We . . . came to an understanding. I didn't shoot her and the guy I took out at the door. She's leaving me and mine alone. Our friendship is dead, but whatever. She had me abducted and nearly killed. I wasn't getting her a birthday gift."

"I appreciate the heads up. Still . . . I think I'm going to stay out of town a couple more days. You might trust Gabriella, but I don't."

"All right. Be safe."

"You too," he said and hung up.

I hoped I could manage it.

———

My only contact with the Frederick County Sheriff's Office remained Deputy Dunn. I didn't even know his first name. We'd briefly collaborated the prior year. He probably came away with the impression Rich and I weren't impressed with the county's police work, and he wouldn't be wrong. Still, I needed local support, so I reached out, and he told me when I could come by the nearest office.

It was about a ten-minute drive from RTP—most destinations in Frederick took this much time to reach—and looked like a new building. It stood a single story high, featured unmarred tan siding, and even the windows were clean. I walked in and found Dunn sitting at a small but tidy desk near the back. He was a middle-aged fellow built kind of like me, but with a head which looked a little small for his body. His short hair was a mix of brown and gray, and the same color combination played out in his trimmed goatee. I rubbed my chin. "New look."

"I needed a change," he said without any humor. "What can I do for you?"

"I'm looking into the murder of Jason Napier," I said. "His widow hired me, and I'm . . . working at RTP to see what I can learn there."

"So you bypassed a normal investigation and went straight to undercover?"

"The CEO brought me in. He told me he wants to know who killed one of his best employees." I held up a hand to delay Dunn's objection. "I know . . . he could be blowing smoke up my ass. He's not a great CEO, but I think he's sincere in what he wants."

Dunn leaned back and crossed his right leg over his left knee. "You're still basically in the lion's den."

"I know." I declined to tell him just how leonine the place already proved to be.

"You said RTP, right?" Dunn typed on his computer's keyboard. "We had an assault behind a pub a few days ago. Three guys laid out behind the place. One of them said someone at RTP put him up to it, but it never checked out. You know anything?"

"Nope."

"Someone paid with a company card," Dunn continued. "We talked to him, but he said they must've left before shit went down."

"Lucky for them, then." The deputy stared at me. "Whatever impression you got of me before, do you really think I'd take on three guys behind a pub?"

He shrugged. "You'd have to be pretty capable."

"I'm sure whoever did it would appreciate the compliment," I said.

"Uh-huh." Dunn arched one eyebrow but didn't belabor the point. "You found anything in your . . . investigation?"

"Working on it. There's definitely something irregular going on. I can send what I have to you."

"Please do."

"All right." I pulled out my phone.

"You have it on your cell?" Dunn asked.

"No, but I can access it. What's your email?" He told me,

and I sent him the information I'd gathered along with Marvin Bernard's initial conclusions. "Look it over and tell me what you think. Something's going to happen soon, and it'll be nice to have some local support."

"The sheriff's office is always happy to stand behind rogue investigations," he said.

"Glad to hear it," I said. Dunn frowned. "Thanks for your time." I stood and left. It was still early enough to hit traffic on the drive back to Baltimore. As I sat in stop-and-go on the highway later, Dunn replied to my email. I opened and read it. He told me what I'd compiled looked promising, and while they couldn't act on it right now, we were getting close. I smirked at his use of "we" after the rogue investigation comment. It wasn't far off, though. The locals weren't ready to step in yet. I needed to do more and run the continuing risk of getting caught.

In short, I was still on my own.

CHAPTER 20

"I'M WORRIED ABOUT YOU." Gloria frowned as she scrutinized my face. Her fingertips brushed a bruise on my cheekbone.

"My makeup skills are pretty good," I said.

She gave me an appreciative nod. "Above average for your first try. I wish you didn't need to put it on, though."

I opened my mouth and showed her my missing tooth. Thankfully, it was on the side, so it wouldn't be obvious. Gloria grimaced. "I told Gabriella I'm sending her the bill. I mean it."

"I don't know how you didn't shoot her." It was a sentiment I'd never heard from Gloria before, accompanied by a rare flash of anger in her hazel eyes.

"It was tempting," I admitted. "In the end, we've been friends for decades. I guess it still carries some weight, even though I certainly wouldn't use the word to describe her now."

The doorbell rang. Gloria moved to answer it, but I put my hand up. We were at her house, so someone would need to know who she was and where she lived. These were surmountable obstacles, though. I went to the door with my right hand on my pistol. A young man of maybe twenty stood on the porch with a burgeoning food bag in his hands. "She tip in the app?" I asked.

"Yeah," he said.

"Good. You can just set it down. Thanks."

He did and walked away without incident. I waited for his small Hyundai to leave the driveway before I picked up the bag and brought it inside to place on Gloria's kitchen counter. I would happily cook every day in this space. By contrast, Gloria carried in most food because she couldn't be trusted to do more than boil water without needing the fire department. "The delivery guy wasn't a paid killer?" she said with a grin as she walked in.

"Maybe he poisoned our food," I said. "Let's ask someone we don't like to come by and taste it."

Gloria swatted me on the shoulder and got two plates down. I didn't know what she ordered, though the smells wafting from the bag suggested meat, cheese, corn, and fragrant spices. Probably Mexican. The containers I opened confirmed my guess. Always nice to work on my powers of observation. Gloria got beef enchiladas for both of us, and I moved them to a couple of plates. I added some rice to my own, along with the restaurant's fresh and crispy tortilla chips. She dressed her plate similarly, then dumped the guacamole into a bowl, and we took them to her large dining room table. A baseball team could enjoy a meal if they packed their chairs a little tight. We sat together with several feet of open dark wood on either side.

"I'm putting my certificate to use," Gloria said after we'd each eaten for a few minutes. Almost a third of my entree was gone, plus all my rice. Most of her food remained intact. It tasted too delicious to consume slowly.

"Very nice," I said. "You already have a fundraising client?"

"I do." She paused, and I wondered why until she continued. "It's your parents' foundation."

"I'm sure you'll do great work for them. Just make sure you get everything in writing."

Gloria frowned. "You're being unfair to them."

I thought about it and offered a small nod. "Probably. I guess I'm still salty about how everything shook out. Don't let me be a wet blanket for you." I squeezed her hand. "They do important work, and I know you'll help them raise a lot of money."

"You know we're both going to the eventual banquet, right?"

"Wouldn't miss it," I said.

"Good." Gloria cut a small piece of enchilada. It made a perfectly-sized bite for a rabbit. "I know you believe in me, and I love it, but I can't help thinking they hired me because they know me."

"Of course they did." She pursed her lips, and I gave her hand another squeeze. "Someone you know opening a door for you isn't a bad thing. It's how a lot of the world works. What matters is the work you do to justify their trust in you . . . and I know you'll hit it out of the park."

"Thanks." Gloria smiled. "I guess I needed to hear you say it."

"Can we have this Mexican food at the gala?" I asked.

"I doubt it."

"I'm not sure I can make it, then."

"I'll have your secretary clear your calendar," Gloria said.

"At this rate, you might need a secretary of your own."

"Can I poach T.J.?"

"No," I said.

The next morning at my fake job, I closed a few quick requests in the queue and then focused on the data dump from Jason's old computer. So far, I'd focused on databases and spreadsheets as they were the most likely to be relevant to the case. They didn't paint a complete picture, however, and I wanted to wrap this up so I could stop driving to and from Frederick every day. And for Jason's widow.

The local admin account coupled with my knowledge of how RTP formed its usernames allowed me to map Jason's personal network drive. Most of it consisted of backups of data I'd already uncovered. The rest was abandoned projects, none of which applied to the current case. I broke the connection and returned to what I'd taken from his hard drive.

Jason made clever use of the Temp folder. He stored a bunch of text files in it. All of them were small, only a few kilobytes each. Individually, they served as short notes, reminders, and the like. Aggregated, they began to tell a story, and it was an unflattering one for RTP. I sorted them into date order and opened each to read the contents.

I don't understand why a technology company is getting into mergers and acquisitions.

What's the deal with Pat's husband? He turns up every now and then with flowers and leaves? Creepy!

Some of the companies we're signing on to help will be lucky to last a year.

For a CFO, Pat doesn't seem too interested in what the mergers guys do. They're not even here half the time.

Today, a small airplane parts company who hired us six months ago folded. We ended up with some computer assets and sold a bunch for cash. Is this what Louie's group is working on? How is this worth it to the company?

Louie's kind of an asshole. He doesn't like people asking questions about what his team does or who he answers to. Is he protecting Pat?

A restaurant supply company we're supporting got sold today. Louie seems happy about it.

The computer graveyard is getting fuller. It's a good use of a big refrigerated room, but why are we taking other firms' old PCs?

Another contract partner sold off today. I'm starting to see a pattern. Do we sign on to help failing companies and try to get some benefit out of it when they fold or get bought by someone bigger?

Louie and his boys seem happy whenever this happens. Pat acts like she doesn't know or doesn't care. I don't get it.

I didn't get it, either, but I'd given up trying to understand Pat Ritter. Jason's use of the tiny files was clever. A larger Word document might get scanned by an automated system especially if he tried to email it to himself. Plain text files, by contrast, might slip under the size threshold. A clever person could always fool an automated tool if he knew how it worked. I used SFTP to send the files to myself.

Wondering if Jason tried to get this information out of the company gnawed at me. Sure, it was in his head—and on his hard drive—but he backed everything up. I remotely connected to the email server, tried the same local account credentials, and breathed a sigh of relief when they worked. I could have gotten in another way, but on a monitored network PC, my actions might've thrown an alarm. Despite his account being marked as inactive, I could still see Jason's emails. He'd never used the company resources to send the files to himself. Smart man. Even if they didn't get scanned, someone could've picked up a usage pattern.

I texted T.J. to grab the files and send them to Marvin Bernard. They didn't constitute hard data, but they added context. Maybe this additional information would get him to tell me we had something worth reporting. I logged off the email server and closed all my open Notepad windows. A couple minutes later, I heard footsteps approach.

Louie and Corey glared at me from my cubicle door.

———

I crossed my arms and stared back. "Can I help you clowns?" They didn't say anything. "Any more happy hours you want to invite me to?"

"Bryce is fine by the way," Corey said.

"I don't remember asking," I said. I figured he would be, but it was still good to hear, even if I wouldn't give Corey the satisfaction of further acknowledgement. The encounter with Bryce and his fellow failed tough guys reminded me to take a breath. This situation didn't threaten me . . . at least not yet. I could dial back the aggression which might seem out of place for DBA Trent.

Louie jabbed a finger in my direction. "We're on to you." He turned red-faced as he spoke. "We're keeping an eye on you."

"Which one is it?"

"What?"

"Being on to me and keeping an eye on me are two different things," I said. "The second might lead to the first. You guys want to walk a lap around the floor to get your story straight?"

"Piss off, Trent," Louie said. "We add a lot more value to

this company than a keyboard jockey like you ever will. Don't think it won't matter one day . . . maybe even soon."

I held up my steady right hand. "Look at me shaking."

Before either of them could issue further nonspecific threats, another voice joined the chorus. "Don't you two have anything better to do?" Pat Ritter appeared behind them. "My DBAs aren't interested in things like added value. Maybe you could put a presentation together for the next all-hands, Louie. I'm sure we'd all love a refresher on concepts like ROI."

"See you around, Trent." Louie bobbed his head to the side, and Corey followed him away from my cubicle.

"What were they harassing you about?" Pat asked as she stepped into the place they'd vacated.

"My guess is some inter-team rivalry," I said.

"You know . . . Jason didn't much care for those guys, either. I tried to tell him they have high-pressure jobs and work hard, but he didn't like them."

I feigned surprise as best I could. When in doubt, widen the eyes and offer a slight nod. "Really? Interesting. Maybe he was on to something."

Pat waved a hand. "They're not so bad."

"They work for you, right?"

"They do," she said, "though I sometimes wonder if their true allegiance is to Devon Knott."

As much as I normally didn't like talking to Pat, I wasn't going to shoo her away when she promised to spill the corporate tea. Anything to help my investigation, even if it led to Knott's door. "What do you mean?"

"My husband works in finance on a larger big-corporation level. He proposed the idea of mergers and acquisitions to Devon. Prior to that, we'd just been a technology services company. The research part died with Wikipedia."

"So Knott stood the team up?"

Pat nodded. "It's a financial service, so he organized them under me as CFO. I . . . think it's kind of a mixed bag. Louie can tell you every penny he's added to the company ledger, but I picked my ROI comment on purpose. I don't know if the return justifies the work. His team is only here maybe half the time. They work from home a day or two a week, and they spend time scouting companies and doing on-site research."

Or so they told Pat at least. "How do they determine which companies RTP is going to try and acquire?" I asked.

"You'd probably have to ask them the specifics," Pat said. "They email me about a bunch of little businesses. I don't even reply most of the time because I don't think it's worth it. Maybe I should. Anyway, I usually don't find out until a few weeks later. Louie tells me we're spending money to buy some company." She paused. "The weird thing is, we sell a lot of them off. Or at least their assets."

"Sounds like a cash grab."

"Basically. Like I said, I don't think the time it takes to do everything justifies the man-hours we spend. Knott seems to like it, though, so it stays." Her voice took on a resigned tone. "He doesn't listen to me when I say I think the whole thing is superfluous."

She'd handed me a bunch of ammo I could take to Marvin Bernard. In conjunction with the financial documents and text files, it must have painted some sort of actionable picture. Maybe I'd been wrong about Pat. Unless she told me all this to throw suspicion off herself, it looked like Louie and Devon Knott were the ones in the soup. As Pat wished me a good day and walked away, I wondered how to navigate the case if I ended up investigating the man who hired me.

When Pat took off early, I followed a few minutes later. I called T.J. on my way back and asked her if she could get Marvin Bernard to the office. Rolling out ahead of schedule made my commute easier. I made it to downtown Baltimore in about fifty minutes. When I walked in, T.J. smiled at me. It marked the first time she'd seen me in a week. "You're not dead," she said.

"Maybe I am," I said. "My ghost is haunting you for all the cheap shots you took about my potential demise."

She wrinkled her nose. "That's all bullshit."

I smiled. "We agree. Any word from Marvin?"

"He told me he can't stop by," T.J. said. "We can call him when you're ready, though."

"Did you send him everything I forwarded to you?" I asked. She nodded. "Good. I hope he's had a chance to review it."

"I'll get him on the line." T.J. put her cell on speaker and called the accountant.

"Seems like you've found some interesting things," Marvin Bernard said after the brief round of introductions.

"I have," I said. "In isolation, they may not mean a lot, but when you put all of Jason's notes together, a picture emerges. I had a conversation with my boss in Frederick today, too. She also oversees the mergers team."

"I'm listening."

"Her husband is some corporate finance guy and suggested the whole mergers and acquisitions thing to the CEO, who signed off on it. I get the feeling Pat wasn't too keen on it then, but she got outranked. The guys visit sites here and there, send her emails about companies they think RTP should target, and all. A lot of them are small, and many of them go on to fail. RTP gets some assets out of the deal. It doesn't seem worth it to me, and I think Pat agrees. The team doesn't seem to care what her opinion is, though. I get the feeling she thinks they're bypassing her and going to the CEO."

"Hmm." Marvin paused. "It's all adding up."

"To what?"

"Let me give you some good and bad news. The bad news is you haven't told me or handed me anything which implicates one specific person. Louie . . . I think his name is . . . sounds slimy, and he probably is. The CEO might be mixed up in it, too. Your case is stronger now, but we don't have evidence which leads to one culprit or mastermind."

"What's the good news?" I said.

"I see a pattern, especially with the added information you got from your boss. It sounds like RTP is buying up struggling companies and hoping for a dead cat bounce. You'll recall this was my guess when we spoke last."

"I do."

"I'd venture it's more than a guess now," Marvin said. "Taking everything into account, I'm certain this is what they're doing. Selling off assets or trying to turn a quick profit. They're probably buying these other places with debt and trying to leverage it quickly. Done right, it can make some money. It sounds like your boss is concerned about the ROI, which is fair. On a small scale with little local companies, you need a lot of churn to really add to the bottom line. And if one deal blows up, it can set you back months."

"None of this is illegal, though?" T.J. wanted to know.

"On the surface, no. Like with most things, the crime is in the details. If you wanted me to speculate, I would say your dead man got wind of what was going on and threatened to blow the whistle."

"My suspicion, too," I said.

"We're close," Marvin said. "There's something shady going on. I'm certain of it. Maybe there's data to be uncovered in the companies RTP has acquired. An official investigation at this point might turn up the ringleader, but I think it's still a little early. See if you can find something definitive."

I hadn't thought of looking at their targets. It sounded like a good idea. "I'll see what I can do. These guys are assholes, but they're not idiots. They probably didn't leave a smoking gun on the network, but I'll do some more digging."

"Good. I'll be happy to look over whatever else you might have."

We thanked Marvin for his time and hung up. "I guess I'm still a DBA for now," I grumbled.

"If you're getting close, they must be getting suspicious." T.J. frowned.

"They are. A couple of them came to my cubicle and tried to stare me down. It didn't go so well. Pat chased them off, and then she spilled the tea about the group."

"Maybe she's on your side after all."

"Possibly," I said. "I thought Knott really wanted to know who killed Jason. I hope it's still true. He could simply be loyal to the bottom line, though."

"Be careful," T.J. said. "You know I don't really want you to die, right?"

"Sure. Finding a new job is a hassle."

She punched me in the shoulder. "I mean it."

I grinned. "I know. My ghost would totally haunt you, though. You've made enough jokes."

"Good thing I think ghosts are bullshit, then."

"Good thing," I agreed.

CHAPTER 21

I WOKE up early the next morning. As much as I disliked it, doing so served a few purposes. It put me ahead of traffic, so my commute to Frederick felt more normal. It meant I could leave earlier at the end of the day. Additionally, starting early meant I might crack the case before lunch, and I could speed away from RTP and vow never to return. My face looked more normal than the prior couple days, so I didn't bother covering any lingering marks with cosmetics.

The third floor was mostly empty as I sat at my desk. My pilfered local administrator credential proved useful again as it allowed me to access the mergers and acquisition team's network folder. They didn't keep a lot of info online where it might be discovered. Clever, even if it pointed the finger at them a little more. It also meant I'd need to go hunting for the really good stuff if I required it. Louie struck me as smart enough to keep it offline and encrypted, and even if I solved the first part, the second would tie me up indefinitely.

Among the data they'd put in their shared drive was a list of their successes. These were the companies RTP acquired under their watch. I'd never heard of any of them. Quick online research of the first two revealed them to be small, the transactions low-level, and the assets sold for a modest profit. Trumpeting these moves as successes strained the definition of the word, but Louie seemed to enjoy the blessings of the CEO.

The other businesses got a folder each, and I could drill down for more information. Organization charts. Emails relating to the acquisition. I could search the contents of the folders, but I also didn't want to miss anything. Going through all this stuff by hand would take a while. "Good thing I came in early," I muttered to my empty gray cubicle walls.

It took a while to find anything promising. I'd already finished my coffee and considered where I might go for another cup. Deep in the email exchanges with a company called Triangle Tech, I unearthed a potential gem: *I don't know how Irish will take the news.* If this referred to the man who first came to my office with a seemingly implausible story, I knew how: poorly. No other references appeared anywhere else in the folder.

The sale took place eight months ago. Triangle Tech's website was defunct, and the page told me I could buy the domain if I wanted. I did not. I did, however, use the Internet Archive to visit a past copy of the company's site. Thankfully, the individual pages worked. Triangle had been a small technology services company in southern Maryland. They did similar work to RTP, but contracts dried up, money grew tight, and they accepted a buyout offer. Under the Executives tab, I found bios for the men and women who ran the operation.

Their number included Danny Mahoney, whose writeup referred to him as "Irish." The picture matched the man who came to see T.J. and me if I mentally added a few months of hard living. "Son of a bitch," I said. Irish's bio told the story of him being one of Triangle's first employees, how he rose through the ranks, and the pride he felt at delivering services to his community. It all explained why he didn't like RTP and kept on them even after they'd tossed Triangle onto the trash heap of local history.

I fired off a quick text to my secretary. *Irish might be crazy, but I know who he is now. He worked for a place RTP bought and discarded. I'm going to try and find him.*

T.J. sent a response quickly. *Wow! I'll check the police report and see if there's any info on him.*

A few minutes later, she posted a cell phone number. I walked up to the fourth floor. Devon Knott sat behind his desk. He bade me enter when I knocked. "I might've found something," I said. "Someone, really. I need to go and check it out. You'll have to provide some cover for me with Pat."

He nodded. "Sounds promising. Good luck. I'll take care of Pat. Don't worry about her."

I left his office and sprinted down the stairs.

———

By the time I reached my car, T.J. had texted. *Found a cell number in the police report. Might be bullshit, but you can try it.* 410-555-9313. I sent my thanks in reply and dialed the number. It rang six times and went to voicemail. Maybe Irish screened his calls . . . if this were even his phone. Did the police verify the info, or did he just make something up when they booked him? I hoped for the former.

I declined to leave a voicemail and instead thumbed a quick text. *If this is Irish, you told me about a man in Frederick recently. It's taken a while, but I know some things. Call me back at this number.* I started the S4 and drove out of the parking lot. Danny Mahoney hailed from southern Maryland, but he found me in Baltimore and learned about RTP in Frederick. Just this activity covered a lot of ground. He could be anywhere.

A few minutes later, my phone rang. I diverted into a strip mall to stop and talk. "Hello?"

"You the detective?"

"You Irish?" I asked, though the voice I heard sounded like I remembered his.

"I told you to call me by it," he said.

"I also learned your actual name. Which would you rather go by?"

"Let's stick with Irish. I've come to like it."

So far, he hadn't said anything weird. Maybe he was under a lot of stress the day he dropped in to the office. Or off his meds. I didn't even know if the man actually lived anywhere. A little more research might have been a better tactic than sprinting from the building, but here I was. "All right. I think we should meet somewhere and talk. I've learned a lot, but I don't know everything. Maybe you can help."

"I told you they weren't just a tech company," he said.

"I believe you."

"Why'd you call the cops on me, then?"

"I didn't," I said.

"Don't bullshit me."

"I'm not. My secretary did. She felt unsafe. I thought we had things under control, but it was her decision, and I'm not going to fault her for it. You came in with wild eyes and said a lot of really random stuff."

Irish didn't answer for several seconds. Eventually, he said, "It wasn't one of my best days. Ain't had a lot of good ones recently, if I'm being honest." He sighed. "All right. Let's talk. Where are you?"

"Not far from RTP."

"I'm near Security Square Mall. I'll text you the address." He hung up before I could say anything else. A moment later, my phone lit up with a message. I entered the data into the GPS and set off. The mall sat right off I-70 near its junction with the Baltimore Beltway. As with any such place, I felt surprised it was still open. It would be a long way from southern Maryland, but it afforded Irish easier access to Frederick.

I took the dedicated exit for the mall at the end of I-70 and worked my way into the surrounding neighborhood. The address Irish gave me resolved to a simple brick house. None of the homes on the street looked to be in good repair. I parked in the driveway, got out, and approached. Window blinds drew back as I walked up, and before I could knock on the door, Irish opened it. He looked much like when he came to my office, even if his eyes focused on me a lot more consistently than in our first meeting. "Were you followed?"

"No," I said.

"Thanks for coming," he said. "I know I didn't make a great first impression." He ushered me inside and locked up.

"Honestly . . . we thought you were a nut." The inside of the house wasn't in much better shape. Too many years of use left the carpet thin. The walls all needed paint. None of the furniture went together. The living room was a hodgepodge of brown leather, gray cloth, and plaid. Whoever lived here probably grabbed pieces they could afford when they had the money.

Irish took the evaluation well. "You weren't wrong. I'd kinda come to the end of my rope. My uncle—this is his place— he's a nurse, and he got me an appointment. I'm not back to where I was before this whole mess began, but I'm better than I've been in a while."

"Good," I said. "How come you never got back to me?"

"I left with the cops," he said. "I figured you didn't take me seriously."

"I thought there might've been an actual true story under whatever you told us. We didn't have much luck ferreting out the details, however. Before long, a woman came to the office and wanted me to look into her husband's murder."

"He was the guy killed in Frederick?"

I nodded. "Good timing on her part. Even as I figured out more about what happened, though, I didn't have a way to reach you. Eventually, I came across your name and alias in a company RTP acquired."

"Sons of bitches," Irish muttered. "Triangle did good work for people who needed it."

"So far, you're the only person I've tracked down who's been on the wrong end of one of RTP's acquisitions. What can you tell me about it?"

"I don't know if I have the full picture." Irish frowned. "I was involved, but I wasn't the president of the company."

"I'm sure it's still useful," I said.

My host leaned back in the shopworn recliner. "It started when we lost our IT guys. We were a small outfit, so we only had two . . . a father and son. Good workers. Knew their stuff. The dad got cancer and then needed to stop working, and his son went on leave to take care of him. Sad, really." I nodded my agreement, and Irish continued. "We needed someone to take over, and we ended up picking RTP. They weren't the closest place, but they offered experienced folks and put a good package together."

"Did the whole thing not go well?"

"They were fine. It's hard to recover from losing so much knowledge, but their people did the best they could. At first, at least. Pretty soon, some other guy started coming with them. He . . . kept looking at everything. Checking it out. I thought he might have been taking inventory, but I suspect he was evaluating the assets."

"What did he look like?" I asked.

Irish shrugged. "I dunno. Not too tall. Kind of a meathead, though. Looked like he spent a couple hours in the gym after work. I never got a name, though."

It sounded like Louie, but I didn't press Irish on the mystery man's identity. "What happened next?"

"Their people spent more time on the phone . . . with the home office, I guess. The other guy especially. I'm not sure who they talked to. I heard a woman's voice sometimes. I think she was in finance."

"Probably Pat," I said. "She's the CFO. Technically, I work for her as a DBA."

"I got to know the CEO's voice, too," Irish said. "Their people took over one of our conference rooms whenever they needed it, and they weren't shy about using the speaker phones. He didn't seem like he wanted to be involved. I never knew a CEO who didn't care a lot about money."

"Did they ever talk to anyone else?"

"There was another guy." Irish leaned forward. "He's the one I didn't know. Only heard him once or twice. Smooth talker. Seemed to know his way around money. I think the meathead listened to him more than the CFO and CEO."

I'd never met another financial decision maker at RTP. Who would have been on the other end of the line when Louie and the team posed questions? "I'll have to work on who he is. Let's keep going. I guess they bought you out next?"

"Yeah," Irish confirmed. "It was a shit offer, I thought, but Triangle wasn't making a lot of money toward the end. RTP fired everyone, kept some of the computers, sold off the others, and leased the building. In the end, they turned a profit, which I guess was their goal all along."

"The whole thing must've left a bad taste in your mouth," I said.

He bobbed his head. "Yeah. I was out of a job, and it wasn't a great market. Still ain't. I kept tabs on them. It was hard from down south, so I came to my uncle's place. Being so close to Seventy helps. Straight shot to Frederick." Irish jerked his thumb over his shoulder toward a room I hadn't seen yet. "I got a directional mic on the dining room table in there." He snorted. "Between it and a strong Wi-Fi antenna, I tried to keep an eye on things. Never managed to learn a lot. Then, I met Jason. He found me nearby one day. He was suspicious of some things, too."

"You worked together?"

"More or less. He used ProtonMail to send me some info here and there." Irish took a deep breath. "One day, he was going to meet me after work. Never did. I drove up and nosed around. It's when I saw them bring his body out. His arm looked frostbitten."

On my first day, Devon Knott mentioned a meat packer once owned the RTP building. The basement still housed a refrigerated area which served as a graveyard for old computers. Did Louie keep Jason in there until he died of hypothermia? On whose orders did he do it? "I'm glad you're able to tell me all this," I said. "I'm not sure who I should be suspicious of now, though."

"All of them," Irish said. "Bastards. The place is rotten to the core. You said the CEO hired you to figure out what happened?"

"Yeah," I said.

"Not sure I'd feel so good about it. He might not be the ring-leader, but the buck woulda stopped with him."

"It usually does."

"Don't get caught up in too much," Irish said. "Looks like you already went a couple rounds with someone."

"Unrelated, but thanks." While I still bore some bruises from Gabriella's goons, the prior two times I needed to use my fists recently had been very related to RTP. Maybe I'd get to pin those on Louie before this case concluded.

This proved to be an illuminating conversation. I thanked Irish for his time and left. I didn't know who I could trust inside RTP's walls now—if anyone. Wrapping things up quickly would be important. I didn't want to take the same trip to the computer graveyard Jason Napier did.

———

I drove home feeling a little drained after my talk with Irish. In reality, my recent night of not sleeping was probably still playing havoc with me. Still, questions remained after our conversation. He'd cleared a few things up, but he also muddied the waters. Once in my house, I ordered pizza to be delivered. No more trips onto the mean streets of Federal Hill for a while. Not until I knew Gabriella really would leave me alone—and especially not with a resolution to this case feeling closer than ever.

As I waited for dinner, I sat at my laptop and did some digging. Irish's former company got bought and trashed by RTP. They weren't the only ones out there. Ever since the mergers team began its work, other firms met similar fates. I searched for them thanks in part to the records Jason kept along with the Maryland Chamber of Commerce, who probably never envisioned their website being used the way I did.

I compiled a list of a few former companies. All their websites were defunct. As before, the Internet Archive let me browse them as they existed months or years ago. It made some of my advanced Google searches harder, but I still found the information I wanted. Organization charts, Word documents which should have been kept internal, and employee rosters in spreadsheet form remained out there. Sometimes, the "hacker" is merely the person who gets blamed for finding the data an idiot should have protected.

Thankfully, idiots remained in generous supply.

I assembled a list of people who might've been in position to interact with the RTP team and know what happened. My pizza remained en route, so I called the first person on my sheet, a man named Vance Gordon. We talked for a few minutes, but he couldn't tell me much apart from the volume of dislike for RTP. It proved to be a similar story to Triangle Tech. Gordon's erstwhile firm hired RTP to manage their IT systems and services. Within a few months, business was down, RTP made an offer, and the owner took it. Ninety people hit the unemployment line, a bunch of computers and furniture joined the open market, and a developer bought the building. Before we hung up, Gordon told me it's now a restaurant, and he refuses to eat there. I couldn't blame him.

The brief mention of an eatery made me hungry, and my two pizzas arrived a minute later. I made a small salad and wolfed down four slices. The remaining pie and a half would be leftovers. Maybe I could wrap this case up soon, and Gloria would be back to help me eat them. She'd wrinkle her nose at the idea of eating two-day-old reheated pizza, but in the end, she'd enjoy it just the same.

A few more post-dinner conversations turned up similar results. One showed an actual dead cat bounce. RTP bought into the business, it improved, and then the whole operation got sold at a profit. While everyone I talked to landed somewhere on the bitter scale, none of them could tell me anyone got harmed or died as a result of the takeovers. My last call went to a woman named Kendall Leonard. She served as the vice president of a company in Hagerstown called Burchard Farms. "The land is still there," she told me. "People still work it . . . but all the goods go somewhere else."

"What happened when RTP came in?" I asked.

"They seemed a little skeptical at first. A lot of people think farming is all about roosters crowing, milking the cows, planting the crops . . . whatever. That's all part of it, but you have to do something with the milk, the corn, and all. You need to keep track of it."

"It makes sense. A small family farm might be able to do a lot by hand, but a larger and more professional operation needs computers."

"Right," she said. "We didn't have a ton of equipment. A small staff in the office. We ran our website off a server in the old barn. Still, when our IT manager retired, they sent us a couple capable guys to fill in. It was supposed to be until we found someone else, but they did a good job. I wanted to keep them on."

"Let me guess," I said. "Something happened, and they bought out the company."

"Oh, something happened, all right. Some weird shit." She snorted. "Bastards. No one even looked into it. First, a body turns up in the fields. Some unsolved killing. Business took a hit. Places didn't want to buy from the Murder Farm."

"You think RTP planted the body?"

"The deputies said the guy wasn't killed there." Last week, I would have thought the idea RTP killed a man and dumped his body in a farm they wanted to acquire on the cheap a fantasy. Tonight, I was all in on the idea. "Nobody knows who the man was to this day. The last theory I heard was it was a homeless guy. I don't think there was ever a suspect."

"Did RTP move in right away?" I said.

Kendall sighed. "No. Another guy started showing up at first. He didn't look like an IT guy. Then again, I don't look like a farm worker. I think his name was Lou."

"Louie. I know who you're talking about. He's the head of the mergers and acquisitions team."

"What the hell does a tech company need a mergers and acquisitions team for?" Kendall said.

"A lot of people share your skepticism," I said. "Me included."

"Anyway, Louie was always on the phone. I don't know who he talked to. He never stuck around if I was nearby. RTP offered us a loan to keep meeting expenses. Soon, they made an offer for everything. The owners sold for too little, but I think they'd lost their stomach for the business. The farm hadn't been in the original family for years. The value of the land alone was high. I'm sure they made a nice profit on the sale."

"Do you have any proof anyone connected with RTP put a corpse in the field?" I wanted to know.

"Of course not," Kendall said. "They were careful. You ask me, some bastard who works for them did it. Maybe Louie. Hell, I don't know. I found a job pretty quickly, but I'm still salty about what happened. It didn't need to go down like that."

"No, it didn't." I thanked Kendall for her time and ended the call. Over the course of the day, the unflattering picture of RTP I'd formed in my head grew a lot worse. I needed to talk with Pat Ritter and Devon Knott in the morning. They wouldn't like the conversation. I hoped I would survive the aftermath.

CHAPTER 22

I TRIED to get up early the next morning. The spirit was willing, but the flesh was weak. In the end, I hit snooze on my phone alarm five times, took my fastest shower in years, and grabbed whatever clothes were in easy reach. Thankfully, I've always been fashionable enough to avoid a disaster here. J. Crew wouldn't be calling to photograph me for an upcoming catalog, but I also wouldn't embarrass myself. The black turtleneck and medium blue jeans made for fine office attire. Downstairs, I heated up a frozen burrito, poured a tall to-go mug of coffee, and headed to the car.

Thanks to my late start, I sat in traffic at several points. The slowdowns gave me a chance to eat breakfast and drink my java. I arrived at RTP a few minutes late, got some more coffee from the break room, and sat at my desk. Pat's office door was open. I called Knott, got his secretary, and asked to be connected to the main man. A couple minutes later, he came on the line. "Meet me in Pat's office," I said.

"Can it wait?" he asked.

"Depends. Based on what I've learned about how the company operates, you might have some interested parties crawling all over this place by noon if I make a phone call. You wanted the truth. I bet it'll come out anyway if you ignore me."

"All right . . . all right. I'll be there in a few minutes." He hung up. I walked down the hall, knocked on Pat's open door, and walked in without waiting for her to invite me.

"Just come on in," she said, frowning.

"I will. Thanks." I dropped into one of her guest chairs.

"You all right?"

"Sure."

"You look like you've been in a fight recently," Pat said.

"A few days ago," I said. "You should see the other guys, but if you want to, you'll need to do it during visiting hours."

"Something I can help you with, Trent?"

"Knott's on his way. I think we're all going to have a very interesting chat."

She narrowed her eyes at me. "What are you up to?"

"At the moment, I'm waiting for a meeting . . . one which is probably overdue."

"Overdue, huh?" Pat scoffed. "You haven't even been here two weeks, and you're already demanding time with me and the CEO." She paused and stared at me. "Are you after my job?"

I laughed. "Get real. I'm sure I could do it better than you, but I have less than zero interest."

"Let me guess. You think you can do a better job because you're a man."

"No," I said. "It's because your personality isn't well-suited to being a manager. Mine isn't, either. I'm simply more aware of my limitations and, in this case, not eager to remedy them."

Pat scowled, but before she could say anything else, Devon Knott walked in. He closed the door behind himself and sat in the other guest chair. "Does she know?" he asked.

"Know what?" Pat demanded. "What do you two have going on?"

"I'm not a DBA," I said, "and I'm not Trent Gustaffson. I'm certainly qualified to do the job, but I'm really a private investigator from Baltimore. My actual name is C.T. Ferguson."

"I brought him in," Knott said. "Jason's widow reached out to me. I feel terrible about what happened to him, and I wanted to get to the bottom of it. She also contacted C.T., so it seemed like a good move to bring him here and let him look around from the inside. I made sure he had the access he needed."

Pat crossed her arms. "You could have told me, Devon. You can't just stick a man on my team and not tell me what's really going on."

"I probably should have. My idea was to make sure as few people as possible knew who C.T. was and what he was really doing here."

"As thrilling as your little back-and-forth is," I said, "we have some things to discuss. Namely, this company is a shady dumpster fire, and both of you bear some of the blame."

Knott frowned and exchanged a glance with Pat. "You're going to need to explain."

"It's the mergers team. They're total wild cards. I'm sure they've added to the bottom line, and it's significant for a smaller, privately-held company. They're leaving a long trail of woe behind them, and it might bring this whole place down."

"I had a bad feeling about them." Knott's bony fingers pinched the bridge of his nose.

"You liked them well enough when my husband proposed the idea," Pat said. Enough accusation dripped from her tone to soak her desk.

"Aaron usually knows what he's talking about," Knott said. He turned to me. "What specifically did you hear?"

I told him about Irish (while leaving his true identity out of things), the other companies who couldn't point bloody fingers at RTP, and finished with the story of Burchard Farms. "I haven't even started investigating the body in the field yet," I said. "I also feel I shouldn't need to. There's enough damning evidence in everything else I've said."

Neither Pat nor Knott said anything for several seconds. I knew my story was a lot to take in. They probably knew bits and pieces of it already. Taken as a whole, the activities of Louie's team painted RTP as major villains. Now, I'd figure out if the CEO and CFO cared about the company's reputation over their own. "We need to see this through," Knott said with a resigned sigh. "It sounds like Jason died because he learned some things he shouldn't have. We owe it to him to finish this."

"I agree," Pat said.

"Great," I said. "Before we break out the pom-poms, though, you both know you might not survive the fallout, right?" Each of them nodded in turn.

Knott tapped his chest. "I'll be sure you have what you need, C.T. I know this case has turned into more than you probably thought it would. Personally, I'm disgusted by some of the things I've heard. They make me question my leadership."

"They should," I concurred.

"You're right. Please see this through to the end. Even if the board gives me the boot for everything, I want to get this company back on the right track."

"Me, too," Pat added.

"All right," I said. "I'll keep looking around. Pat, I'm not going to be doing any stupid DBA tickets. Or any other work, either. You might need to give me some cover with the team."

"I will."

"OK." I stood. "Let's hope we can wrap this up soon. The

drive is bad enough, but I don't want to keep coming here. It's probably hazardous to my health."

"Let's hope it isn't," Knott said.

I would leave the hoping to him.

———

After my meeting with the C suite, I returned to my desk. Pat knew my real identity and why I was really here. If she were complicit in RTP's sins, she might still resent me and try to get rid of me. At least she wouldn't keep pestering me about busy-work. Brent and whoever else worked on the team could handle the menial tasks. For my part, I hoped to be done with this place and see a killer in handcuffs within the next day or two.

My cell phone buzzed on the desk. The name which popped up ranked near the bottom on the list of people I expected to be reaching out—Gabriella Rizzo. *I've had a couple days to process everything. Still think you could've been more honest, but I'm willing to move on. Maybe our friendship is broken. I hope not, but I know it might be. Still . . . Truce?*

I didn't have time for the mob queen and her self-created problems. My reply basically told her as much. *I'm at a critical point in the case right now. Can't worry about other stuff. Let's talk in a few days.* I hoped it would be the end of the conversation. Gabriella could be more productive with her time by visiting Tweedledee and Tweedledum in the hospital. They'd probably still be there. I took a deep breath as my night in their company played in my head.

The hospital. Corey's buddy Bryce would probably still be in a bed, too. I'd given him quite a crack on the head, and he didn't strike me as the type with a lot of brain cells in reserve. I wondered what he knew. Would Corey share details of the company's plan with him? Or was it more along the lines of asking to find a couple friends and beat up some meddlesome but handsome new employee?

Bryce would make a nice catch, but bigger fish awaited me. I didn't know if I could implicate Pat or Knott. Even if I could, I wouldn't be able to make a case against either of them out of the blue. I would need to step my way up to them.

The first face I needed to press under my shoe belonged to Louie.

———

It all came back to the mergers and acquisitions team. Even if they moved to the machinations of a master in the shadows, Louie and the rest of his glorified goons occupied the center of every recent RTP shitstorm. Knott should've concluded they were way more trouble than they were worth, of course, but strong executive leadership didn't seem to be on brand for the company.

Louis Eckert lived in a town called Urbana. It sat off I-270 on the way to Frederick from Baltimore and anywhere to the south or east. Like most areas of suburban sprawl, townhouse communities sprang up around schools and strip malls, and single-family homes lingered nearby to vacuum up the people with an intense dislike of small yards and shared walls.

Louie must have been okay with limited acreage. He lived on a street of recent townhouses. Every time I saw them, I compared them to Baltimore's classic rowhouses, and it wasn't much of a competition. The modern dwellings didn't allow for much character. Builders presented a few options they could easily churn out, and the result was an avenue of homes which looked more or less the same. Louie chose a bay window on the ground level and a different shutter color than his neighbors. It wasn't a ringing endorsement for individuality.

All the houses featured one-car garages and a short driveway. Louie remained at work when I ducked out early to run home, pick up lunch and supplies, and wait for him. He answered his desk phone when I pulled up, so I hadn't missed him. I sat in a visitor parking spot allowing me a clear view of his house. In addition to a turkey sub and chips, I brought a good camera and a directional microphone.

After an hour, I wondered if my decision to come here had been smart. The possibility remained for Louie to come home and spend a quiet evening watching TV and flexing in the mirror during the commercial breaks. If this turned out to be the case, I'd be wasting my time. The likelihood remained on my mind as one hour became two. Dusk approached, and streetlights in the community flickered to life.

Into the third hour of my vigil, Louie pulled up. He must have gotten a loaner BMW from the dealership. This one was a white X3 SUV. The garage door opened, and he steered the crossover inside. So much for jumping into a random pickup truck and smashing it into the Bimmer a few times. Probably for the best. I'd hate to be thought of as unimaginative and repetitive.

I set the mic on my dash and pointed it at his house. The occasional car drove down the street. Workdays were ending. No one took note of me, however. The tint on the S4's windows--which went right up to the legal limit in Maryland-- likely helped. Sure enough, the TV clicked on. Based on what I could hear, Louie watched the local news. A short while later, his phone rang. He muted the broadcast to answer.

"Hello . . . what do you mean? . . . tonight? . . . sure, I'll be home. Bye."

I could only hear one side of the conversation, so I used my vast sleuthing powers to deduce someone would be stopping by. Hopefully soon. I didn't want to miss an incriminating conversation because I needed to find a place to pee. About a half-hour later, a late-model Lincoln Continental drove down the street and pulled into Louie's driveway. It idled there. I used the camera to zoom in and get a shot of the license plate.

Louie came out his front door a minute later. He looked around briefly before opening the driver's side rear door and climbing in. I'd already pointed the mic at the car. "What the hell do you mean they're on to us?" Louie demanded.

"Exactly what I told you," another man said. I couldn't place the voice. "We were always concerned Pat and Devon would figure it out. They managed not to for a while."

"What's changed?"

"The new DBA. He's not who he claims to be."

"Son of a bitch," Louie said. "I thought something seemed weird about him. He took out the first two guys I put on him, and then three at the bar a couple days later. Ain't no DBA who knows how to fight like he does."

While I liked Louie's estimation of my prowess, I didn't want word of who I really was to spread through the company. Only two people knew. I wondered which one gave me up. "It's worse," the mystery man said. "He's a private investigator. Jason's widow hired him, and Knott agreed to use him as a confederate inside the company. He's been nosing into things since he started."

Louie sighed, and both men fell silent. Eventually, he asked, "What do we do about him now? Bastard probably knows everything."

"Maybe not everything, but he's on the right track. We'll have to deal with him."

"I could--"

"No," the other fellow broke in. "You've had two chances to solve the problem. Leave it to me. I have an idea. He doesn't know the whole story yet, and I'm going to make sure he doesn't."

"Fine," Louie said. "We done here?"

"Yes, Louie. Get back to your microwaved dinner and local news."

"Eat shit." Louie opened the door and climbed from the Continental. He walked back to his house as the car backed out of the driveway and left the way it came in. Its windows were darkened, too, and even the help of the camera didn't afford me a look at anyone inside. I did have the plate, though. Using my phone to connect to my main computer, I accessed the BPD's lookup tool.

The Lincoln belonged to Mark Ritter, Pat's brother-in-law. Was he the mystery man pulling the strings? It would make for an interesting day at the office tomorrow. I wondered if his closing threat would see some goons darken my doorstep tonight. I resolved to be armed and vigilant as I drove away from Urbana.

CHAPTER 23

I PARKED behind my house and scanned the area. No one waited to jump out of the shadows at me. I kept my hand on my pistol as I walked to the back door, unlocked it, and went inside. The house looked like I'd left it. If the puppet master knew I was a private investigator, it stood to reason he knew my name. Learning my address from there would be trivial. I peeked out the front window. No unfamiliar cars sat nearby.

Normally, after I arrive home, I kiss my lovely girlfriend and remove my holster and gun. Oh-for-two today. Gloria remained at her house, and I kept the 9MM at my side. To minimize my time standing in the kitchen, I prepared a quick dinner of reheated pizza and a small Caesar salad. As I sat on the couch and ate it, I considered how much I filtered through the lens of not wanting to be put in situations where I might die.

No one wanted to be. I'd been diligent about preventing those scenarios since I got shot. When I found myself in them anyway, I tended to take extreme measures. Clocking Bryce with my billiard-ball sap. Injuring Gabriella's goons. Today, I didn't want to linger in the kitchen because someone might have a shot at me through a window. In the living room, I could sit farther back and be invisible from the road. Taken collectively, this behavior made good sense. I could rationalize it, but I knew I couldn't keep it up. Risks were a part of the job. I would need to come to terms with dangerous scenarios when they happened and not go from zero to a hundred in two seconds.

Those were goals for another day, however. For now, I wanted to wrap up this damned case. I was close, too. I could feel it. Pat's brother-in-law created an unknown variable. I'd presumed either Pat or Knott lied about their knowledge of what went on it. It might still turn out to be the case, but an outside actor also influenced events. Was the CFO in league with her husband's brother?

As I finished my meal, an engine rumbled outside. I set my plate down, put my hand on my gun, and walked to the window. Standing beside it, I crouched and peered out the blinds. A Dodge Charger idled across the street. The illumination from the streetlights didn't allow me to see inside. I slid the pistol from its holster. The car remained in place. A thin cloud of smoke sullied the air behind it.

The driver's door opened, and a man climbed out. He was tall enough for the process to take a few seconds. Once his feet were on the asphalt of Riverside Avenue, he reached back into the car and pulled out an unwieldy plastic bag. The man looked at a paper on the bag, scanned house numbers, and approached a home across the street.

On the tiny chance it was all an elaborate setup, I maintained my post and my vigilance. The fellow turned out to be delivering food after all. A couple minutes later, he returned to his car, folded himself behind the wheel again, and drove away. I slid my gun back into place and stood.

At this rate, it would be a long night.

————

I drove the Caprice to RTP in the morning. In the event Louie and his mystery benefactor escalated things, I wanted the extra protection. I kept a watchful eye on my mirrors throughout the drive, but nothing out of the ordinary transpired. Once I put my bag down at my desk, I walked to Pat's office. She worked with the door open again, and like the previous day, I strode in and sat down without waiting for an invitation.

"Two days in a row," she said without looking over from her monitor. "To what do I owe the pleasure?"

"I have an interesting development. Can you ask Knott to come down?"

"Couldn't you?"

"He tried to blow me off yesterday," I said. "Let's see how he acts with a fellow member of the C suite."

Pat rolled her eyes but made the call. The secretary gatekept her at first, too, but Knott agreed to meet with us as soon as his CFO asked. While we waited, my pretend boss tried to make small talk. "How long have you worked as a private investigator?"

"I'm in my fourth year."

"What did you do before?"

"I split my time between collegiate lacrosse champion, hacker, and playboy," I said.

"Well," Pat said with a frown, "I'm sure that was all very interesting."

"It was."

Mercifully, we earned a reprieve on continuing the conversation when Knott joined us. He closed the door and dropped onto the guest chair beside me. "It sounds like we have another update."

"We do," I said. "When I left yesterday, I surveilled Louie's house. It turned out to be pretty illuminating."

"Do tell," Knott said.

"He got a call while I was on my vigil. I used a directional microphone to listen. I could only hear his side of the conversation, but someone definitely wanted to meet with him."

"Is this all legal?" Pat asked.

"You want to study for the bar exam or solve a murder? I only have time for one."

"Continue, C.T.," Knott said. "Please."

I nodded. "A short while later, a Lincoln Continental drove down the road. New one." Pat's brows knitted as I talked about the car. "It parked in Louie's driveway. Between the streetlights and the window tint, I couldn't see anyone inside. Louie came out, got in the car, and had a chat with someone."

"You know who?" Pat asked. Her voice sounded a little unsteady.

"No," I said. "They talked about this place, though. The jig is up. Louie and the mystery man know who I am. They've figured out what I'm investigating. They also know Amy Napier originally hired me and you two have, to some degree, been supporting my work."

"Are they threatening us?" Knott said.

"Probably. It happens to me a lot in my job. I've gotten used to it. The two of you might want to take precautions, though. Vary your routes to and from work. Come in and leave at different times. Try not to be predictable."

"Are you worried?"

"A little," I admitted. "I still don't know who Louie talked to. Whoever it was said I didn't know everything, and he would handle it. I kept an eye out for tails this morning, but no one followed me. I don't like looking over my shoulder, though, so I'm hoping we can wrap this up soon."

"I think we all want that," Pat said.

I leaned forward and stared at her. She shot me a quizzical look. "You reacted when I described the car."

She shrugged. "Not often you hear about one."

"Maybe you hear about them a little more frequently than the rest of us," I said. "The Continental is registered to your brother-in-law."

"Pat!" Knott said, spreading his hands.

The CFO closed her eyes and rubbed her forehead. "I don't know what Mark does in his free time. If he's involved in any of this, it's the first I've heard of it." She glared at Knott. "Devon, you can't seriously think I'd have anything to do with murdering an employee."

They bickered for a moment while I turned what I knew over in my head. Mark Ritter owned the car. He probably drove it, but he didn't need to be alone. His brother, Pat's husband, was a financial whiz. Someone who would know a thing or two about mergers and acquisitions, dead cat bounces, and all the ways to apply pressure to a flagging company. I'd met him briefly on my first day when he delivered flowers to his wife—according to Brent, this was at least a semi-regular occurrence. Could he be the mastermind? "Where was your husband last night?" I broke in to their squabble.

"What?" Pat frowned. "He was working. Aaron doesn't always keep normal hours because of overseas markets."

"Did you see him?"

"Of course."

I pressed her. "When? What time?"

"When I first got home. I guess it was . . . four o'clock or so.

He said he'd be working for a while, so I left him alone. We had dinner together around seven-thirty."

Three and a half hours. Plenty of time to catch a ride with his brother, chat with Louie, devise a scheme to get a good-looking and persistent PI off everyone's back, and be back home in time to eat. "Where's his office?"

"The basement," Pat said.

"Is there a walk-out?" I asked.

"I really don't see what—"

"Is. There. A walk-out?"

"Yes," she said in a quiet voice.

"So it's possible he left the house between the time you first saw him and when you had dinner." Pat's only reply was a small nod. "Damn. Maybe I should try to pass the bar after all."

"It's not proof of anything," Knott said.

"Pipe down, Matlock," I said. "We're not in court. Maybe Aaron's not involved. It's possible, though, for him to be the guy pulling the strings. He certainly has the financial smarts."

"It's not Aaron," Pat insisted. For his part, Knott pursed his lips and didn't have any words.

"I guess we'll see," I said.

While I liked both Mark and Aaron Ritter to be involved, I couldn't pin anything on them. Louie wouldn't give them up to me. He might to the police, but I knew Dunn would tell me I didn't have enough to build a case yet. My surveillance of Louie's house would be unlikely to sway him as he'd be concerned about using it in court.

I drove to visit someone who might know.

After he got knocked out in a pub parking lot, paramedics

transported Bryce Wahl to Frederick Health Hospital, where he remained. His medical records—way too easy to access from the hospital's website—showed he was admitted with a concussion, a cracked skull, and brain swelling. Surgery fixed the last two, and a few days of rest cleared most symptoms of the first. Now, Bryce remained a guest of the hospital for observation.

I obtained my visitor's pass from the front desk, affixed the sticker to my hoodie, and took the stairs to the fourth floor. Bryce Wahl stayed in room 415. I lingered in the hallway until a cute young nurse passed and then slipped inside. An older man slept in the bed closest to the door. I walked farther into the room. Bryce, his head bandaged, stared at the TV, which played a game show at low volume. His eyes narrowed as he scrutinized me.

Outside the pub, Bryce's bulk was easy to spot. He looked a lot less menacing wearing a gown and lying in a hospital bed. He remained a large man, however, and he took up most of the real estate. A silver handcuff peeked out from his left sleeve, and I spied the other end affixed to a side rail. Bryce's lips turned up in a sneer. "You got a hell of a lot of nerve coming here."

"You had a hell of a lot of nerve jumping me outside a pub with two of your friends," I said as I dropped onto the uncomfortable plastic chair near the window. "Let's say we're both brash and move on."

"The hell do you want?" he grumbled.

"Let me tell you what I know. Corey and his boss got me to the pub that evening under the pretense of taking the new guy out for happy hour. It smelled fishy, though. I saw you and your buddies when I looked out the bathroom window."

"Good for you."

"Sorry to spoil your ambush," I said. "And by sorry, I mean

I'm totally not."

"You gonna apologize for whatever the hell you hit me with?" Bryce asked with a scowl.

"Twelve ball, corner pocket." He frowned. "My dress socks made for a nice sap. I wasn't walking into a three-on-one without some kind of an edge."

"You cracked my skull."

"Let's not pretend a head injury is some kind of lasting damage for you," I said. "You were a small cog in a big wheel. I know Corey put you up to it, but he's not in charge of anything. Louie might've leaned on him, I suppose. My suspicion is it goes higher. They're both assholes, and I doubt they're making a lot of decisions."

Bryce looked away and stared at the ceiling. "I didn't talk to anyone but Corey."

"You're a bad liar." He didn't even glance at me. "I suspect you were even before I scrambled your brain."

"Eat shit," he said.

"I've seen hospital chocolate pudding," I said. "It's pretty close." No reaction. "All right. I'll take you at your word for now. Who did Corey talk to?"

"You think he'd tell me?"

"I don't think he's had an original idea since he started working for Louie." Bryce remained silent. "They're throwing you to the wolves. Why are you helping them?"

Bryce turned his head and tried to glare at me. It would have been ineffective even without the gauze wrap. "What are you talking about?"

"The police have obviously been here." I pointed toward the handcuffs. "I've seen both Corey and Louie in the office the past couple days. You're not snitching on them, which I'm sure they appreciate. They're not helping you, though."

"Who says I need their help?"

"You have a lawyer?" He didn't answer. "I'll presume no. So a county public defender. I don't know what charges you're facing." I paused and considered the situation. No one saw me take on Bryce and his goonish friends. Corey and Louie sped off before we got down to business. No camera was there to catch us. First responders would've rolled up and seen three guys on the asphalt. They wouldn't have connected the dots to presume Bryce and company were the aggressors unless someone told them. "Somebody gave you up, though."

He scoffed. "How do you figure?"

"Think about it. When the ambulance and police got there, you and your friends looked like victims, not perpetrators."

"We *were* victims," Bryce said.

"Hand me a bandage," I said. "My heart bleeds for you."

"Piss off."

"My point is you wouldn't be wearing the silver bracelet now unless someone tipped off the sheriff's office as to what happened. Maybe one of your friends did."

"No way." Bryce shook his head. "We don't rat on each other."

"The only other people who could've were Corey, Louie, or Eric."

"What about you?"

"I called nine-one-one," I said. "I didn't tell them what went down, though. You guys needed an ambulance."

Bryce lapsed into silence again. I'd dropped a lot on his lap, and I doubted he'd process it quickly even if he didn't suffer a recent head injury. "You might be onto something."

"I usually am."

"Corey didn't seem to care what happened afterwards. Prick didn't even check in to make sure we were okay."

"You'd served your purpose," I said. "He didn't have any use for you."

"Louie put him up to it," Bryce told me. "He was concerned some new guy was more than he let on. I guess he meant you."

"Just like Optimus Prime, I'm more than meets the eye."

"They paid us. We were supposed to rough you up. Put you in the hospital. They wanted you out of whatever they were doing."

"They didn't tell you what it was?" I asked.

"No," he said, "and I wasn't gonna press them on it. The less I know, the lower the chance they're going to come after me later if shit goes sideways."

"It went sideways. They might not have come after you, but the cops seem to know what happened."

"It wasn't Louie. We take care of each other."

"How do you mean?" I said.

"Me and Louie . . . we been gym buddies for years. He even put me up when my house flooded out last year. I'd do the same for him if he needed it."

"One of them dimed you out, though."

"Bastards," Bryce said.

I didn't know if he meant Corey and Louie or the deputies who visited and slapped the handcuffs on him. Probably both. I only cared about the first set. "I'm working with some deputies," I said as I stood. "I'll mention you cooperated today. Maybe it'll help you down the line."

"Who are you really?" Bryce asked.

I affected a growly voice. "I'm Batman." He blinked in confusion as I left the room.

———

I returned to RTP and wondered what I could find about Louie, Corey, and the rest of the mergers and acquisitions team. With Pat in the loop as to my real identity and reason for being here, I could drop the pretense of caring about the database administration side of things. Brent seemed capable enough to pick up the slack. I used the administrative credentials I swiped from the helpdesk guy last week to map their local hard drives.

Louie and Corey were assholes, but they were smart. They didn't leave anything incriminating in plain view. Still, an accountant like Marvin Bernard could use some of the documents they'd collected to keep building a case. I copied a trove from both of them, sent them on their way via SFTP, and told T.J. to be on the lookout for them.

It took a while to collect and pass on all the information. Marvin would need time to look at everything, analyze it, and tell me how it all fit into the big picture. I didn't want to make another trip from Baltimore to Frederick, but I got the feeling at least one more commute would be in my future. As the afternoon wore on, the third floor grew more empty. An email from Pat popped up in my inbox.

C.T.,

There are some more developments you need to be aware of.

Let's talk, but not in my office and not in view of other people. Devon and I want to keep this away from everyone else if we can.

I'm in the basement. Can you meet me down here?

Thanks,

Pat

I stood up and checked out her office. It was empty with the door locked. She could have been downstairs. The whole thing smelled fishy. Lot of it going around recently. I popped into my cubicle long enough to tuck my gun into my waistband, and then I took the stairs to the bottom level. As soon as I opened the door, I felt the temperature drop at least ten degrees. The basement lacked whatever charm the upper floors possessed. It looked industrial. Bare white walls. Tile floors. Knott told me a meat packer used to own the building. The aesthetic—such as it was—made sense.

As I walked along and passed a few closed doors, I didn't see Pat anywhere. Ahead, a man stepped out of a room on the right. Louie. "Look who it is." He moved to block the hallway. "I knew you weren't a DBA. Didn't figure you for a private eye, though. Couldn't cut it as a cop?"

"Never tried," I said. I kept my right hand at my side. The weight of the 9MM at my back reminded me it was there. I hoped I wouldn't need it.

"You think you're smart, huh?"

"Louie, please. I'm smarter than you and everyone else on your team. You had a good run, but your days of scheming and killing are over. Make it easy on yourself and come quietly."

I heard two sets of footsteps behind me. They must have hidden in one of the other rooms. Louie grabbed my right arm as someone else seized the left. I struggled in their combined grip, and then I felt something sharp bite into my neck. I fought against the two men restraining me, but whatever they injected me with soon made me light-headed.

"Make it easy on yourself and come quietly," Louie taunted as he drew his fist back and walloped me in the stomach. The guys holding me let go, and I sank to the floor. Darkness crept in, and my limbs felt heavy. Corey moved beside his boss. My vision grew blurry, but another man stood with them. "Get the wife," the stranger said, and before I could offer a rebuttal, the lights went out.

CHAPTER 24

AT SOME POINT LATER, consciousness returned. It came in bits and pieces, though it allowed me enough awareness to keep my eyes closed. I got the sensation I was tied up and prone, but what I mostly felt was cold. Voices talked nearby. "We've set everything up." It sounded like Corey.

"Now, we wait for them." Louie. I knew they were involved. Who was the unknown man whose voice I heard before blacking out? I wouldn't learn it without looking around, so I opened my eyes. Sure enough, I lay on a carpeted floor. Louie and Corey stood nearby. My hands were bound behind my back. Worst of all, I was mostly naked. Someone stripped me down to my boxers. I wanted to hunch up against the falling temperatures, but I couldn't.

"What are you doing with us?" a woman asked. A memory flashed in my head. Someone gave an instruction of, "Get the wife" before whatever drugs these assholes gave me knocked me out. I had a sinking feeling I knew who it was, and I rolled over to see Amy Napier in much the same predicament. Her hands were tied, as well, and she'd been reduced to a bra and a pair of bike shorts.

Louie stood over me. "Look who's awake." He drew his foot back and kicked me in the stomach. I sputtered and coughed. "Not so tough now, are you?" He crouched, grabbed a handful of my hair, and gave me a short jab to the face. Pain flared along my jaw.

"Enough," another voice said. I glanced around the room. It came from a speaker mounted on the wall. Louie stood. "The two of you have messed around in something you don't understand." I couldn't identify the man speaking. "I'd hoped we wouldn't need to do this again . . . especially not so soon." Amy choked and started to cry. "This is a useful room. It used to be a giant refrigerator."

"You're gonna freeze to death just like your husband, you nosy bitch," Louie said. He and Corey opened the door, walked out, and closed it again. Two locks clicked into place.

The original voice spoke again as I moved closer to Amy Napier. Tears ran down her face. "We have a good arrangement going. No one here really understands it, and it needs to stay this way. Once you're dead, it will. It's nothing personal. Depending exactly how fast the temperature drops, you probably have an hour before you get frostbite, another hour before you get delusional, and . . . well, death probably not too much longer from there. We'll check on you tonight." A brief burst of static came through the speaker, and then silence prevailed.

An hour until we got frostbite. It felt close to freezing in the room, but I knew my lack of clothing contributed to how I perceived the temperature. The area was big, covered with carpet, and filled with old computers, equipment, and desks. If the flooring were made of astroturf, the place would have made a nice lacrosse practice field. "The PC graveyard," I said. A battered clock above a server rack told me it was five after six. I made sure the second hand still turned.

"Is this where Jason died?" Amy asked.

"I think so, yes."

She sobbed anew. If I could get free, I could use a computer to get a message out. I stood up and moved throughout the large room, surveying the inventory. It didn't look good. Most of the PCs were old junkers. No intact systems remained. Desktops and servers lay with the covers opened and useful parts scavenged. Or sold as part of the scheme. Large cardboard boxes, broken down and flattened, stood propped up in a corner near the largest desk. Its surface held a hodgepodge of supplies. Anti-static bags. Duct tape. Screwdrivers. I considered using one of those to try and slice my bonds before my eyes landed on a box cutter.

I backed up to the desk, felt around for the tool, and picked it up when my left hand closed on the cold metal. As I fumbled around for a moment until I found the switch which would extend the blade, I wondered if Jason Napier tried this, too. With the razor out, I flipped the tool in my hands and steered it to the rope. Working it back and forth proved challenging at first. I wasn't used to working blind. The grip I needed to use felt strange. Still, I made a little progress.

While I worked, I pondered the whole mess. Louie might have dragged us in here, but he still wasn't the one calling the shots. The meeting at his house proved he was a lackey. Who was the mystery man? The voice we heard a few minutes ago didn't belong to Devon Knott. His was lighter and quieter. I couldn't place it as one I'd heard much during my time at RTP.

My brain kept spinning even as my body shivered. I could figure this out. Going back to the beginning of the case injected too much noise into the signal. I focused on the current predicament. Knott and Pat knew who I really was, and both insisted they wanted me to get to the bottom of who killed

Jason. I knew Louie and his team were involved, but someone pulled their strings. Pat sent me the email to lure me here. When I looked in her office right after, she wasn't there. Gone for the day. I remembered the last time I'd heard from her at an odd hour. She looked at me like I accused her of kicking her dog.

Once I'm off the clock, I don't do work.

Someone sent the email on her behalf, then. Whoever did it would need to be able to access her account and delete the messages before she saw them. Adam the tech guy would have the right privileges, but he didn't strike me as the type to be involved. Sitting on the wrong end of a gun, however, has forced many people to compromise their principles over the years. Still, I ruled him out for now. Who else? Brent? He also didn't seem like the type to help Louie willingly. I thought about the things Brent had told me since I came to RTP. One stuck out in my mind.

You're kind of lucky, I guess. You started on password change day.

I didn't feel especially lucky right now. My first day had been busy in terms of going everywhere in the building. I thought about the many people I'd met. My bosses. Coworkers. The person who issued my badge. All the people upstairs. A realization hit me a moment later, and the razor bit into my skin. "Shit," I said as I steered it back to the ropes. Warm liquid hit my hand a moment later.

"Are you all right?" Amy wanted to know.

"I'm fine." I worked the box cutter back and forth in a steady rhythm, and about a minute later, I'd managed to free myself from the bonds. I looked at the cut on my left wrist. It was just above where I'd been tied up. While it bled, it didn't look especially long or deep. I walked over to where Amy stood.

"Turn around. I'll cut you free." She did, and I sawed through her ropes in a few seconds.

"Now what?" She rubbed her wrists and her eyes focused on my injury. "You cut yourself."

"It's no big deal," I said. "We need to concentrate on getting out of here before the cold becomes too much for us." The largest desk was cluttered with parts and other detritus. A smaller one against the far wall in the middle of the room was clear except for a monitor, keyboard, and mouse. A whiteboard hung nearby.

"How do we do it?" Her eyes welled again, and her voice cracked. "The door is locked, and the only people who know we're here don't care."

She was right. We wouldn't batter the door down. Covering the vents with computer boxes might buy us some time, but it would only prolong the inevitable. A mountain of technology surrounded us. Desktops and laptops lay in various states of repair and completeness. In some ways, it felt like being at a computer expo at the state fairgrounds. "We're going to get the word out. We'll build a computer out of these parts and send a message."

"I don't know how to do that," she said.

"I do." I found a roll of paper towels and pressed one to my cut. "Can you grab the duct tape?" I jerked my head in the direction of the large table. Amy retrieved the tape and stretched a length around my wrist. It combined with the towel to form a large improvised Band-Aid.

Amy looked around the area. "Even if we get out of here, we need to know who killed Jason."

"I'm pretty sure I've figured it out," I said. "Let's get to work. If we freeze to death, none of it's going to matter."

"Tell me who it is," Amy insisted.

"Priorities. First, we need to focus on getting out of here alive. If we do, I'll tell everyone I can."

Amy crossed her arms and eventually nodded in assent. "Fine."

CHAPTER 25

"WHERE DO WE EVEN BEGIN?" Amy asked. She spread her hands and looked around the massive room. "There are a million pieces of junk in here."

"A lot of these computers don't work anymore," I admitted. "It's kind of like an auto junkyard . . . just because a car gets scrapped, doesn't mean you can't harvest some useful parts. Same thing here." I pointed to the mostly empty desk. A few components dotted its surface, and a cable hung from a network jack nearby. "We can work there. You'll probably need to help with some things because of the time crunch."

"I don't know how—"

"It's not hard. If you can push, pull, and use a screwdriver, you can assist with building a computer." I took in the collection of discarded equipment. We would need a desktop. Laptops featured too many parts soldered to the motherboard. "The first thing we need is power. I'll find a rig which still turns on. We'll go from there." Sifting through the off-white and dark gray cases, I figured a few years' worth of enterprise computer refreshes lay here in disuse. Some featured barcodes stuck on a side, and others were bare. Considering all the companies and IT assets RTP acquired, I was surprised they didn't have more.

The first one I tried didn't even turn on. I swapped out the power cable for another but got the same result. Next, I used a different outlet on the wall. Always start with electrons. If they're not flowing, the rest is irrelevant. Still nothing. I set the case back down and tried another. No juice. The third was the charm. It fired up, and the hard drive spun. The computer was missing a few necessary components, though, so I turned it off. "We'll build with this one," I said. I looked at the back of the mini-tower. The electric cable went in at the top. The bottom featured three expansion bays. All were empty. USB and networking ports occupied the middle. "The next thing we need is video."

"What about the network?" Amy said. "Don't we need to get the word out?"

"We do, but we need to see the screen to make anything happen. Computers go through something called BIOS when they boot. They'll beep in certain patterns if things are missing. The big two are standard input and standard output . . . a keyboard and video. The former is easy. There are hundreds of them strewn around the room. One of them is bound to work if the one on the desk doesn't. We need a card to manage the display, though." I checked the plug on the monitor's cable and then turned the PC case around so Amy could see the inside and pointed to the expansion slots. "It'll go in there. We'll have to scavenge one from another machine. Let's get a few so we increase our odds of finding a good one."

I led Amy to the large desk. We each grabbed a Phillips screwdriver. I instructed her to start with one pile, and I would take the other. I showed her how to check which display connection we needed, then how to remove the card. Once I unscrewed it from the case, I rocked it back and forth while gently pulling up until it popped out. Amy told me she could do it, and we got to work. "My hands are cold," she said as she rubbed them together.

"I know. Mine, too. Sit on them for a minute if you need to."

"How are you so calm?"

I smirked as I heard my pulse in my ears. "I'm as nervous as a cat in a kennel. I got shot a few months ago and almost died. I've tried to keep myself out of these situations since." Amy started to say something—probably an apology—but I put up a hand. "It's fine. Like I said, I'm nervous, too, but I'm concentrating on what we need to do. Besides, working with computer parts takes me back to my younger days."

Starting when I was about eleven, I'd built several high-end desktop rigs. They were great for gaming, but more importantly, they taught me how everything fit together, along with a troubleshooting process to resolve issues. While I hadn't actually assembled a PC since before I went to Hong Kong, the skills never went away. A few minutes later, I felt a little colder, but we each had a few display boards to try.

It ended up being a good thing. The first three were duds. Nothing outputted to the screen. I'd plugged the keyboard in to eliminate it from the power-on self-test. We got a short series of angry beeps each time. "Why aren't you screwing the cards in?" Amy asked as I tossed the third aside and tried the fourth.

"No point unless we know it works." The fourth one made the monitor flicker to life. I watched the derelict computer do its initial self-assessment. It counted eight gigabytes of RAM, which made our lives a little easier. "The memory is good. If it hadn't been, we would've had to salvage some." I powered the computer off and turned it around so we could see the rear of the case. "The next hurdle is networking. All the machines I've seen here have the ports built in."

"Isn't that a good thing?" Amy wanted to know.

"Depends," I said. "For our purposes, no. It means the connection is hard-wired into the motherboard. Those take too much time to replace. If it doesn't work, we'll need to find a new PC. The one tool I didn't see on the other desk is a connectivity tester. We'll just have to plug the cable in and hope for the best." I connected the RJ-45 to the appropriate port. "There are two small lights near where the plug goes in. If they come to life after a minute or two, we're good."

"And if not, we're screwed?"

"Pretty much."

Amy crossed her fingers. "Fire it up, then."

———

I pushed the small circular button. The fan whirred to life. A few seconds later, the hard drive spun up. The monitor displayed the BIOS as it counted the RAM and performed other basic self-tests. We heard no beep codes. On the back of the computer, two tiny green lights near the network cable blinked. Amy and I both released deep breaths.

"We did it," she said, smiling in spite of the dire circumstances.

"We did, but it's only one mile marker. I still need to figure out how to login." I could try my own account, but if our adversaries were clever, they would have ordered someone to disable it as a precaution. There was also the possibility this computer came from a company RTP Hoovered up, and it may not have the right domain settings. I remembered the local administrator password, but this PC had been offline for a while. It would almost certainly have a different credential stored. "We'll need to keep warm even if this works."

"What do you mean?"

"Let's presume this plan succeeds. It takes time for law enforcement to respond, especially if they're also bringing paramedics. Whoever comes will probably get snowed by the people remaining upstairs. It won't work for long, but it'll cost a minute or two, and they all matter at this point. It's getting colder in here. We'll need to keep warm."

Amy turned up her hands. "They didn't leave us anything."

I pondered everything I'd seen in here and how we might MacGyver something to fend off the chill. "Maybe they did." The Windows splash screen loaded. The boot process had been slow, but it moved forward. "See those boxes along the far wall?" She looked in the right direction and bobbed her head. "They're big enough to basically fit a person inside. Maybe two. Look on the desk over there. You'll see a bunch of silver-gray bags. They're designed to prevent static electricity from damaging components, but we might be able to use them as insulation."

Her eyes lit up. Having something to do which might help our chances of survival tended to have this effect. "There's duct tape over there, too, right?"

"Yes," I said. "See if you have enough stuff to make one. Two would be ideal, but we can huddle together in one. It might keep us warmer, anyway."

"All right," Amy said, and she jogged off toward the large desk. A Windows login screen stared back at me. I looked at the whiteboard. A network diagram consumed the right side of it. The left contained a bunch of random character strings with no other information. I guessed them to be administrator passwords. None matched the credential I knew, so they were all older. So was the computer I used. It would be a matter of matching the password before any setting limiting the number of incorrect logins kicked in.

Brent told me passwords changed for all users every two months. It was a pretty aggressive policy but a good one. The key issue was how often the built-in admin account changed. It was a local account rather than a domain one, so it wouldn't necessarily be subjected to the same policies. Refreshing it periodically made for a good security practice, however. Maybe RTP required it to change every four months.

This still left two questions: how old was the computer I used, and when did the list of passwords on the whiteboard begin? I didn't have any good way to answer either. Might as well start in the middle. I picked the sixth string out of the eleven recorded and entered it. No dice. I tried the seventh. Same result. Ditto the eighth and ninth.

Was I moving in the wrong direction? Would my fifth failed attempt lock the account on this computer? If it did, I'd need to transfer the working components to a different case. It would take time . . . during which the room would grow colder. I already shivered as I sat in the chair. Executive decision time. Instead of trying the tenth password on the list, I moved up to number five. The computer looked old enough to justify the guess. I keyed in the characters, closed one eye, and pressed Enter.

Welcome to Windows.

I breathed a sigh of relief as the desktop populated with icons. "Did you get in?" Amy called from across the room.

"Finally, yes," I said. My next worry was network access control. Did RTP monitor the enterprise for unknown devices? Would this computer count as one? I figured I had a couple minutes. Automated tools would detect an incident. Some could also take actions based on defined protocols. I probably had two to three minutes at most if this turned out to be the case. If an intrusion required human intervention, the result would be more time for the home team.

I opened Internet Explorer while also scoffing at its presence on the computer. It took about thirty seconds, but the browser opened to the internal RTP homepage. Before cell phones became ubiquitous, carriers set up websites to allow people to send messages from a computer. While they didn't get used much anymore, they still existed. I entered the site for T.J.'s carrier and keyed in her number. A box opened, ready to accept my input. I needed to be quick.

In RTP basement with Amy. Cold room. Freezing. Send cops and ambulance ASAP.

I clicked the SEND button. The browser spun for a moment, and then a dialog box popped up.

Your message has been sent.

I let out a deep breath I didn't know I'd been holding. A few seconds later, another prompt filled my screen. *Your PC is out of compliance. You will be restricted to internal RTP resources until this is resolved. Patches should be deployed automatically. If you have any questions, please contact the help desk.* I got up and walked to where Amy worked. She'd taped a bunch of anti-static bags into a large cardboard box. It looked like the world's worst and least comfortable sleeping bag, but if it kept us warm long enough for help to arrive, it would be great. "Did you send a message?" she asked.

I nodded. "Just in time. The network didn't like an old PC being online."

"So now we wait."

"Now we wait," I repeated. "Need any help?"

"I think I'm almost done." Amy extended a length of tape

and ripped it, affixing a bag to the inside of the box. There are only a couple of these things left."

"Good." I let Amy finish and moved to a small rack. It still held five older servers. A peek at the back showed they remained plugged in. There was plenty of room behind them. I blew hot breath into my hands and powered all of them on. One remained off, but the other four fired up.

"What are you doing with those?" Amy wanted to know.

"They put out warm air," I said. "We need all the help we can get."

"All right." She taped one more bag into place. "I think this is done."

I took the makeshift blanket and set it on the floor behind the rack. "You go first." I lifted the top layer of cardboard.

"You sure?"

"Go ahead," I said.

Amy dropped to the carpet and slid inside the box. She scooted over as far as she could. There would be room for me. The servers weren't putting out much warm air yet, but it had only been a couple minutes. I climbed inside. The anti-static bags felt scratchy against my skin. The makeshift blanket covered me from my shins to the top of my chest. It would need to be good enough.

"I hope the police come soon," Amy said.

I drew my arms around myself. Her body put out a little heat, too, but it grew colder by the minute in this room. I didn't know how long our combined warmth would last. "Me, too," I said.

We'd made the best of a terrible situation. Now, we needed to hope T.J. received my message and got the word out in time.

CHAPTER 26

THE SERVER FANS provided minimal warmth. There simply weren't enough of them. In a data center, with racks lined up in rows, the aisles behind the machines were warm. Here, not so much. Only four computers turned on, and I didn't know how well they worked. Amy and I huddled closer as the improvised blanket proved inadequate to keep out most of the cold. "I know this is awkward," she said.

I stopped my teeth from chattering long enough to reply. "Yeah, it is." Our barely-clothed bodies were pressed together, but I knew I was focused solely on surviving. I figured Amy felt the same.

"Thanks for not being a creep about the situation."

"If we survive this," I said, "I'll add 'not a creep' to my business cards."

Amy let out a light chuckle. "I mean it."

"I know. I think we're both just looking to make it out of this alive."

We lapsed into silence for a few minutes. My teeth chattered, and my feet were well past the point of being called cold. I needed to be concerned about frostbite if we stayed in here much longer. Amy, being shorter, fit inside the cardboard better than I did. "You married?" she asked out of the blue.

"No."

"Girlfriend?"

"Yes," I said.

"How long have you been together?"

"We've known each other a little over three years." I recalled meeting Gloria at an art show during my first case. "I guess we've officially been a couple for a little over two."

"You should marry her," Amy said.

"If we get out of this room alive, I'll think about it."

"I'm serious. Jason and I dated for about two years. I wondered when he would pop the question. There were a few great moments for it, but they passed by." She paused, and her voice cracked when she spoke again. "He surprised me. It was a totally mundane moment . . . after dinner one night in his apartment. Somehow despite a lack of romantic trappings, it was exactly right."

"I'm not sure either of us are the marrying type." This had been true at the beginning. Gloria and I enjoyed a relationship of fun and convenience. Over time, though, it evolved. For all practical purposes, we lived together, and our partnership remained strong. My mother periodically nagged me about ring shopping. Maybe I would really need to consider it. Talking to Gloria would have made the most sense, but I knew it was a conversation I'd never initiate.

"Figure it out," Amy said. "I can't imagine my life if I hadn't married Jason." She fell silent again, and I understood why. With her husband dead, she would need to reimagine the next fifty years or so. Presuming we got out of here, and the oppressive cold reminded me this remained far from a certainty. We fell silent again. I wished I could stay warm. Huddling inside the box might have bought us a few extra minutes. Soon, Amy's rhythmic breathing told me she'd fallen asleep. I felt tired, too, but I needed to remain awake.

The chill made it difficult. Drifting off would feel nice, but I worried I might never wake up again. We couldn't see the clock from where we lay, so I had no idea how much time elapsed from when I sent the message to T.J. The website told me it went through. What if she didn't see it for fifteen minutes? What if her phone battery died? Maybe I should have texted Rich, too. As quick a typist as I am, the network compliance check might still have booted me off before I could.

As I struggled to stay warm and keep my eyes open, I thought I heard a noise from outside the room. Did Louie and Corey come back to check on us—and finish us off if the conditions didn't do it for them? In my current state, I doubted I would mount much of a defense. A man's voice said something from the other side of the door. The optimist in me—making a rare appearance—allowed for the possibility our rescuers could be here.

A loud thud rocked the door and jolted Amy awake. "Huh? What's going on?"

Another bang thundered throughout the room, and the door collapsed inward. Footsteps reverberated on the raised flooring. Deputy Dunn and a few of his FCSO colleagues rushed toward us. A pair of paramedics trailed behind them. "Your secretary told me you'd be here," Dunn said. He looked around and shook his head. "I almost didn't believe her."

"I'm glad you did," I said.

———

"We've turned the temperature up," another deputy said. "The controls were in a closet just outside this room."

The EMTs, a burly blond man and a tall dark-haired woman, moved around the deputies and helped Amy and me out of our improvised blanket. They brought the real things, and I wrapped one around me. "You should probably go to the hospital," he said.

"No time," I said, making sure my feet were wrapped up, as well. "I'll warm up, but then I need to get back to my case."

"Let's go to another area," Dunn suggested. It was the best idea I'd heard in a while. We all followed him out. Amy and the female paramedic walked into a room across the hall, followed by two of the deputies. The blond fellow, Dunn, and I moved next door.

Another deputy poked his head in. "We found their stuff. We'll bring it in a minute."

The room we were in probably served as a small office in a past life. The carpet grew shabby from disuse. I sat in an uncomfortable but functional chair. Another one about ten feet away and a desk were the only furniture. Dunn dropped down and wheeled himself closer. "What the hell happened?"

"I would say I flew too close to the sun, but I'd welcome the heat right about now," I said. When his response consisted of an annoyed stare, I elaborated. "This company is involved in a lot of bad shit. I've been trying to tell you."

"Maybe I'm listening now."

"I sure as hell hope so. The long and short of it is they bought up smaller places, sold off the assets, fired people, and waited for profit. A lot of it is probably legal, but it's all scummy when you put it together. One of their employees figured it out, and they froze him to death in the next room."

"You got proof of all this?" Dunn asked.

"Working on it," I said. "I have more than I did when I talked to you last time."

Additional footsteps rushed down the hallway. Rich stopped, looked into the room, and came in. "T.J. told me you were here," he said. The deputy who popped in before returned carrying my clothes and shoes. Conspicuous by its absence was my gun.

"I'd like to report a missing firearm," I said. I tossed the blanket down and slipped my socks on first.

"They took your gun?" Dunn said.

"Yeah. I can get you the information on it." I felt my jeans. My wallet and phone were still there. I put the rest of my clothes on. The deep chill was gone, but I still felt cold. "Do we need to stay down here? There are break rooms upstairs. I'd love to warm up with some coffee."

"You should get checked out at a hospital," Rich said.

"Pass. I want to wrap this up."

He pointed at my arm, where the duct tape bandage remained visible past my sleeve. "Do you need stitches?"

I shook my head. "I don't think it's bad enough. Neosporin will do the trick." Dunn's phone rang, and he stepped into the hallway to take the call.

Amy shuffled by a moment later. "I'm going to ride to the hospital." She inclined her head toward the EMT. "She talked me into it. I'm sure you're not coming along, but I wanted to thank you for getting us out of there."

"Glad I could," I said. "I'll bring it home from here." Once Amy and the paramedic left the area, I walked out into the hallway and headed for the stairs. Rich followed, and Dunn— still on the phone—trotted behind us. I pushed open the first-floor door and found the kitchen area. With the exception of a few offices, each level of the building featured an identical layout. I set a pot of coffee to brew, figuring I wouldn't be the only one partaking. You can always count on cops to want a cup.

Dunn slipped his cell back into his pocket. "We rounded up a couple guys . . . Eric LaFave and Corey Young. I suggested they come here for questioning." Rich frowned. "It's a little irregular," Dunn continued, "but it gives us all a chance to ask our questions."

"I'm sure the java here is better than at your place," I added.

While we waited, I checked my mobile. Three missed calls and several worried texts from Gloria, plus a couple from T.J. I sent my girlfriend a message first. *I'm all right. Had a complication in the case, but I think we're in the homestretch. Will tell you more later. Hoping to wrap it up tonight.* I tapped out a quick response to T.J. next. *We're good. Cavalry arrived on time. Thanks. I'm not dead. #sorrynotsorry.* "Millennials and their phones," Dunn said with a grin.

"I'm hoping for a neural implant in a few years. Typing is *so* last decade."

He laughed, and Rich offered a knowing wag of his head. When the caffeine finished, we each poured ourselves a cup. I shuddered after my first sip. The coffee felt super warm going down, but a lingering cold remained in my body. Still, I felt a lot better than I had on the floor in the PC graveyard. A few minutes later, four deputies herded Eric and Corey into the room. Both stared at me with wide eyes. "We're good here," Dunn told them. "Make sure no one else comes in." The quartet dispersed.

After the last one cleared the threshold, I strode to Corey and clobbered him in the stomach. He folded in half and sputtered. I looked at Eric, drew my fist back, and he flinched. No one tried to stop me. "How the hell . . . did you get out?" Corey wheezed.

"You left me a room full of equipment. I built a working computer out of it."

"Son of a bitch." He struggled back to a standing position. "You gonna keep picking on a handcuffed man?"

"After you tried to freeze Amy and me to death?" I said. "Be glad the two cops in this room wouldn't allow me to beat you to a pulp."

"Let's get down to business," Dunn said. "C.T. here has been building a case for a while. Neither of you look like management material to me. Who put you up to it?"

"I work for Louie," Corey offered. "I followed his orders. He's the one you should be talking to."

"Where is he, anyway?" Eric said.

Dunn spread his hands. "We haven't found him yet. Just you two clowns. We can pin it all on you. Be glad Maryland doesn't have the death penalty."

"None of this was my idea." Corey snorted. "You ain't pinning this on me. It goes higher than Louie. We took our orders from Pat Ritter. She's the CFO."

"He's lying," I said.

"No, I ain't," Corey said. "We reported to her. Kept her in the loop at every step of the way. She's responsible for everything."

Dunn jotted a note. "All right. We'll bring Miss Ritter in for questioning."

"He's lying," I repeated. "It was her husband. I don't think Pat knew what was going on."

Dunn crossed his arms. "Explain."

"Her husband Aaron works in finance. He's the one who pushed for RTP to have a mergers and acquisitions department. Somehow, the CEO signed off on it. Pat doesn't do work after hours. She told me at least once. I got emails from her twice when she wasn't here."

"Not unusual by itself," Dunn said.

"There's more. Aaron was here on my first day. It happened to be when everyone was required to change their passwords. He brought flowers for Pat, but he also stood behind her desk. It would have been easy to see what she typed. Another guy told me he came by every couple months or so. I'll bet my nice German car he always came when she needed to make a new password. Then, he used her email account off hours."

"You got anything to say?" Dunn asked Corey and Eric.

"Our team worked for Pat," the latter said.

"Give me a little time, and I'll be able to prove it," I said. "It's the husband."

"All right." Dunn looked at his watch. "You have ninety minutes."

"I'll give you a hand," Rich said.

"With this kind of deadline, I think I'm going to need it."

CHAPTER 27

I CLIMBED INTO MY CAR, and Rich sat in the passenger's seat. Dunn planned to arrest Pat if I couldn't clear her name. While I didn't like her very much, I also didn't want to see her hauled off to jail for something her husband did. I texted her a heads-up, letting her know what was going on and asking if she could tell me anything to help me—and herself. "What are you thinking?" my cousin asked.

"We need to find Louie."

"Why's he so important?"

"He was the head of the mergers and acquisitions team," I said. "In theory, he reported to Pat. In reality, I think he worked for her husband."

"You have a financial link between them?"

I shook my head. "Not yet, but it'll turn up. Louie is too self-interested to go down as the ringleader of all this. He'll sing, and he'll name Aaron in every chorus."

"All right," Rich said. "Where are we headed? You're on a ticking clock."

"I'm aware." Dunn and his fellow deputies would've checked all the obvious places. Louie's house. The rest of the

RTP campus. Any family members who might put him up. I could ignore all those. He wouldn't be with Aaron Ritter. Neither would want to create a single point of failure where they could both be snatched up at the same time. Besides, I figured Aaron was the type to leave Louie to the wolves. All the more reason for him to narc on everyone.

Where would he be hiding? I couldn't check all the hotels and motels in the area. The sheriff's office was better equipped for such a task—if they even bothered once they arrested Pat. Louie tried to freeze Amy Napier and me to death, and he probably played a significant role in Jason's demise. I couldn't let him wriggle off the hook. I closed my eyes and tried to remember conversations with other people about Louie.

Most of the time, I called him an asshole, and anyone who didn't work for him more or less agreed. Bryce stood out as the sole exception. He liked Louie. *We been gym buddies for years.* He also expressed a willingness to help him in dire circumstances. *He even put me up when my house flooded out last year. I'd do the same for him if he needed it.*

"I think I know where he is," I said as I took my phone from my pocket. Neither Bryce nor Wahl were common names, and the combination proved rare and easy to isolate. Only one man with the moniker lived in the area. While he remained in the hospital, I guessed Louie would be holed up in his house. "You riding with me or taking your own car?"

"I'm good to ride shotgun," Rich said. "Let's go."

I used the GPS to navigate to Bryce's home. He lived about ten minutes from the heart of Frederick just off one of the county's many two-lane roads. The place in question sat on a mostly flat acre of land. A rambler sat in the center of the lot. The driveway was long and covered in gravel. Even if I killed the lights, the tires would give me away. I wanted to retain the advantage of surprise, so I drove a bit farther and pulled onto the grass in front of a split-rail fence.

Before I could get out, Rich grabbed my forearm. "He probably has your gun."

"I'm guessing it's not the only one in the house."

He frowned. "I wish I could give you mine, but I'd get really jammed up if you needed to use it."

"It's all good," I said. "Louie's a meathead." I paused. I'd categorized him correctly, but he knew the layout of the house, and he could avail himself of at least one gun. He held a few significant advantages. "Give me five minutes once I reach the house. If I'm not back by then, call Dunn and come in."

"All right." Rich's sour expression told me what he thought of the plan, but it was the best one we had. My cousin was way out of his jurisdiction here. Dunn told me he would arrest Pat based on what Eric and Corey told him. My only chance to ensure the right people paid for what they did required me to go into Bryce's house. Louie wouldn't open up willingly, so I grabbed my snap gun from the floor behind the passenger's seat.

I closed my door as quietly as I could, hopped the fence, and kept low as I padded across the grass.

———

The only lights on the property came from inside the house. I couldn't see much in front of me, but I kept moving in the right direction. I flattened myself against the beige siding at one end of the structure. The window near my head showed some illumination from inside. A quick peek told me no one waited behind the glass. I kept in a crouch and moved along. A small porch about six inches high led to the dark red front door.

I remained low and tried the knob. Locked. No dog came barking, so at least I'd only need to deal with Louie . . . and whatever weapons he carried. I stayed in place for a moment. Footsteps approached from inside the house. I folded myself up as small as I could and waited. The only sound I heard was my own heartbeat. After a few seconds, Louie moved away from the door.

The snap gun would make noise, too. If Louie remained near the front, he'd hear it. I waited a minute in the hopes he would be deeper inside the home. The tool popped the lock in a few seconds. Footfalls rushed closer again. The deadbolt thunked open. I stood and positioned myself on the far side of the door. Louie opened it a crack, and he held a pistol—mine—out before him. I rocked back and drove my shoulder into the door. It slammed into Louie's forearm. He yelped and dropped the gun.

I moved to the opening. Louie glanced down at the fumbled pistol and then glowered at me. "You found me."

"Brilliant deduction," I said. "In other news, water is wet."

He backed up a few steps, putting himself in the house's entryway. "Come and get me, then."

I stepped over the threshold. Louie tried to catch me by surprise with a quick punch, but I turned it away. He stepped to the side and went on the attack again. While his bulk gave him power, he lacked finesse. I blunted each of his strikes and hit him with a short elbow in the gut after the last one. It didn't hurt him much, but it forced him back a step. "You ain't so tough," he said. "No weapons. No ambushes. Just you against me."

"You haven't even hit me yet," I pointed out. "Are you waiting for an invitation?"

Louie threw a couple punches as he backed down the

central hallway. We ended up in the kitchen, which was a wide open space leading to a living room. After I blocked a kick, Louie sprinted a few steps to the counter and slid a long knife out of a block. "So much for no weapons," I said. "And here I thought we could punch each other like gentlemen."

"Piss off. You're not taking me in." I picked up a chair from the breakfast nook as he came forward. One of the legs blocked his first swing. Another handled the second. Small bits of wood splintered off from the impact. Louie tried to go low, but I moved the seat down and turned his arm and weapon aside. Before he could recover, I jabbed him in the throat with the top rail. His left hand went to his neck as he coughed.

I drew the chair back and clobbered him with it. It broke into pieces as Louie hit the floor hard, white wooden legs landing all around him. I kicked the knife away, and it slid across the floor under the refrigerator. Louie struggled to all fours. I hoisted him to his feet, put him in a hammerlock, and steered him to the counter away from any other knives or small appliances. "Give it up."

He shook his head, probably half in defiance and the rest to try and clear the cobwebs after getting walloped with a chair. "You can't overpower me." He struggled in the hammerlock. Louie could shame me on a bench press or a bicep curl competition. I understood holds and leverage, however, and I twisted his wrist a little harder. He howled in pain and stopped fighting.

"This isn't a gym, Louie," I said. "We're not maxing out on the squat rack." With my left hand, I took a zip tie out of my pocket. I grabbed his free arm and pulled. He fought me, but a twist in the right place took the power out of him. I zip-tied his hands behind his back.

"You all good in here?" Rich called from the front of the house.

"Yes," I said. "He's subdued."

"Deputies are on their way."

Louie lapsed into a scowling silence even as Frederick County's finest rolled in. They read him his Miranda rights, and he took advantage of remaining silent. I answered a few questions, and the deputies soon left with Louie in tow. "You think he'll talk?" Rich asked as we walked back to the car.

"He's not going to get painted as the mastermind," I said. "It might take a little while, but he'll give up Aaron."

Rich glanced at his watch. "You're still on the clock, y'know. It's under an hour. He can probably hold out."

We climbed back into the S4. I blew out a long breath. How did Aaron—and then Louie and the rest of the lackeys—learn about me. They went from being skeptical of Trent the DBA to knowing who I was and actively trying to kill me over a short period of time. Something changed. But what? "I want to go back to RTP," I said as I fired up the engine. "I think there's something there we're missing."

"What do you think it is?"

"No idea." I swung the car around and got on the gas. "I hope I know it when I see it."

Deputies still maintained a presence at RTP. The basement was vast beyond just the cold room Amy and I had been imprisoned inside. They could be processing the scene for hours more. They let Rich and I back in as we approached the front door. My cousin followed me to the third floor. Out of habit, I headed toward my own cubicle.

"This is where you've been working for a couple weeks?" he said.

"Yep."

"Who knew you'd be an office drone?"

"Not anymore," I said. "I insisted on a clause in my contract forbidding the company from trying to kill me. Looks like I'm a free agent again."

"You figured out what we're looking for?" Rich asked.

"Not yet. Somehow, Aaron and his cronies learned the truth about me really fast."

"Maybe someone told them."

I shrugged. "Maybe. If so, I don't think it was Pat. Devon Knott . . . the CEO . . . I'm less sure about."

"You want to look around his office?"

"I doubt it," I said. "He's on the top floor. I doubt he left an obvious paper trail for us to find regardless."

"All right," Rich said. "Maybe someone put a bug in your cube."

"It's possible." I nodded in appreciation of the good idea while wondering why I didn't think of it first. I checked the desk and the tall storage cabinet while Rich looked under the chair. "Nothing here." I moved on to the IT equipment. Another swing and a miss. Maybe they'd used a small device and hidden it well. I took out my phone and opened an app.

"What are you doing?"

"Scanning for things like bugs," I said. "There are a few good apps for it now."

"Of course you would have one," Rich muttered.

"Right. The guy who cares about privacy and being spied on is the asshole." Nothing anomalous showed up in my cubicle. Where else could I look? I'd been careful to keep up the wall between Trent and the real me. The only place I dropped it was in Pat's office once events started spiraling out of control. I jogged to her door. Locked. My snap gun was in the car.

Rich stood behind me. "You think they listened to you in here?"

"It's the only place I know I talked to Pat and Knott about who I really am," I said. "It makes the most sense." The lock didn't look very strong. I used an old credit card to get past it in about ten seconds. My app lit up with a red blob when I pointed it at Pat's desk. "I think there's something in here."

I moved to the U-shaped desk. Pat's monitor sat in the center section, along with a docking station, keyboard, and mouse. The longer parts served as file storage. The red light on my screen grew brighter as I neared the monitor. A search of the desktop and equipment turned up nothing. I dropped to the floor and looked on the underside.

Bingo.

A device which looked like a tiny flash drive was affixed with tape. A small antenna jutted from one end. Inside its clear case, a miniature green LED flashed at regular intervals. I found a stack of napkins on Pat's small side table and used one to pluck the bug free. I held it up to show Rich. "I guess nothing's here after all."

"We'll search somewhere else, then," he said, playing along. I handed him the listening device and jerked my head toward the door. Rich left the office. I searched the rest of the room with the app and found nothing else of interest. Then, I called Dunn. "You're almost out of time," he said.

"I wanted to wait until there was one second on the clock," I said, "but you'd just accuse me of being dramatic."

"You got something?"

"I do. There was a bug in Pat's office at RTP. It was where I told her and Knott who I was and what I'd found. Whoever listened on the other end would've heard it all."

"I'm going to presume you have a guess who it would be," he said.

"Sure. Her husband Aaron."

"We're at their house now. I figured I'd arrest her if you didn't come through."

"Is Aaron there?" I asked.

"Yeah," Dunn said. "He's angry but complying with our warrant."

"Pat told me his office is in the basement."

"We'll check it out. I'll get back to you." He hung up.

Rich held the device inside the napkin. "We'll need to turn this over to the deputies."

"Of course," I said. "Dunn is checking Aaron's office. They must've gotten a warrant pretty fast."

"It's usually easier in a county setting," Rich said.

"Do I detect a note of jealousy?"

"Maybe."

We left the building and climbed back into the car. Dunn called a moment later. "We found an app on his tablet," he said. "Pretty nice shit. It saves recordings and even makes a transcript."

"We'll swing by and drop off the bug," I said.

"We'll be here." Dunn broke the connection again.

"Looks like you got Pat off the hook," Rich said.

"More importantly, Aaron's going to jail for a long time. He and his cronies."

"Not bad for a long-haired DBA."

"Piss off," I said.

CHAPTER 28

I DROPPED Rich off at his car. "Thanks for coming tonight," I told him. "I know this isn't exactly your beat."

"Dunn called me. I'm glad he did. You had a pretty rough go of it."

"I finally feel warm. It took a while." I shuddered at the memory of being so cold. "I can't imagine freezing to death in the PC graveyard. Horrible."

"You got them all," Rich said. "Justice will be done."

"Unless your system lets someone get off." Rich rolled his eyes. "You know it's possible. Aaron has money. His odds of getting slapped on the wrist are the best."

"You and I can't control what happens in court. I know it sucks sometimes. I had to learn it the hard way when I first became a cop."

The conversation bordered on unproductive at this point, so we both said goodbye. Rich climbed into his blue Camaro, fired up its throaty V8, gave me a wave, and drove off. Despite the late hour, I called Gloria as I headed back toward Baltimore. She sounded tired but insisted I didn't wake her up. "It's good to hear your voice," she said.

"Yours, too." Especially because I wasn't sure I'd ever hear it again as recently as a few hours ago.

"What complication did you have?"

"The people who killed Jason tried to freeze Amy and me to death, too," I said.

"You call that a complication?"

"I guess it's a significant one. We're fine now. I got us out of there."

"Thank goodness," Gloria said.

"It's all wrapped up now except for the legal crap. If you want to come by tonight, I'd love to see you."

"I'll be there."

I smiled for the first time in a while. The thought of seeing Gloria compelled me to push the accelerator a little harder. I made excellent time on the drive back from Frederick. When I swung my car onto the concrete parking pad, Gloria's coupe already sat there. As I got out, my phone vibrated in my pocket. Its screen showed a message from Pat Ritter. *I know it's late. I've been questioned and released. Aaron is being held. I think the cops are going to arrest Devon, too. I wish I'd known what my own husband was up to. Feel like a fool. Thanks for getting to the bottom of it all.*

Still standing on my parking pad, I replied. *You shouldn't feel bad. People like Aaron are good at deceiving even those close to them. I'll keep an eye on how things unfold. Good luck.* I put my phone away once I sent the message. Whatever else Pat needed to tell me could wait. I unlocked the door, walked inside, and saw Gloria sitting on the couch. She shot to her feet, wrapped me in a tight hug, and planted a long kiss on me.

"Missed you, too," I said.

"Shut up and come upstairs with me." She grabbed my arm. My rule of never arguing with a woman who wanted to take me to bed remained intact. Later, we lay beside each other. Gloria propped herself up on one elbow and stared at my wrist. "You've gotten a lot of cuts and bruises from this one."

"Not to mention a missing tooth," I said. My tongue found it out of habit. I hoped my dental insurance would cover most of the bills. Then again, let them nickel and dime me. I'd mail the balance to Gabriella Rizzo. Maybe she could take it out of the Chads' paychecks.

"It sounds like you got everyone," she said.

"So far. Marvin Bernard still needs to go over everything. The sheriff's office might use their own person, too. Depending on what the accounting turns up, more people could land in the soup. The CEO got arrested."

Gloria's eyes widened. "Wow. I thought he was on your side."

"He was," I said. "Nominally, at least. Ultimately, he's in charge, so a rogue team which aggressively buys up companies and murders the employee who finds out is going to land on his doorstep. If I had to guess, I don't think he'll be charged, but he'll resign over the whole mess."

"Maybe he should."

I nodded. "I don't think he was up to the job."

Gloria extended a leg and climbed on top of me. "Speaking of being up to the job . . ." She leaned down and kissed me.

"Now and forever," I said.

———

The next morning after Gloria showed me how much she missed me for a third time, I walked downstairs. I set a pot of coffee to brew and looked in my fridge. Not being home as much left my stock in a sorry state. Still, my eggs were good for a few more days, and my bread didn't show any green spots, so I got to cooking. As usual, the smells from the kitchen wafted upstairs and roused Gloria from her slumber. Her feet hit the floor, and she joined me downstairs a few minutes later. "I've missed having you cook breakfast for me," she said after greeting me with a minty kiss.

"Me, too. Maybe you can be in charge of keeping fresh supplies in the house."

"I'll setup a delivery for later today."

I made over hard eggs and sourdough toast. It wouldn't win any awards for innovation or plating, but it got the job done. As I ate, T.J. texted me to see where I was. I told her I'd be in soon. Gloria cut her eggs into pieces so tiny I wondered if she'd let in a stray Chihuahua. I sliced mine into man-sized chunks. The toast came out a little dry due to the age of the bread, but overall, I counted the meal as a win. "I'm going back to my own office today," I said when I'd cleared the majority of my plate. "It'll feel good to be in the friendly confines."

"And it's a much shorter drive," Gloria added. She trailed me by a significant margin in amount of breakfast consumed. A while ago, she'd incorporated smaller bites and eating slower into her training for tennis. It paid off—both in her level of play and overall fitness—but it also meant I lapped her when we dined together, and I'd never considered myself a fast eater.

I polished off my toast. "Might as well get started," I said. "I wonder how disappointed T.J. will be when she realizes I'm not dead."

Gloria grinned. "She likes you. You're the one who gave her a chance. She'd never wish harm on you."

"I know, but her ghoulish moments shine through." I kissed Gloria and went upstairs to get dressed while she finished eating. I also put a proper wrap on my wrist. The cut was too long for my largest Band-Aids, but a gauze pad and some tape did the trick. A few minutes later, I came down in dark blue jeans and a red quarter-zip sweater. Gloria gave me her best wolf whistle. It wasn't very good, but I appreciated the effort. We locked lips again on my way out the door, and I drove the S4 a much shorter distance to my office.

When I opened the door, T.J. shot up, ran to me, and gave me a hug. "I'm glad you're not dead," she said, her voice muffled by my shoulder. "Don't tell anyone."

"Your secret is safe with me," I said. I dropped into my familiar leather executive chair, and it felt about a million times better than the crappy one foisted upon me at RTP. "Anything new?"

"Not really." T.J. took up her station as well. "I told a bunch of people to buzz off. A few others will probably call back in the next couple days if they still need something." She grimaced. "I wish I could have a few new prospective clients lined up for you."

I shrugged. "They'll come. Amy found us." A thought occurred to me. "So did Irish. Remind me later I need to update him. Turns out he's not a nut."

"No shit?"

"No shit," I said. "Just a guy who wound up on the wrong end of an RTP buyout, nosed around, and took it all pretty hard."

Before my secretary could say anything, my cell phone rang. I looked at the caller ID. Amy Napier's name appeared, so I answered. "Amy . . . you all right?"

"I'm good," she said. Her voice sounded tired. "They kept me overnight at the hospital as a precaution. You probably should've gone, too." I didn't say anything. She filled the conversational gap capably. "I'm home now. Probably going to take it easy the rest of the day."

"You should," I said. "You've had a rough couple days."

"So have you. How are you holding up?"

"I was cold for a while, but coffee, clothes, and a blanket helped. Today, I'm back to work. No rest for the wicked and all." T.J. rolled her eyes.

"I can come in later," Amy said. "I know we need to settle up."

"It doesn't need to be today," I said. "Rest. Take care of yourself. Come by in a day or two. We'll still be here."

"All right. Thanks again. I don't know what I expected when I hired you, but this is the best outcome I could've hoped for."

"I'll make sure we quote you on the billboard." We said our adieus and hung up.

"We can't afford a billboard," T.J. pointed out.

"Skywriting?" I asked. She smiled and shook her head. "Guy with one of those clamshell signs over him?" Another head shake. "Oh, well. We'll figure it out."

———

Around the middle of the day, Gloria reminded me we were going to the first fundraiser organized by her new company tonight. I told her of course I remembered even though I obviously hadn't, and she told me she believed me even though she obviously didn't. This is how adult relationships work. The beneficiary was my parents' foundation, so we would also see them tonight. I hoped the bar maintained a good stock.

The rest of the work day passed uneventfully. T.J. told a couple people concerned about their possibly cheating spouses not to call back and used even stronger language when an insurance agent reached out. She was doing great. I left a little early to get ready for the soiree. My facial bruises were no longer visible, at least, so I wouldn't lose time pancaking over them with Gloria's makeup.

We needed to arrive before all the guests. "The organizer can't be late," Gloria said as she eyed me up and down while I got dressed. "Unfortunately."

"Does she also need to stay until the room is empty?" Gloria grinned and shook her head. "Let's not be the last ones to leave, then." Even if we dashed out at the first opportunity, getting out of our clothes would take a while. I wore a black Armani three-piece suit. Gloria's dark blue gown almost reached the floor. Her necklace and shoes were the same color, and I wore a tie to match. Silver earrings completed her look.

As usual when we went to a fancy function, we took Gloria's Mercedes coupe. I drove while she checked her makeup in the vanity mirror and reapplied a few bits. It was a short jaunt to the Pier Five Hotel across the harbor. I barely even got to open the throttle before I handed the keys to a valet who looked very eager to climb behind the wheel of an AMG. I couldn't blame the fellow. If I were in college and got the opportunity to drive a rocket—even for a short time—I would take it.

Inside, workers put the finishing touches on the ballroom. The round tables were set with classic white cloths and black napkins. A banner for the Robert and June Ferguson Foundation hung along the front wall. Whoever spoke at the podium would stand around the center of it. Several months passed since I worked for the foundation. In retrospect, it had never been a good fit. My parents did a lot of good for people in bad circumstances, but a *pro bono* PI service represented an outlier.

Even though I remained bitter at how they ended the arrangement, I felt grateful they'd thrown me the bone when I needed it.

"Hello, Coningsby," my mother said, making me jump. "You seem to have the jitters, dear. Is everything all right?"

I recovered and buttoned the top button of my jacket. "Sure. Nice to see you, Mom."

"Gloria, dear." My girlfriend and mother embraced and exchanged air kisses on the cheeks. It must have made them feel European. Thankfully, no one attempted a bad accent. "Thank you for putting this together. Everything looks great." My mother wore a powder blue ball gown, earrings to match, and a pearl necklace.

"Son." My father offered his hand, and I shook it. He came in a tuxedo with his bowtie and pocket square going with my mother's gown. Gloria and I walked into the hall while my parents remained at the door to greet people as they came in. I dropped into my assigned seat while my girlfriend conferred with the venue staff. Ten chairs ringed every table, and my parents would be sitting with us. I didn't recognize any other names typed on the small folded cards.

I split my time between watching Gloria work the room—she was a natural—and keeping an eye on people filing in. When I first met her, Gloria was a socialite. Over the last three years, she grew more serious about using her time, money, and connections for good. It was terrific to see. She beamed a smile for everyone who approached her, but she also understood logistics and spent time talking to staffers all over the venue. At some point, she'd need to learn the power of delegating, but for her first proper event under her own banner, she was already a star.

Everything ran smoothly apart from a few audio glitches

with the mic. Gloria seethed each time the person at the podium had a hint of trouble. When not busy stewing over the vagaries of technology, she introduced me to the other people at the table. They didn't know my parents but got their placements thanks to their donations. "What do you do?" a graying sixtyish man asked as he peered down his glasses at me.

"Trophy boyfriend for the organizer," I said, patting Gloria's hand.

"Seriously," he insisted. Sussing out my job was apparently a Big Deal to this man.

"I'm a freezer inspector."

He blinked a few times before showing me a rehearsed smile. "Well, someone has to do it."

"If your servants have the night off," I said, "and you get stuck in a cold walk-in, you'll thank me."

The man scrutinized me for a few seconds before turning back to his wife. Gloria elbowed me in the side. "He's a major donor," she whispered in my ear. "Be nice."

I put a hand on my chest to feign indignation. "I don't know any other way to be."

My parents each gave speeches after we all ate a steak dinner, the emcee solicited a new round of donations following dessert, and even those lighter in the wallet appeared happy at the end of the night. Gloria fluttered around the hall again, talking to various venue employees as the room emptied. "It was a success," I said as I caught her en route to another conversation. "You did great. Be happy. Everyone else is."

She smiled. "I am. I just want to know what we might be able to do better next time. Give me a few minutes."

While I waited, I caught up with my folks outside the ballroom. "Tell Gloria she was terrific," my mother said.

"I usually do," I said, "just not in this context."

My father smirked while my mother rolled her eyes. "We're tired, son," he said. "Let's talk soon, however, about what we were discussing before."

I still didn't know how I felt about my parents possibly serving as gatekeepers for potential clients. Still, it would keep people coming in, and infusions of clients and cash would only be good for my business. "Sure."

Gloria popped out into the hall a few minutes later. A few hairs looked out of place, but otherwise, her appearance hadn't changed since we walked in hours before. "Ready to go?"

I leaned in closer as we headed for the door. "We getting out of these clothes right away?"

"After tonight? You bet."

"I've never been gladder for a short drive in your car," I said.

CHAPTER 29

WE REACHED my house in a few minutes and ran upstairs. The problem with putting on fancy clothes was the time it took to get undressed. I slept better than I had in a week, and even though I woke up around eight-thirty, I still felt refreshed. I needed a run, though, so I left Gloria sleeping, changed into my workout attire, and headed outside. Fog hung over the area, and it misted as I walked to Federal Hill Park to begin my laps.

Thirty minutes later, I hoofed it back up Riverside Avenue, wet from more than honest sweat. In my house, I headed upstairs, peeled damp clothes off, and took a shower. Gloria stirred when I got dressed, but she remained asleep as I headed downstairs. A trip to the grocery store never materialized—and Gloria didn't arrange a delivery yet—so the food situation remained suboptimal. I looked in the pantry, found a tub of oatmeal, and put a pot on to cook.

As usual, Gloria came downstairs a few minutes later. She kissed me good morning, poured herself some coffee, and checked out the oatmeal. I'd added a diced apple and cinnamon before the water boiled, and a little brown sugar after the fact made for a tasty bowl. Gloria added maple syrup, also. To each their own. After polishing off a bowl and a half—along with a second cup of coffee—I bade Gloria adieu and drove to my office.

"Amy called," T.J. said before I even closed the door.

"Good morning to you, too."

"Good morning. Amy called." She grinned.

"Did she say anything?" I asked, feeling a bit like I was pulling teeth to get information.

"She'll be here in about a half-hour," my secretary said. "I told her you were checking something out on your way in."

"Yes." I walked to my desk and sat. "I was examining the effects of a second cup of coffee. It's an ongoing study."

"Any progress?"

"Yes," I said. "I think I'll need a third at some point."

A short while later, the exterior door opened, and Amy Napier walked in. At first blush, she looked fully recovered from our ordeal in the RTP basement. She offered a tentative smile as she approached the desk. I walked around to greet her, and she pulled me into a hug. She maintained it for a full minute, and I didn't resist. "Thank you for everything," she said as we both sat.

"I'm glad you were able to get justice." I didn't mention almost freezing to death. Amy could do without another reminder of her husband's demise.

"Me, too. I'm keeping an eye on what happens at RTP. I'm pretty sure Devon Knott is going to step down."

"He probably should," I said.

"Enough about that damn company." Amy took a checkbook out of her purse. "We need to settle up. I paid you a deposit when this all started . . . before I knew what a mess it would become."

"Wasn't your fault," I said. "Each case is a unique animal."

"Still, I feel like I owe you extra for all you did. Risking your life . . . saving us both."

While I was normally glad to hear a list of my accomplishments read aloud, I didn't want Amy to pay more than she could afford. "I don't know your financial situation," I said, "and I don't need to. It's your business. Pay me what you think my time was worth." T.J. frowned at her desk, but I ignored her. I appreciated her focus on the bottom line—we needed to make money, after all—but I wouldn't fatten my account by playing into a widow's good feelings toward me.

"You sure?"

"Positive. Don't put yourself out for me."

"All right," Amy said. She wrote a check for a reasonable amount and handed it to me. I accepted it and set it on my desktop. "Thanks again for everything. If you need a testimonial, I'll be happy to provide one."

"I'll have my billboard people call your people," I said.

She smiled, wished us a good day, and left. I handed the check to T.J. She pursed her lips as she looked at it. "Not bad. I think it could be a little higher, but this is all right."

"I see you're auditioning for your role as CFO."

"Can I still wear jeans if I have a fancy title?" she said.

I patted my own blue denim. "As long as I do, you can."

———

The morning went on with no new prospective clients dropping by. T.J. fielded a few phone calls, and she said one could be promising. The door opened around eleven-thirty. Gabriella Rizzo and one of her goons walked in. The organized crime queen offered me a tentative and small smile. "Why don't you get a coffee?" I said to T.J. "Or go to lunch. Bring me back something if you do."

She looked between me and the newcomers and frowned. I bobbed my head once. "All right." She slipped her jacket on and walked out. I listened for her shoes hitting the metal stairs on the way down. "Your guy can leave, too."

"He should stay," Gabriella said. The enforcer, for his part, crossed his beefy arms. "You took a shot at me."

"And if I feel the need to again, I'm smart enough to plug him first." Now, he frowned. "Did you come to talk?" She nodded. "I don't see how he helps, then. Is he your unusually muscular dialogue coach?"

Gabriella turned to her goon and jerked her head toward the door. When he frowned again and didn't move, she repeated it with a little more verve. He took the hint, walking outside without a word. The steps clanged with his heavy footfalls. "Fine. We're alone." She hung her tan coat on the rack near the door and then extended a hand toward one of my guest chairs. "May I sit?"

"Sure," I said. Gabriella wore a black turtleneck sweater and tight jeans. As usual, she looked terrific. She also didn't appear to be carrying a gun. The extra bulge would've been noticeable in her getup. "What do you want to talk about? The weather? The Orioles' chances this coming season?"

"I think we both know," she said. "The air is pretty thick between us, and I don't like it. My dad could compartmentalize things like this. I can, too, but I've known you most of my life. I don't want to think we're enemies."

"It's hard to be my BFF when you have two guys abduct me and promise they'd beat me to death."

Gabriella crossed one leg over the other. "You can't get past that, can you?"

"You shouldn't be throwing stones here," I pointed out. "Why did they grab me in the first place? Because you couldn't get past the idea I knew more about your father's death than I let on."

"I was right, wasn't I?" she asked.

Even though it was a rhetorical question, I answered. "Sure. Look what it got you. Nothing you didn't already know, and you converted a lifelong friend into someone who wouldn't piss on you if you were on fire. Good job. If there's a job opening for bridge burner, you might want to apply."

"All right." Gabriella put up her hands. "I get it. I was pissed at you. Now, you're pissed at me. I can honestly say I didn't tell those two to work you over like they did, but it doesn't matter. You probably wouldn't believe me, and in the end, they worked for me. It was my fault."

"Nice to see you own it, at least," I said.

"You try now. You could've been honest with me from the start."

"What would you have gained? Everything in the police report—which I know you read as soon as it was available—was accurate. Sure, I was there. Your dad and I talked. In the end, it doesn't change anything about what happened. I don't have any piercing insight to offer you. He was old and sick and took a less painful way out. Even at the end, however, he was concerned about you."

A single tear ran down Gabriella's right cheek. She didn't move to wipe it away. "I would've been happy hearing even that. I might've been pissed about you professing ignorance, but I'd get over it. Why didn't you just tell me?"

"I didn't know how you'd react," I said. "Your dad paid someone to kill me, and he damn near succeeded. I couldn't deal with it again. I couldn't put my family through the wringer a second time."

"You think I would've sent someone after you?" Gabriella wiped her eyes as a few more tears welled.

"We've been friends for years. You're a lot of things, but first and foremost, you're your father's daughter."

She put her tissue away and bobbed her head slightly. "That's fair. Even so, we're different in a few ways. I think he overreacted to slights in his last months." Gabriella spread her hands. "C.T., I wouldn't have gone after you." When I didn't reply, she added, "Do you believe me?"

"I'm not sure," I said. "A big point of evidence to the contrary is the fact you *did* go after me recently, and I was lucky to get away alive."

Gabriella sat in silence, and I did, too. It wasn't collegial, because we each stewed for different reasons. Eventually, she said, "How do we get past this?"

I shrugged. "I'm honestly not sure we do."

"You've been a good friend over the years. I'd hate to lose it." She paused, and before I could rebut, Gabriella continued. "I know what you're going to say. I shouldn't have sent two guys after you. I know. I think I got too focused on learning everything I could about my dad's final hours. Didn't you want to know as much as possible about your sister?"

I narrowed my eyes at Gabriella. "Don't you dare compare Samantha to your father."

We lapsed into silence again. As before, my old friend broke it. "A truce, then. If our friendship is broken, I'll have to wear it . . . but I don't want to be at odds with you all the time."

"How does this truce work?" I said.

"For the most part, we leave each other alone. I won't bother you, and you won't bother me. Maybe we can get back to sharing an occasional meal at the restaurant. For now, let's be friendly from a distance."

"How about indifferent from the same distance?"

She shrugged and nodded. "I guess I'll take it."

"All right. I don't trust you, Gabriella. Truce or not, you broke a vital part of our friendship. I'm not sure it'll ever come back."

"We'll see if we can rebuild the bridge with time." She stood and offered me her hand. I thought about it for a second before accepting. "Thanks, C.T. Take care of yourself."

"You, too." Gabriella left. I listened to her footsteps on the stairs before I dropped back into my chair.

CHAPTER 30

T.J. RETURNED with lunch a few minutes later. She dropped a McDonald's bag on my desk. Inside were a chicken sandwich and large fries, a portion of which were missing and presumably eaten by the young lady who delivered the meal. "Thanks," I said as I took the food out.

"Sure." She sat at her own desk. "If you want a higher class of lunch, you need to pay me a higher class of wage."

I grinned. "We'll talk to Melinda when your evaluation period is up."

"You know you'll be footing my bill solo after that," she said.

"I know. You saw the check from Amy Napier. If we get a client like her every month, you can spring for Chipotle when the mob queen of Baltimore drops by for a chat."

"I thought about rates and billing when I was out."

"Of course you did," I said as I unwrapped the sandwich. It featured a large chicken fillet with lettuce and tomato. I could've lived without the mayo, but I didn't exactly tell T.J. what I wanted.

"You want to hear my idea?" she said. I nodded around a

mouthful of food. "You'd need to maintain it in secret. Don't publish a rate schedule or anything. You and I would know about it. Individual clients pay one rate. Businesses pay a higher one."

It was simple and elegant. The idea allowed me to work with people who needed my services but didn't have a large bank account at their disposal. On the other hand, companies who enjoyed a good balance on their ledger could afford to pay a little extra. "I like it," I said after I finished my bite.

T.J. smiled. "Really? I hoped you would."

"Yes. Let's implement it. From this moment forward, our double-secret rate plan is in place." I knocked on my desk like a judge banging a gavel. "You need to get me a crab mallet one of these days."

"You think I can afford seafood on my salary?" T.J. said.

"If you keep coming up with ideas like this, I might have to keep you around."

"If you keep me on and give me a raise, I might have to stop making jokes about you dying on the job."

I took another bite of my sandwich. "Let's not get ahead of ourselves," I said.

———

Later, we were about to close up shop after another day of no new clients when the front door opened, and my parents walked in. T.J. shot me an inquisitive look. I shrugged. "Mom, Dad. This is an unexpected visit."

"We were in the neighborhood," my father said.

"You're aware I know where you live, right?"

"We came by to talk to you, Coningsby," my mother said.

She smiled at my secretary. "Although we'd prefer to do it somewhere else."

T.J. stood and slung her purse over her shoulder. "I can go."

"No," I said. "Stay."

"Coningsby, this is about—"

"Are you planning on talking about what we discussed a few days ago?" My mother bobbed her head. "If it affects the business, it affects T.J., too. She should be a part of it."

"Can you keep talking about her in the third person, too?" T.J. asked. "She just loves it."

"If you think it's best, son," my father said. "We'll order something for four. Not much difference from three."

"I feel like pizza," I said. T.J. nodded her concurrence. "There you go. We have paper plates, napkins, coffee, and water. All we need is a meal."

"All right." My father took his phone out of his pocket. "I'm sure there's a good local place."

"Brick Oven isn't far," I offered. "Except, they don't deliver."

My mother started to object, but my father cut her off. "Fine. We'll pick some up and come back."

"And some salad, too," my mother added as they walked back out the door.

T.J. raised an eyebrow. "You weren't expecting them to come by?"

"Nope."

"What did you mean that something's going to affect me, too?"

"You know I used to work for their foundation, right?"

"You might have mentioned being salty about it a few dozen times."

"I guess I did," I said. "Anyway, they threw me a bone a few years ago when I got back from Hong Kong. My job didn't really fit their charitable work then, and I'm not sure it does today, but they seem to be interested in some form of revival. I figured it can't hurt to hear them out."

"All right." T.J. dropped back into her chair. "You might need to hire an accountant."

"You might need to take an accounting class."

"You paying?"

"Sure," I said. "Community college all the way."

"Could be the way to go. You might be on to something."

"Don't you know by now I usually am?"

My parents returned about forty minutes later with three pizzas and a large container of salad. Despite telling them I had all the accessories on hand, they also carried a small stack of paper plates, a six-pack of Coke, and a baggie of cheap white plastic utensils I would've paid to watch my mother try to use. I set some paper towels on my desk, and my father placed the food atop them. They'd brought a cheese, a pepperoni, and a vegetable pie. I snagged a slice of each and crammed a little salad onto the plate. My mother frowned and sniffed when she saw it.

After a couple minutes, they sat in my guest chairs, and we all enjoyed dinner. "Let's get down to brass tacks," my father said as he polished off his second piece. "I know we left you high and dry a couple months ago."

I raised a can of Coke in his direction. "Nice of you to admit it."

"We realize you took it personally," my mother said. She made a game attempt at her salad, but the flimsy fork betrayed her. I fought a laugh as she grimaced. "We were trying to protect you."

"I don't need your protection, Mom. It's a dangerous job. I knew the possibilities when I got my license."

"We've been thinking for a while," my dad said. "Things haven't been great between us since all this happened. We kind of shoe-horned what you did into the foundation's expenses. It wasn't a great fit." He snorted. "The damn accountant certainly told us enough times. We've been focusing more on individuals rather than other charities in any event. A lot of people have had a rough time of things. Maybe we're filling a gap."

"We think some of them could use what you do, Coningsby," my mother said. "They're all in a bad way, but it's not always their fault."

"How many really need a PI versus an avenging angel?" I asked. "However much I might sympathize, I'm not going to take a check to settle the score for a battered woman."

My father shook his head. "We're not going to ask you to, son. Our charity isn't about beating people up . . . even if they deserve it." He paused and sighed. "I know this is something we don't experience, but it's hard to be poor. Even trying to move through the system costs time and money. You have to go to court. You need a computer or a cell phone. There are people who simply don't have those things."

"I know," I said. "I've probably helped some of them already."

"Maybe you can continue to." My mother gave up on the greens and set her fork down. "If we think someone needs your help, we want to be able to refer them to you."

"This all sounds good," T.J. said. "How do we get paid?" I covered my smile by wiping my mouth.

"We'll pay your rate," my father said. "A retainer when you take a case we send your way, and then we'll settle up the difference at the end."

I ruminated as I ate my salad. The idea sounded good. Originally, I helped people who couldn't afford the services of a private investigator, and my parents paid me for completing a case. It worked well for both of us—they got to help folks who needed it, and I made more in my contracted arrangement with them than I would've on my own. I liked the freedom to pick and choose who I worked for, however, and I didn't trust my parents to vet people like I would. "I'm concerned about the gatekeeping."

My father spread his hands. "Explain."

"I selected my clients before. I do now. Would I need to accept someone solely because you sent them to me?"

"I don't think so," he said. "You'd need to use your judgment of course. We're not going to send you frivolous cases."

I harbored some doubts, but on the surface, the arrangement sounded good. If nothing else, we'd get an infusion of clients and money, and I could afford to keep T.J. on even after the deal with Melinda ended. "All right," I said. "Let's try it and see how it goes. We should evaluate it periodically to make sure everyone's getting what they need from it."

"Coningsby, you sound so professional," my mother said.

"Don't tell anyone. I don't want to have to wear a tie." She smiled.

"All right," my father said. "We'll draw it up. An official contract this time."

"Sounds good," I said.

They left a short while later. T.J. put a mix of pizza slices into a box. "You don't care if I take some home, do you?"

"Not at all."

"How do you feel about this?"

"Cautiously optimistic."

"I think it'll be good," she said.

"Maybe," I said. "I hope you're right."

She grinned. "Don't you know by now I usually am?"

"You're fired," I said.

END of Novel #11

Thanks for reading Dead Cat Bounce. *C.T. Ferguson will be back in a new adventure around the summer of 2022. In the meantime, if this is your first time reading the series, you can start at the beginning with* The Reluctant Detective—*available by itself or as part of a three-novel box set.*

THE END

AFTERWORD

Thanks for checking out this novel! I hope you enjoyed reading the book as much as I enjoyed writing it.

I write mysteries and thrillers with action, snark, and flawed heroes. If this sounds like something you like, you can check out my catalog below.

The C.T. Ferguson Crime Novels:

1. The Reluctant Detective
2. The Unknown Devil
3. The Workers of Iniquity
4. Already Guilty
5. Daughters and Sons
6. A March from Innocence
7. Inside Cut
8. The Next Girl
9. In the Blood
10. Right as Rain
11. Dead Cat Bounce

12. Don't Say Her Name (Summer 2022)

The John Tyler Action Thrillers

1. The Mechanic
2. White Lines
3. Lost Highway
4. Four on the Floor (Spring 2022)

(Note: C.T. Ferguson appears in *White Lines*.)

While these are the suggested reading sequences, each novel is a standalone mystery or thriller, and the books can be enjoyed in whatever order you happen upon them.

Connect with me:

For the many ways of finding and reaching me online, please visit https://tomfowlerwrites.com/contact. I'm always happy to talk to readers.

This is a work of fiction. Characters and places are either fictitious or used in a fictitious manner.

"Self-publishing" is something of a misnomer. This book would not have been possible without the contributions of many people.

- The great cover design team at 100 Covers.
- My editor extraordinaire, Chase Nottingham.
- My wonderful advance reader team, the Fell Street Irregulars.

www.ingramcontent.com/pod-product-compliance
Lightning Source LLC
Chambersburg PA
CBHW010843190726
48286CB00012BA/2972